"So," Sam said. "Do you want to stop and think?"

Tension crackled between them, but Rebecca refused to let her gaze waver. "No," she said baldly. "If I'd wanted to stop and think, I'd have done it a long time ago. Now I just want to...feel."

The muscles in Sam's jaw clenched as he stared her down. "I don't seem to be popular with your family," he said at last.

For the first time, Rebecca let her gaze drop from his. She examined the top button of his shirt while she said awkwardly, "My mother is a worrier. She's just being...protective."

"Do you still feel the need to be protected?" Sam said.

He still sounded angry, and Rebecca couldn't blame him. She sensed that she was on the edge of a chasm, but she didn't hesitate. "No," she whispered. "Not from you."

"Then to hell with your family," he growled, and swept her into his arms.

Dear Reader,

Four more fabulous WOMEN WHO DARE are heading your way!

In May, you'll thrill to the time-travel tale Lynn Erickson spins in *Paradox*. When loan executive Emily Jacoby is catapulted back in time during a train wreck, she is thoroughly unnerved by the fate that awaits her. In 1893, Colorado is a harsh and rugged land. Women's rights have yet to be invented, and Will Dutcher, Emily's reluctant host, is making her question her desire to return to her own time.

In June, you'll be reminded that courage can strike at any age. Our heroine in Peg Sutherland's *Late Bloomer* discovers unplumbed depths at the age of forty. After a lifetime of living for others, she realizes that she wants something for herself—college, a career, a *life*. But when a mysterious stranger drifts into town, she discovers to her shock that she also wants *him!*

Sharon Brondos introduces us to spunky Allison Ford in our July WOMEN WHO DARE title, *The Marriage Ticket*. Allison stands up for what she believes in. And she believes in playing fair. Unfortunately, some of her community's leaders don't have the same scruples, and going head-to-head with them lands her in serious trouble.

You'll never forget Leah Temple, the heroine of August's *Another Woman*, by Margot Dalton. This riveting tale of a wife with her husband's murder on her mind will hold you spellbound . . . and surprised! Don't miss it!

Some of your favorite Superromance authors have also contributed to our spring and summer lineup. Look for books by Pamela Bauer, Debbi Bedford, Dawn Stewardson, Jane Silverwood, Sally Garrett, Bobby Hutchinson and Judith Arnold . . . to name just a few! Some wonderful Superromance reading awaits you!

Marsha Zinberg
Senior Editor

P.S. Don't forget that you can write to your favorite author

c/o Harlequin Reader Service,
P.O. Box 1297
Buffalo, New York
14240 U.S.A.

JANICE KAY JOHNSON

HOME AGAIN

Harlequin Books

TORONTO • NEW YORK • LONDON
AMSTERDAM • PARIS • SYDNEY • HAMBURG
STOCKHOLM • ATHENS • TOKYO • MILAN
MADRID • WARSAW • BUDAPEST • AUCKLAND

Published August 1993

ISBN 0-373-70561-1

HOME AGAIN

ABOUT THE AUTHOR

As the author of several young-adult novels, Janice brings a wonderful sense of authenticity to the character of Alan in her latest Superromance novel, *Home Again*. She accurately depicts parent-teenage relationships and adds her own special brand of warmth and humor to the mix. The result is a touching romance with characters you will remember long after you've turned the last page.

Janice has written more than twenty books, and has already gained Superromance fans around the world. She lives in Washington State with her two daughters, two dogs and five cats.

Books by Janice Kay Johnson

HARLEQUIN SUPERROMANCE
483—SEIZE THE DAY

HARLEQUIN TEMPTATION
149—NIGHT AND DAY

HARLEQUIN REGENCY ROMANCE
13—THE IMPERILED HEIRESS

Don't miss any of our special offers. Write to us at the following address for information on our newest releases.

Harlequin Reader Service
P.O. Box 1397, Buffalo, NY 14240
Canadian address: P.O. Box 603,
Fort Erie, Ont. L2A 5X3

CHAPTER ONE

STILL STEAMING, Alan Halstead tossed his coat into the closet and slammed the door before anything could fall out. "Hey, Mom," he called.

Rebecca Halstead's voice drifted down the stairs, oddly muffled. "Alan, is that you?"

"Do you know what that jerk did today?" he demanded.

He heard a thump and his mother mumble a word he would have sworn she'd never say, before she called, "Come and tell me about it."

Alan took the stairs two at a time. "What're you doing?"

"Trying to fix that damned leaky pipe. As if I know anything about plumbing."

"Why don't you call the plumber?"

"He charges fifty bucks to breathe the air in your living room. It goes up when they step into the bathroom."

"Oh."

He found his mother sitting cross-legged in front of the sink. She was pretty, as mothers went, but dressed in a gray sweatshirt and jeans, barefoot, with her curly brown hair bundled under a scarf, she looked young but plain. And mad.

When he stopped in the doorway, she tossed down the wrench with a *clank* and blew out a heartfelt sigh. "I swear, if I ever marry again it'll be to a man who knows how to fix things."

Alan had heard that one before. Smugly he thought, *check.* Coach James was also the new shop teacher. That must mean he could fix stuff.

"So..." His mom scooted over to lean against the bathtub and her scowl evaporated. "What did The Jerk do today? I assume you mean your boss?"

"He isn't really my boss...."

"Picky, picky. He could fire you, couldn't he?"

"Yeah, I guess," Alan admitted. Actually, he worked ten hours a week for his aunt Jess, who ran a maid and janitorial service. Unfortunately, four of those hours were at a rental store owned by a dour man who frowningly double-checked everything Alan did.

"You know those lawn tractors for sale? The ones lined up by the window?" When she nodded, Alan said, "Today he told me to watch, and he drove 'em one at a time about three feet forward. Then he just stared at the floor. There were a few dust balls. Big deal. So then he wanted to know why I wasn't getting under the tractors."

"Why weren't you?"

He would have been mad, except she sounded inquisitive, not condemning. "Nobody had asked me to. Besides, who cares? I mean, when one of 'em is sold, I clean. It's not like it's a dirty toilet or anything."

Rebecca lifted her eyebrows and glanced at the toilet a few feet away, which was Alan's job to clean.

"I'll do it tomorrow," he said quickly.

"Was he angry at you?"

"No—yes—I don't know. With that stone face, I never can tell what he's thinking."

His mother's blue eyes were steady. "Well, he *is* paying you to do a job. I don't know that having expectations is unreasonable."

"Yeah, but he never tells me when he thinks I've done a good job!" Alan burst out. "He just nods when he comes in, then ignores me unless he has something to complain about."

"What does Aunt Jess say?"

"That I'm doing fine, and I don't have to love him."

"Well, then?"

In frustration he slapped a hand on the door frame. "Well, nothing! I'm just bitching. Can't I do that?"

Her nose crinkled when she grinned. "You bet. So tell me, does this store rent an all-purpose plumbing-problem fix-it-upper?"

"Who knows? I don't know what half the stuff in there does."

"Well, then, you want to lend me a little muscle?"

"Sure, but listen, Mom."

She picked up the wrench again. "Umm?"

"I talked to Dad last night." She didn't say anything, and Alan calculated just the right level of unhappiness to inject into his voice. "He can't come to the father/son banquet."

"Oh, Alan, I'm sorry."

The rush of warm sympathy in her voice made tears prickle uncomfortably in the back of his eyes, and Alan had to remind himself that he had hoped his father *couldn't* come. This was his one and only chance to introduce his pretty, divorced mother to Coach James, the new high-school shop teacher and assistant football coach.

He was the first guy Alan had seen who was right for his mother. It wasn't like she was making any effort to meet men. She didn't seem to understand how lonely she would be when he left for college in a year and a half. Ever since he had realized that she would be better off if she remarried, he'd been keeping a list in his head of her requirements. Most of the time she claimed she wasn't interested in men, period, especially not in marrying another one, but then every once in a while she would toss out a comment like she just had.

"If I ever marry again," she would say, "he'll have to enjoy working around the house." Or, "He won't be the kind you have to nag to do things." That one had struck home, because Alan's father used to take six months to change a simple burned-out headlight on the car. So Alan had kept his list, assigning numbers in order of importance: 1. Likes to work around the house. 2. Can fix anything. 3. Changes headlights, et cetera, without being nagged. 4. Good with teenage boys. 5. Makes a decent living but is *there* when you need him. 6. Sexy.

Half the girls at school thought Coach James was cute, so number six was a cinch. The boys liked him, too, which handled four. Being shop teacher took care of most of the rest, though Alan couldn't be sure about the nagging part.

If Alan could just get James and his mother together, she would admit that he was perfect. The annual father/son banquet for varsity and junior-varsity football players couldn't be more opportune. The fact that she wasn't his father was the only catch.

Now he said quickly, "Do you think you could come, instead?"

Alarm widened Rebecca's eyes. "No way! If you think I'm going to be the only woman there..."

"Hey, half the guys have parents who are divorced!" he argued. "Some of them never even see their dads. Coach Kowalski says any relative is okay."

"You're *sure?*"

The coach *had* said that. Unfortunately, Alan didn't know anybody else who was actually bringing a mother or an aunt or a grandmother. But somebody else would, he reassured himself. Colin Hughes, for example. His dad was dead, and he never mentioned an uncle or anybody. His mom would be coming for sure.

He tried to look offended. "Do you think I'm lying or something?"

"No, of course not, but..." Rebecca bit her lip. "Alan, I'll bet Uncle Joe would go with you."

"He's okay, but I really want you to come."

He could see her scrambling for an excuse, but he had her over a barrel. She said weakly, "You're sure I won't be the only woman there?"

"Cross my heart and hope to die." He crossed his fingers, too, just in case, but she didn't see that part.

She sighed again. "Oh, all right. Now, come here and hold this."

TEN PACES inside the banquet room, Rebecca stopped dead. Long, white-covered tables made the room a maze. It was already jammed with fathers and sons. She saw one set of broad shoulders after another and heard the rumble of masculine voices. As she searched the room hopefully, her nervousness grew into panic.

There were gray sport coats, brown, blue and tan. Shaggy blond and brown heads next to thinning or graying ones. Snugly knotted ties that made the boys look terribly young and their fathers solemn. Shined shoes. Pressed creases.

Not a single woman was there.

Men were already turning to stare. She stuck out like an ornamental fountain in the middle of a smoothly cropped lawn. Worse, because she hadn't worn the discreet black turtleneck dress she'd picked out, which at least would have blended with the neutral, masculine colors. No, her son—her *darling* son—had wanted her to knock 'em out. So now she had on her highest heels and a sapphire blue silk number just a shade shorter than she liked.

Yep. She might as well have jumped up on one of the long tables and wriggled her hips.

Beside her Alan cleared his throat. "Uh, we're supposed to sit up here...."

"I'm going to kill you," Rebecca snarled between gritted teeth.

He took a step back. "Maybe we're just early."

"We're ten minutes late."

"It's no big deal if you're the only mother. You're the one who always says men aren't any better than women."

"We're not talking better or worse here. We're talking *different!*" She spit the last word. Her pink cheeks betrayed just how conspicuous she felt.

Alan was flushed a dull red, too. He lowered his voice. "Here comes Coach Kowalski. Will you *please...?*"

"What? Act as if my son hasn't just embarrassed me?" But she turned and managed a smile for the burly coach, whom she had met several times before.

"Mrs. Halstead."

He didn't have to sound so surprised, she thought tartly. For Alan's sake, she tried for an air of maidenly confusion. "Mr. Kowalski, am I hopelessly out of place here?"

"No, no," he said unconvincingly. "Of course not. We're happy to have you."

"Dad couldn't come," Alan contributed.

"No uncles or grandfathers, eh? Well," the graying coach said heartily, "why don't you go ahead and find your places?"

"We'll do that," Rebecca said. After he'd moved away, she whispered, "For heaven's sake, let's at least sit down! Maybe nobody will notice me."

Alan clutched her arm. "But, Mom, I want you to meet Coach James first."

"Later." She started toward the tables, but Alan dragged her to a stop.

"Please, Mom. I really like him. This is important."

"We can't do it another time?" Seeing the expression on his face, she gave one last longing look toward the table Coach Kowalski had indicated, then sighed. "Okay. Where is he?"

Naturally, the coach who'd won her son's adoration was on the other side of the room, which necessitated circum-navigating it to the accompaniment of silence.

By the time they reached the small group around the as-sistant coach, every muscle in Rebecca's body was rigid. Her smile felt like a death mask, and the way back to their table loomed as grim as the path to the underworld in Greek mythology.

Blond, fresh-faced and cocky, the young coach turned to greet them, his smile deepening dimples in his ruddy cheeks. If Alan had been a girl, Rebecca would have un-derstood his devotion. At sixteen, she herself might have had a crush on him. Well, maybe not. His thick neck didn't do much for her, though it probably wasn't a drawback for a football coach.

What depressed her now was how young he looked. She was used to feeling like a contemporary of her son's teachers. This one looked more like *Alan's* contemporary. Only a few lines around his eyes gave away the extra years he had on the kids he taught.

"Hi," she said, holding out her hand. "I'm Alan's mother."

He threw back his head and laughed as though she'd said something incredibly witty. "Believe it or not, I noticed you aren't his father!"

Stiffly, she replied, "Alan's father couldn't come."

"My parents are divorced," Alan supplied helpfully. "And since Mom's single, I don't have a stepfather or anything."

Of course, he did have three uncles, any one of whom would have been happy to accompany him tonight. But, no, he had to have his mother, Rebecca thought in exasperation, letting her hand drop.

"Not for lack of offers, I'm sure," the coach said with what he undoubtedly intended to be a friendly leer.

"Mom hardly ever dates," Alan assured him. He avoided his mother's gaze, but even through the sport coat he had to feel the sharp pinch she gave to his arm. His cheeks reddened again and he added hurriedly, "She could if she wanted to. I mean, she's always turning guys down—"

Rebecca interrupted. "Alan, your coach has absolutely no interest in my dating habits." She forced a smile. "Mr. James, I just wanted to tell you how much Alan is enjoying football this year."

The coach touched her nearly bare shoulder and lowered his voice. "Glad to hear it. Alan has what it takes to play this game. He could make it big time if he concentrated a little more. Yeah, the books are important, but the lucky kid who has the athletic ability needs to make choices sometimes. I've been telling him what a great program Northern State has—"

"I'm hoping for Stanford," Rebecca cut in.

The coach winked at Alan. "Yeah, but the cheerleaders at Northern have more talent, if you know what I mean."

Alan grinned back, but Rebecca was not amused. "Somehow the cheerleaders aren't high on my list of priorities in helping Alan choose a college," she said frostily. She glanced around and saw that people were beginning to sit down. Relieved to have an excuse to end the conversation, she added, "Alan, it looks like it's time to find our seats. Mr. James, nice to meet you."

"Ditto, Mrs. Halstead." He smiled winningly. "Or should I say *Ms.* Halstead?"

"'Ms.' will do very nicely," she agreed. "Alan?"

"Maybe we could sit with Coach James," her son suggested.

"There are name tags at each place," she reminded him, ruthlessly separating him from the coach. Not quite past caring that she was the only woman here, she forged a path between tables until she finally spotted *Halstead* on a crisp white marker.

The rest of the evening passed in a blur. Awards were given out, and she clapped until her hands stung. Most of the presentations reminded her more of a roast than a ceremony, and she began to wonder if male bonding required crude jokes. Thank goodness half the fathers appeared to find the whole thing as juvenile as she did.

The banquet mercifully over, she let Alan drive home. He'd wanted to come in his clunker, but since she had no desire to walk home, she had insisted that they take her car. Now, slumped in the passenger seat, she felt as if she'd been through a wringer. If there were many more evenings like this one in store, she *would* get married just to provide a stepfather to stand in for her.

"Well, what did you think?" Alan asked eagerly.

"Congratulations on your awards. I'm really glad to know that you're not only a great athlete, you take the time to help other kids. You ought to be proud of being voted the most inspirational.''

"Huh? Oh, sure. I really meant about Coach James."

Rebecca turned her head, her attention arrested by something in her son's voice. "He seemed nice," she said.

"He's cool, isn't he?" Alan braked too suddenly for a red light, jerking Rebecca forward. "He isn't married, you know."

Rebecca righted her purse, which had fallen over. "Now, don't get any ideas," she warned. "You know how much I hate dating."

"But if you got married again . . ."

It didn't take a genius to figure out what he was getting at. She grabbed the edge of her seat as they rocketed forward the instant the light turned green. "I wasn't too crazy about being married, either."

"But Coach James isn't like Dad. He's younger, for one thing."

"But I'm not," Rebecca pointed out as gently as she could. "I'm thirty-five. Your coach can't be more than thirty, if that."

"Five years isn't much," Alan insisted. "I mean, you don't have to tell him how old you are."

"Alan." Rebecca waited until her son glanced at her. "Even if I said I was his age, if the man can do elementary subtraction, he can figure it out. Unless I had you when I was fourteen . . ."

Alan turned the car into their driveway and switched off the ignition, then sat in silence for a moment. Rebecca waited. Finally he said, "A few years doesn't have to make any difference. If you really like him—"

Rebecca interrupted again, determined to be kind by being ruthless. She didn't want Alan to continue fantasizing—not on this subject, anyway. "He doesn't appeal to me. I'm sorry, Alan. I know you really like him, but even if I *were* in the market for a husband, he wouldn't be on my list."

There. That ought to do it, she thought, surprised at how cynical she'd sounded. On the other hand, she suspected some divorced or widowed women did approach finding a husband pretty much the way they bought Christmas gifts. You started with a list, but occasionally let sudden impulses sway you. The truth was, Rebecca didn't much like shopping, either.

"But..." Alan stopped, then tried again. "But he's a really cool guy."

She touched her teenage son's arm. "I believe you. I'm glad you have him for a coach. He just isn't for me."

"You didn't even give him a chance!" he said angrily. "That's not fair!"

"Nobody said love was."

"But if you'd just try...!" Alan swore. "Oh, never mind. You aren't going to, are you?" He jumped out of the car and slammed the door.

A headache gripping her temples, Rebecca slowly followed. Single parenthood was so much fun. If she ever did remarry, the man would have to be good with teenage boys.

THERE HAD TO BE some way to make his mother see how wrong she was. Worrying about age was just a smoke screen, Alan figured. Or could she really think she looked old? Sometimes she grumbled about bags under her eyes or how much harder it was to keep the pounds off her hips. Maybe she had quit noticing that she was really pretty.

What better cure than to have a guy five years younger than her have the hots for her? She'd been pretty snippy to Coach James, though. Would he even be interested?

Alan hadn't paid much attention to the coach's reaction. He'd just *assumed* . . . Yeah, well, he'd assumed his mother would be interested, too.

So in the locker room the next day before practice, he sauntered by Coach James's office to find out.

The young defensive coach glanced up from some play diagrams. "Aren't you turning out?"

"Late class. I'm on my way," Alan said. He made his voice casual. "Have fun last night?"

The coach shrugged nonchalantly and leaned back in his chair. "Sure. Hey, you have a nice mother."

"Yeah, she's okay. Beats all the other moms I know."

"How long have your parents been divorced?"

"Three years. I wouldn't mind seeing her marry again."

"With looks like that, she's probably fighting men off."

She wasn't *that* pretty. Not like Julia Roberts or somebody. But the fact that the coach thought so was a good sign.

"You're not married, are you?" he asked as though he didn't know or care.

"Nah. What, you trying to set your mom up or something?"

Alan tried to shrug as nonchalantly as the coach had, but his heart was racing. "She doesn't need me to. I just thought you might be her type."

The coach smiled. "Thanks for the vote of confidence. Now go on, get your butt in gear." He raised his voice. "Five minutes! Let's get to work!"

Alan hurried to his locker and banged it open, satisfied with the conversation. He'd done all he could with the coach. Now he'd approach his mother again.

He waited another day in the hope that she'd forget their earlier conversation. On Wednesday just before he left for work, as he sat in the hall lacing up his high-tops, he said,

"Mom, do you think I could invite somebody to dinner Sunday?"

Sunday dinners were a family tradition. His mom had one sister and two brothers, all but one of whom were married and had kids. Along with Grandma, as many of the aunts and uncles and cousins as could make it got together one Sunday a month. It wasn't a formal occasion. The men would go out and throw the football or play one-on-one basketball; the women would talk mostly, and they'd all eat. Sometimes Alan or one of his cousins would bring a friend, but usually it was just family. For one of the girls to bring a boyfriend or one of the guys to bring a girl took guts; it was like announcing you were engaged.

Right now his mother was in the kitchen; he could see her trekking between the refrigerator and the counter, her hands full.

"I was just talking to your grandma. We're having dinner here this month," she said, distractedly. "And you know we don't have loads of space. Who do you have in mind?"

He'd been hoping she wouldn't ask. If he'd been able to surprise her, she wouldn't have had any choice but to be hospitable. He thought briefly about lying but finally decided against it. Reluctantly he said, "Coach James."

She popped her head around the door frame. "No."

"No?" he repeated incredulously, standing up. "What do you mean, no?"

"I mean no. I usually do when I say it."

"But he doesn't have any family around here. I just thought..."

"My heart bleeds," his mother said. "No."

"Why can't I invite whoever I want?"

"Because I know what you have in mind. If I needed a matchmaker, I'd go to a dating service. I am not, I repeat, *not* interested in your coach. And I won't have you put me on the spot by inviting him here. My answer is no, and that's final." As though to underscore her refusal, she disappeared back into the kitchen.

"But Mom..."

"No!"

"Damn!" He kicked the front door open, then slammed it behind him as hard as he could. What was wrong with her? Why couldn't she see that he was trying to do something *nice?*

He was still mad when he arrived at White Horse Rentals, the store he cleaned two evenings a week. At the sight of the Mercedes out front, he swore again. Why couldn't he be lucky just once?

White Horse Rentals was part of a chain of six stores in the Puget Sound area, all of them locally managed. The owner of the chain, Mr. Ballard, was only there one day a week; it just happened to be one of Alan's days to clean. The store was closed by the time Alan arrived, but Ballard always sat behind the counter, going over figures on the computer. Sometimes the manager was there, too, sometimes not. Either way, Alan would *feel* Ballard's cold gray eyes watching him. It made him clumsy and he didn't like that.

Tonight he was ticked off enough not to care. One word from Ballard—*one word*—and he was out of here. Aunt Jess could send someone else for this job.

When he let himself in, Alan found Ballard running a finger along a shelf. "Dust over here today," he said after a brief nod. "Looks like it's been a while."

Typical, Alan fumed. No hello, just do it. He didn't bother saying hello, either, just said shortly, "Sure."

Didn't the guy have anything better to do? he wondered as he went to the storage closet. Maybe Ballard should wear white gloves so he could make sure every inch of the place was clean. Considering what they rented—chain saws and jigsaws, miter boxes and posthole diggers, lawn mowers and cement mixers—this cleanliness fetish was especially ridiculous. The stuff came back dirty every time, anyhow. It was like trying to keep your garage floor clean enough to eat off of.

Somebody had told Alan that Ballard wasn't married, either. Big surprise. Who could stand him?

The thought made Alan even madder. If his mother passed up someone like the coach, this is what she'd end up stuck with. A jerk.

He froze, his hand suspended above a circular saw. Was there some way he could *show* his mother that? Make her see how great Coach James was in contrast?

Some way he could set it up so that she'd be stuck talking to Mr. Ballard long enough to *realize* what a jerk he was? In fact, now that Alan had thought of it, he could see how perfect Ballard was for the job. The guy sure wasn't good with kids, and Alan couldn't imagine anyone finding that glower sexy. And while Ballard probably *could* fix anything, Alan was pretty sure he wouldn't want to.

He planned while he swept and mopped. How could he get his mother here? How could he *keep* her here long enough?

By the end of the first hour Alan had worked it out. At ten to eight he asked Mr. Ballard if he could use the phone.

The man raised an eyebrow but nodded. "Keep it short."

Alan dialed, then turned his back, but he could feel Ballard watching him.

"Hey, Mom," he said when she answered. "Can you pick me after work? You know how the car hasn't been starting? When I got here I tried to start it again, and it wouldn't."

"Does it need a charge?" she asked.

"We don't have any jumper cables—" He realized his mistake right away. "I could probably borrow some here, but I don't think the battery is the problem. When I turn the key, it kind of clicks. I bet it needs a new starter."

"Sure, I'm on my way."

Satisfied, Alan hung up. "Thanks," he said to Ballard, then started back toward the mop and bucket.

"I'll give you a jump," Ballard offered unexpectedly. "We can see if that works."

Was he hearing things? Alan turned slowly. "Uh, thanks, but I charged the battery this morning. It didn't seem to make any difference."

"I'd be happy to try," Ballard said. "Or I could give you a lift home."

"Thanks," Alan said again, "but I'll take care of the car in the morning. And Mom's probably already on the way." He wrung out the mop and made a couple of slow passes with it until he was out of sight down an aisle.

He'd made sure he was working at the other end of the store. Barely moving the mop, he waited until he heard the sound of a car outside, followed by a knock and Ballard's footsteps as he went to answer it. Then Alan quietly tipped over the bucket and sloshed water across the floor. It'd take him a while to clean up. Maybe ten or fifteen minutes.

Perfect.

CHAPTER TWO

CURIOSITY WAS Rebecca's besetting sin. As her charming ex-husband had put it, she was a nosy broad. Normally when she picked Alan up somewhere, she just leaned on the horn and waited for him to appear. This time she parked and went to the door.

In the six months Alan had worked at the rental store, she hadn't had occasion to meet his boss. Over the months of Alan's grumbling she had put together a picture of the man in her mind, feature by feature.

Permanent frown. Cold eyes. Pursed lips, to go with his nit-picking personality. Short, because short men tended to be the dictatorial ones.

She couldn't wait to see how close she had come.

Half the time she took the guy's side when Alan complained, just because another of her traits was an ability always to see the other side of an argument. Her ex had hated that, too.

Still, just because she sometimes defended Mr. Ballard didn't mean she liked the man. Would it kill him to compliment her son now and then?

She knocked tentatively on the glass door, expecting to see Alan. Instead a tall, dark-haired man appeared. He opened the door and raised an eyebrow.

Rebecca said brightly, ''Oh, hi, I'm here to pick up Alan.''

He looked disconcerted, she thought, and wondered why. Without taking his gaze from her face, he raised his voice. "Alan? Your mother's here."

This couldn't possibly be the ogre. Where were the pursed lips, the glower? Surely Alan would have mentioned that the man was drop-dead handsome. He was easily six-foot-two, rangy, with shoulders wide enough to block her view past him. Wavy hair, Slavic cheekbones, a straight, patrician nose and an incredibly sexy mouth. His penetrating eyes were a clear gray, unusual with such dark hair. She couldn't look away, and barely heard her son's voice call, "I'll be done in a minute."

A couple of creases between the man's dark brows showed that he *could* frown. *Was* he The Jerk? she wondered incredulously.

"Come on in," he suggested, and she found herself staring at his back as he walked over to one of the far aisles. "Why don't you go ahead?" he told Alan.

"I've only got a little to mop up," Alan said. "It won't take me long."

The man glanced back at her. Alan had to be speaking to him; he was the only one here, Rebecca thought wildly. She wanted to say "*You're* Alan's boss?" but heard herself murmuring, "I'll wait out in the car."

"It's cold out there. Why don't you have a seat," he said.

The only chairs were behind the counter, where he had presumably been working. Rebecca felt ridiculously breathless. It was just the shock, she told herself. The contrast. She couldn't believe her mental picture was so totally out of whack.

"Well...thank you."

There was one of those awkward pauses before he held out his hand.

"Sam Ballard."

His hand was warm, and large enough to engulf hers. "Rebecca Halstead," she managed.

"You don't look old enough to have a son Alan's age."

Surprised by the abrupt remark, she said again, "Thank you. I got married at eighteen." Ruefully she added, "Much too young."

Rebecca glanced down the aisle to see Alan mopping up what looked like a sea of soapy water. What on earth was he doing? Scrubbing the floor clean with a tidal wave?

Sam Ballard followed her gaze and she saw him raise his eyebrows, but he made no comment. She clutched her purse and trailed him around the counter. "I'm sorry," she said. "Are we holding you up?"

"No, I'm usually here until close to nine."

"Well, don't let me keep you from your work."

"No problem."

Now what? She perched on a chair and avoided meeting his eyes by glancing around at the clutter of phone messages, receipts impaled on a spindle and stacked green-and-white computer paper behind the small dot-matrix printer. He pulled out an office chair and sat, too, stretching long legs out, his gaze still on her. Despite his businessman's attire of wool slacks, a tie pulled loose at his throat and a white shirt wrinkled after a long day, Rebecca was aware of the easy play of muscle when he shifted, and of the large hand that picked up a pencil and fiddled with it. Appearing supremely relaxed, he studied her with no apparent interest in making conversation.

Under that clear gaze, Rebecca felt frumpy and self-conscious. Why hadn't Alan warned her? She would at least have brushed her hair and changed shirts before coming down here. As it was, she had on her usual evening nobody-will-see-me-anyway costume—jeans, a faded, baggy purple sweatshirt, canvas tennis shoes and no socks. She didn't look young, she looked like someone who'd been shopping in the junior department instead of where she belonged.

When she couldn't stand the silence for another second, she lied, "Umm, Alan has enjoyed working here."

An eyebrow went up, and she'd have sworn humor lurked in his eyes.

"Really."

She moistened her lips, which had become even drier when his gaze had lowered to her mouth. "I hope he's done a good job for you."

"He's fine." Silence. Just as she began to squirm, he added, "I could drop the boy off at home when he's done if you don't want to wait."

"I don't want to put you to the trouble now that I'm here. Maybe I should go out and see if I can start his car."

Both were startled by a knock on the door. Sam rose in one smooth motion and strode to answer it. "Yes?"

"Uh, is Alan still here?" a teenage boy asked. "I saw his car— Oh, hi, Mrs. Halstead."

"Geoff! What are you doing here?"

"The high-school gym is open till nine. I thought I'd go shoot some hoops, see if Alan wanted to come with me."

Alan appeared with astonishing speed, bucket in hand and the mop handle poking out. What had he been doing, hiding around the corner? "You don't mind, do you, Mom?"

"Well, I guess—"

She didn't even have a chance to finish her sentence.

"Give me a sec," Alan said, and disappeared in the back room. Not a minute later, he and the other boy were out the door, her son with his coat slung over his shoulder. His voice came back on the chill night air. "Hey, let's see if we can get my car started." He jumped into the old beater, his buddy leaning against the open door. With a throaty cough the engine leaped to life.

Rebecca was left standing openmouthed inside the door of White Horse Rentals watching two sets of taillights disappear. She threw up her hands in exasperation. "For crying out loud! After dragging me down here... Oh, well. I might as well get out of your hair, Mr. Ballard."

"Sam."

"Sam," she agreed, then smiled apologetically. "Nice to meet you."

His mouth curled into the shadow of a smile. "I was just getting hungry. Any chance you'd like to share a pizza?" He nodded toward the Alfy's across the street.

She'd had more exciting offers. So why had her heart just skipped a beat? "I haven't exactly had dinner...." Her words trailed off, then she said impulsively, "Sure, what the heck. My house is empty, anyway. I wouldn't mind a bite to eat myself."

THE PIZZA PARLOR was romantically dim and blessedly silent without the teenagers who crowded it on Friday and Saturday nights. They agreed on a pile-everything-on pizza and took two mugs of beer to their table.

Rebecca was very conscious of the man who sat across from her. His eyes were shadowed, his strong cheekbones even more prominent in the flickering light from the candle that burned in a glass jar on their table. He was a big man, solid enough to dwarf her small frame.

She had a moment of panic, wondering what she had gotten herself into. For heaven's sake, what would they talk about? Chitchat didn't seem to be his style.

She was still racking her brains for a topic when he said, "I gather it's Alan's aunt who owns the cleaning business."

"Yes, my sister." As she always did when she was nervous, Rebecca rattled on. "Jess used to be a beautician. She always complained about being on her feet all day, so what does she do? Starts a housecleaning service." Rebecca shook her head. "But it's been a huge success. Do you have any idea how hard it is to get someone to clean your house who does a good job and is reliable? Not that I'd know. I can't afford it. But Jess tells me people would pay her the moon. Anyway, she hired another woman, then a couple more. Next thing I knew she'd expanded to janitorial service, like for you here. That's when Alan started working for her."

Rebecca finally shut up. God. Had she told him her whole life history?

"Anybody ever called you Becky?" he asked.

"Not and lived to tell about it," she replied, surprised at his question.

That very expressive dark eyebrow rose inquiringly.

"It's okay for a five year old, not for a grown woman. I mean, how would you like to go through life as Sammy?"

One corner of his mouth curled in a half smile. "I see what you mean. So tell me, what do you do for a living?"

She wondered what he would look like if he really smiled, or even laughed. *Did* he ever laugh?

"We're an entrepreneurial family," she said cheerfully. "One of my brothers has a treetopping service. You know, stump grinding and the whole shebang. And Lee has the auto-body shop on Third. Since I hate housecleaning and I couldn't quite see myself shinnying up trees, I rented a corner at Browder's Flooring and started selling wallpaper, then doing custom hanging, too. That went well, so I expanded into ceramic tile and window treatments. You know, blinds and valances and what have you. I enjoy my work."

"Interesting."

The work? Or her runaway mouth? But she could hardly ask: Instead she said, "How about you? How'd you get into the rental business?"

He shrugged. "About like you. When I was a teenager I mowed lawns for people, did yard work. Got enough money ahead to rent equipment to some of the guys who wanted to do the same. Next thing I knew..." He shrugged again.

His few brief sentences didn't exactly equal her family history but told her quite a bit nonetheless. It was a rare teenager who was so ambitious. Rebecca had always suspected that kind of drive showed a powerful need to assert independence. She wanted to ask more but didn't quite dare.

"Well, your store is a real boon to White Horse," she admitted. "I'm always needing some dumb thing I don't own, and who wants to buy a plumbing snake when you use it about once every ten years? If only you were open in the middle of the night or Sundays, when I really need you!"

He sounded wry when he said, "I work enough hours already."

"Surely you don't work until nine every night?"

"Near enough."

"You're not very talkative, are you?" she said. "And don't just raise your eyebrow at me."

Again his mouth twitched with humor. "All right," he said obligingly. "No, I guess I'm not."

"Why?" she asked.

He shrugged with a straight face. Then, at her expression, he grinned. His smile lit his eyes and carved lines in his cheeks. It was so wickedly sexy, so devastating, she was stunned. "You can smile," she said foolishly.

The smile faded until it had become a memory, but his eyes lingered on hers. "Umm." He glanced toward the kitchen. "That's our number."

Rebecca watched him slide out of the booth and walk over to the counter. He moved with the natural grace of an athlete, his long legs covering the distance in a few strides. She took pleasure in savoring the sight of him unobserved. She couldn't remember the last time she had so enjoyed just looking at a man.

That was when it occurred to her to wonder if he was married. If so, why had he asked her to share a pizza? Why had he smiled at her like that? No, scratch that, she thought ruefully. She doubted if he'd intended his smile to raise her blood pressure.

Over the pizza she continued to chatter. As a rule she didn't mind silence, not if she knew, or could take a decent guess at, what the other person was thinking. But she didn't have a clue about Sam Ballard, and she knew she'd be squirming if he sat quietly regarding her.

Besides, she was a talker. Maybe it came with having a large family. During her childhood silence had been a rare commodity. Somebody had always been in the mood to talk.

Rebecca couldn't tell if Sam minded. He chewed and nodded and interjected an occasional one- or two-word remark, which made her even more nervous and talkative.

When he nodded at her empty beer mug, she shook her head. "Thanks, but I'm not much for drinking. For one thing, it loosens what little restraint I have on my tongue. People think I'm drunk when I've had two beers.''

Amusement glinted in his eyes. ''Makes you want to talk, huh?''

She wrinkled her nose impudently. ''Whatever would make you think that?''

His mouth curled into that smile of astonishing sensuality and…sweetness. What an odd word to come to mind! she thought. Sam Ballard might be many things, but she doubted that sweet was one of them.

''Well, I'd better be getting home,'' she said. ''Alan will be there by now and wonder what happened to me.''

He didn't move. ''No other kids?''

''Just Alan.'' The words *I'm divorced* were on the tip of her tongue, but she managed to haul them back in. They would sound like a come-on if she'd ever heard one.

Then his eyes met hers. This was one of those crystal-clear moments when she knew something important was about to happen. ''Are you married?'' he asked.

Just as quietly, she answered, ''I've been divorced for three years. How about you?''

''Never married.''

''Well, my marriage was no great shakes,'' she admitted, ''but I wouldn't trade having Alan for anything, so I guess I don't regret it.''

Sam didn't comment, just said, ''Can I talk you into having dinner with me? Friday or Saturday night?''

One of those irresistible impulses grabbed Rebecca and she teased, ''Sure, go ahead. Talk me into it.''

It took him a second to remember what he'd said, then he smiled again. Rebecca's heart did a somersault. ''Please,'' he said softly, the rasp in his voice warming her blood a degree or two. ''Have dinner with me.''

She capitulated. ''I'd love to.''

"Good." He wasn't smiling now, but his voice was. "Maybe I'll talk you into two beers. Discover all your secrets."

"Why bother?" she said ruefully. "You know everything about me already."

His gaze flicked down to where the sweatshirt hid her curves, extra five pounds and all. "Not quite," he said without inflection.

He lifted his eyes to hers again and they looked at each other for an unnerving moment before Rebecca broke contact. "Really I've got to go," she babbled, grabbing her purse. "Thanks for the pizza. Here's my card—my home address is on the back."

"Six o'clock Friday evening?" he asked.

"Six is great. Alan may meet you with a shotgun, but you've got steady nerves, right?"

An eyebrow rose. "Your son doesn't like you dating?"

"Just kidding," she assured him, though she was far from sure how Alan *would* feel about her date with The Jerk. Would he understand?

She was still wondering when she got home. By the time she drove into the garage, Alan was standing with the kitchen door open.

"Where have you been?" he demanded. "The Jerk hold you hostage or something?"

"No, I just got a bite to eat," she said, edging past him to drop her purse on the maple kitchen table. "Besides, I didn't think he was so bad."

Alan followed her. "Give me a break. You didn't like him, did you?"

"As a matter of fact, I did." She faced him, chin up, wishing he weren't so much larger than she was. She often suffered from a feeling of disorientation. Where had that chunky little boy gone? Turned into a football player is where, she reminded herself.

"You *liked* him?"

"Gee, I seem to be repeating myself a lot lately. Yes, I liked him. He's very pleasant. Just kind of quiet."

"Quiet!" Alan shook his head in disbelief. "Next you're going to tell me he's shy."

"Well, that's a possibility, I guess." Rebecca took a deep breath, wishing she felt less like a teenager telling a stern father her plans. For all her effort at casualness, she sounded defiant when she said, "He asked me to dinner Friday night."

"Dinner!"

"Alan!"

"But jeez, Mom." He shoved fingers through his short hair, the same light brown as hers. His blue eyes were baffled. "You didn't say yes, did you?"

"Sure I did. Why shouldn't I?"

"But I've told you what a jerk he is—"

"A grown woman and a teenage boy have slightly different perspectives," she told him gently. "He's a very attractive man. In fact," she added, remembering her annoyance, "why didn't you *tell* me how handsome he is? How do you think I felt showing up in this?" Rebecca held out her arms.

Alan didn't pay any attention to her purple sweatshirt. *"Handsome!"*

She pretended to glower at him. "Has your vocabulary shrunk?"

Looking dazed, he shook his head and sank onto a kitchen chair. "I can't believe this is happening. I was sure you'd hate him."

"You were sure... Wait a minute." She grabbed his chin and lifted it so he had to meet her eyes. "What are you talking about?"

"Nothing!" She waited, and his eyes shifted uneasily. "I just... Well, I thought..."

"You thought..." she prompted.

"I just thought you'd see what a jerk Ballard is compared to Coach James," he said in a rush.

Rebecca released his chin and sank down herself into another chair. "But... why?"

He ducked his head and wouldn't look at her. "I just... I don't want you to be alone when I leave for college. And since you didn't seem to be doing anything about finding a husband, I thought maybe I'd help. But I don't want you to go out with Mr. Ballard! I mean, this evening was like a joke. You were just supposed to see..."

"Yes, so you said." She searched what was visible of his averted face. Right now he looked like the child she remembered, not the man he was becoming. Tenderness washed painfully over her, and she said softly, "It's too late for you to find another father, Alan."

Alan's head shot up. "What are you talking about? I don't want another father! I love Dad and... and he loves me! So don't try to suggest—"

"I'm sorry." She swallowed the lump in her throat and prayed she wouldn't cry. Rebecca had never hated her ex-husband more than at this moment. How could he disappoint Alan so? How could he not love his own son enough to meet his needs? For Alan's sake she lied, "That wasn't what I meant. It's just that you must wish your dad were here sometimes. Seeing him once in a while isn't the same."

She was horrified when he angrily wiped a tear off his cheek. "I do miss Dad," Alan confessed, his voice muffled.

"I know." Rebecca stood up and wrapped her arms around her son's broad shoulders, pressing a kiss to the top of his head. "I know, sweetie."

For just a moment he let her hold him, before he drew back and sniffed. "Don't call me 'sweetie' in front of the guys."

Rebecca gave a watery chuckle. "I wouldn't think of it."

They let the subject rest there, though Rebecca didn't put it out of her mind. Should she date Sam Ballard at all if Alan hated the idea so much? She reminded herself that she had a right to a life after her son was gone. She couldn't let a teenage boy determine what men she saw.

Besides, either Alan was wrong about Sam or she was. Either way, it would turn out okay.

ALAN WAS AWAY at the library the next evening when Rebecca's mother called, as she did every day or so. They had always been close, but even more so since her father's death four years earlier from a heart attack and then her own divorce. Left a single parent, she'd found it natural to turn to her mother for advice, a patient ear and an occasional hug, which she reciprocated often enough to keep her from feeling like a leech. She *needed* someone else, especially if she was to resist the temptation to treat Alan like another adult.

So she told her mother about The Jerk and the date she had agreed to. "I'm confused," she finished. "I don't want to make Alan mad, but..."

"Dear, I don't know that I'd even discuss a romantic involvement with him. It's really not his business. I'm surprised he thought it was."

"What do you suggest I do, not tell him where I'm going?"

"Well, of course you can't do that."

"The last thing I want is for him to answer the door Friday and be in for a surprise. He has pretty good manners, but I don't know if they're up to that big a challenge."

"Alan is a nice boy," her mother agreed. "In fact, has it occurred to you that he might be right about this—what did you say his name is?"

"Sam Ballard. And yes, of course it's occurred to me." Rebecca shifted to a more comfortable position in her overstuffed armchair. "But he's an attractive man. And there's only one way to find out, right?"

"I suppose so." Her mother sounded reserved. "Just don't jump into anything, Rebecca."

"You mean on the rebound?" Rebecca laughed. "Mom, I've been separated for four years, divorced for three. I've dated, what, six or eight times? This hardly qualifies as jumping."

"Just promise me you'll reserve judgment."

Rebecca rolled her eyes. "I promise."

"You're not going to bring this man Sunday, are you?"

"Of course not!" Rebecca was rarely so reminded that they were mother and daughter, not best friends. This was one of those times.

She changed the subject, hoping she wasn't being too obvious. Somehow this conversation hadn't helped her state of mind. She almost hoped she *didn't* enjoy Friday evening. Life would be simpler if she, too, decided Sam Ballard was a jerk.

CHAPTER THREE

THIS WAS THE HOUSE. Even in the dusk, Sam didn't need the address to confirm he'd found the right place. The boy's old Chevy in front worked like a sign, albeit a battered and faded one.

Sam half hoped the kid wouldn't be here. As teenagers went, Halstead was okay. He did the job as long as he had someone standing over him. At least he had been reliable about showing up, which was more than you could say for most employees.

Sam was the first to admit he didn't understand teenage boys, even though he'd been one himself. But he hadn't had the time to play jock or hang out at the pool hall. Hadn't wanted to spend the money for faddish clothes or music, either. What he made mowing lawns went right back into the business. It had worked for him then, and it worked for him now. So what did he have in common with a kid like Alan Halstead? Nothing, that's what.

Which made him wonder what he was doing, picking up the boy's mother for a date. He sure as hell wasn't interested in becoming Alan Halstead's stepfather. The house she and her son lived in pointed out the gulf between his life and theirs. The white clapboard structure was probably eighty years old. It had a certain charm, if you liked sagging front porches and wood-framed, single-pane windows that might as well be wide open on a cold day for all the warmth they held in. Sam didn't. He had never had any ambition to spend Sundays sanding old wood floors or shoring up rotting beams.

Well, he shouldn't jump to conclusions. Maybe the interior had been restored. He couldn't see the house that well in the gathering darkness. Hell, maybe Rebecca Halstead hated the place. It might even be a rental, though somehow he didn't think so.

Almost reluctantly, he got out of the car and walked up to the porch, which definitely listed. He knocked firmly on the solid front door, hoping Rebecca's face would be the one to appear in the oval, beveled glass.

It was, and when she opened the door he remembered immediately why he had asked her out. She wasn't a stunning beauty, which wouldn't have attracted him anyway. What she was, was vibrantly alive. And, he realized, she *was* pretty in a quiet sort of way. Her curly mane of hair was light brown threaded with something richer—maybe auburn or mahogany or gold. He'd had a powerful impulse to slide his fingers through it the minute she'd stepped into his store. Now he wondered if it was silky and if it would curl around his fingers.

Her eyes were wide and blue, full of intelligence, her lashes fair, so that her gaze seemed somehow defenseless. Her face was softly sculpted, with a gently rounded chin and small straight nose.

And then there was her body. He didn't let himself take more than one casual glance, though he wanted to. God, he wanted to. Tonight she wore a deep rose turtleneck dress that clung to her full breasts and curvaceous hips.

She was gazing expectantly at him, and he realized she must have greeted him. Damn. He felt like . . . With sudden amusement, he identified it. He felt like a teenage boy confronted with his erotic fantasy. Hell, maybe he understood teenagers after all.

"You're beautiful," he said simply.

Her eyes widened and she betrayed her self-consciousness by moistening her dry lips with her tongue. "Thank you. Why don't you come in."

He followed her through the hall and under an arch into a high-ceilinged living room, which he took in at a glance. The handsome molding had obviously been refinished, and the floor was gleaming maple. The windows begged for replacement, though, and a carved fireplace mantel desperately needed to be stripped of the layers of paint that had built up through the years.

He'd been right. She did spend her Sundays scraping paint and repairing plaster.

"Let me get my coat," she said, and disappeared back into the hall. He heard her call "Alan, I'm leaving now. Expect me when you see me."

When she returned with her coat, Sam helped her into it, trying not to think about her nearness. A moment later they were out the door, without—thank God—running into her son.

In his car, Sam turned to her as he started it. "La-Conner too far?"

"Heavens, no. What a nice idea."

Actually, he was starving, and wished he'd planned something closer. The picturesque small town of La-Conner was forty-five minutes away. What with problems at his Everett store, Sam had skipped lunch. If he had a decent assistant manager there, he'd be tempted to fire the manager. As it was, however, he had nobody ready to move up, which meant the one store was taking more time than he should spare from the others.

He'd sworn not to brood about it tonight, however. Once in a while even he needed a rest from work.

"No shotgun," he observed to Rebecca, who flashed him an impish smile.

"I hid it."

Sam braked at a stoplight. "Don't tell me the kid really has one."

This time she chuckled, a low delicious sound. "No, you're in luck. I hate guns, so I refused to let him have even a BB gun. Alan was mad about it a couple of years ago when his friends started hunting with their dads, but he's forgiven me."

Just to keep her talking he ventured, "His dad doesn't hunt?"

Her expression seemed to close, though she continued willingly enough. "He used to, which was a source of conflict between us, needless to say. He always made a big deal out of donating the meat to the food bank, as if hunting were some noble cause. Actually, I refused to cook it."

"You're a vegetarian?" Sam asked, ready to drastically alter his choice of restaurant.

She made a face. "I should be, I know that. I must sound like an awful hypocrite. But really, the meat wasn't the issue. It was the fact that Bruce's idea of a good time was killing something. I find that appalling." She darted a quick look at Sam. "Have I put my foot in it? Don't tell me you hunt."

He grinned, wondering how often she did put her foot in it. "Nah. Never appealed to me."

"So what do you do for fun?"

Fun? He went blank, which wasn't a good sign. Maybe he'd better take more time off this winter.

"Would you believe slaughter employees?" he asked with a wry smile.

"Well, Alan thinks so," she admitted.

"Does he really?"

"Boy, I have a big mouth," she said, sounding cheerfully repentant. "No, of course he doesn't. He just wishes...well, that you'd praise him more often. He doesn't think *you* think that he does a good job."

"He does fine," Sam said, surprised. "I'd chew him out if he didn't."

Rebecca slanted a stern look at him. "What a negative way to see things! Don't you ever thank people for doing something right or using their initiative?"

"Using their initiative, sure," he said defensively. "If they're just doing the job..." He shrugged. "That's what I pay them for."

She gave an indignant snort, which amused Sam, even as he was aware of how close to home this conversation struck. Was she actually criticizing him? Did she take what a sixteen-year-old kid said that seriously?

"Honest to goodness," she said. "Don't you like to hear praise?"

"At work? The balance sheet is praise enough for me."

Like a pit bull with something in its teeth, Rebecca stuck to it. "What about the rest of the time? I liked having you tell me I was beautiful. Don't you like compliments?"

He couldn't remember the last time he'd heard one. "I'm not beautiful."

"You're a hunk," she said matter-of-factly. "I could hardly believe Alan's boss looked the way you do."

He damn near blushed. He didn't know whether to be flattered or stunned. Did she mean it? Where the hell did she get the confidence that allowed her to say something like that?

"You ever been shy?" he asked.

Again she chuckled. "Yep. When I went to pick up Alan the other night. I was dumbstruck. I kept thinking, why didn't Alan *tell* me? I'd have dressed to the nines."

"You didn't have to," Sam said. "Nothing like tight jeans and an oversize shirt to make a man want to know what's under it."

He couldn't tell whether she was blushing in turn, but for once he'd momentarily silenced her.

But she didn't sound even the least bit ruffled when she admitted, "The jeans wouldn't be tight if it wasn't for that five pounds I keep swearing to lose."

"I'll bet you wouldn't find a man who thinks you ought to lose it."

"Don't say that until you've seen me—" She clapped a hand over her mouth. "Never mind."

Naked. He had no trouble finishing the sentence. *Until he'd seen her naked.* Just like that he was hard. He wanted to do a hell of a lot more than see her.

"That a promise?" he asked, his voice rough.

"I didn't mean it. I mean, it just slipped out.... Oh, God. Now I've done it."

The casual touches people used to communicate didn't come easily to Sam, but without thinking he reached out and took her hand in his. "Hey. Don't worry. I was kidding. But you know something?"

She curled her fingers trustingly around his. "What?"

"I'll bet I'll like every pound of you then, too."

"I think that's the sweetest thing anybody has ever said to me," Rebecca announced. "Now if you can just think of something sweet to say to Alan the next time you see him..."

Sam released her hand. "Incorrigible," he muttered.

"Alan?"

"Nope. You."

"Stubborn," she said, that smile in her voice. "He's a nice kid. Tell him so."

Sam grunted.

DINNER WAS A JOY. Rebecca couldn't remember when she'd liked anybody, man or woman, so much. Of course, she did most of the talking, but Sam didn't mind, she could tell. And he had a sense of humor! How many men really had one? Especially concerning themselves?

She'd noticed before that women's humor tended to be self-deprecating, men's egotistical. Women laughed at themselves, men at each other. Or maybe she was prejudiced.

She'd tried to teach her son to see the humor in his own mistakes, which might be one reason he was more pleasant to live with than the average teenage boy. He didn't automatically assume the world had ended because he had humiliated himself. Well, maybe for an hour or two he thought so, then he realized he'd live. Usually by dinnertime he could tell her about whatever had happened and even laugh a little.

She had hoped he would get over his anger about her going out with Sam by the time she actually did, but so far no cigar. He had admitted to the razzing he had earned by taking her to the father/son banquet, though. Screwball as the whole idea of setting her up with his football coach had been, Rebecca was glad Alan had had the confidence to try it. How many sixteen-year-old boys would have taken their mothers, whatever their motive?

Now all she had to do was figure out a way to reconcile him to Sam's presence in her life, she decided on the way home. Assuming he would *be* in her life. And she was pretty sure he would. She'd be able to tell for sure from their parting.

If he didn't kiss her at all . . . Well, that meant so long, I have your phone number, but don't hold your breath. On the other hand, if he proved too determined to see those extra five pounds, then he wasn't the man for her. She thought that was unlikely. It was awfully hard to picture this dark, self-contained man grappling with a reluctant woman in the cramped confines of a car.

The kiss would have to have a certain fervency, however, to convince her of his sincerity. The car was dark, but she sneaked a glance at his profile. Would he be passionate? Tender? Gentle? Rough? Or would he be as guarded physically as she suspected he was emotionally?

The anticipation was almost killing her. She was glad they had lapsed into silence, because it was a little hard to think of light conversation when her mind had jumped about five minutes ahead.

Rebecca was hardly ever nervous, but by the time Sam turned the car into her driveway and switched off the engine, her heart was drumming in her ears. Alan had left some downstairs lights on for her. She only wished the porch light reached the driveway better. She could barely make out Sam's face through the shadows.

"Would you like to come in for coffee?" she asked, too quickly.

"In a minute."

"In a—" Her voice died when he cupped her chin and he slid his fingers through her hair. How had he moved without her realizing it?

She still couldn't see him well enough to judge his expression, but that hint of humor was in his voice, edged with something darker. "I'd just as soon not have an audience."

"Audience?" Lord. She was starting to sound like her son.

Sam brushed his thumb over her lips. "Maybe he borrowed a shotgun."

She'd have said "Shotgun?" just as inanely, if her lips had been willing to cooperate. But the sensations awakened by the rough pad of his thumb on her lower lip were too overwhelming. If Alan had appeared right this second with that gun, she'd have turned it on him for interrupting them. She wanted Sam Ballard to kiss her as she had never wanted anything else.

He bent his head so slowly she could have screamed. That hard, sexy mouth touched hers gently, even tentatively. What it did to her was shocking. She was so flooded with heat and hunger, she almost shuddered with pleasure.

Rebecca never knew how she responded, whether her lips parted or she sagged against him or what, but suddenly he wasn't gentle. Or tentative. He was thorough, passionate, sensual. He nipped her, tasted her, savored her. One hand cupped the back of her head where his fingers tangled in her curly hair. The other gripped her shoulder and pulled her closer.

Whereupon she bumped against the gear stick. There was no way to get closer to him. His mouth stilled, then his fingers tightened on her upper arm in a spasm of frustration before he lifted his head and made a sound somewhere between a groan and a muttered, "Just as well."

Shaken, Rebecca struggled to collect herself. Good Lord. She'd been necking as mindlessly as some teenager, and outside her own house! Horror of horrors, what if Alan had seen her?

"Do you, umm, still want that coffee?" she asked in a voice she didn't recognize. Too late, she realized how some men would take that.

She needn't have worried. He said dispassionately, "I'm not sure that's a good idea. I'll walk you to the door, though."

Perversely, that annoyed her. Why not a good idea? Did Sam mean the obvious or that he wasn't interested?

Damn it, she was too old to suffer these agonies of uncertainty. She'd forgotten how miserable falling in love was.

Except, thank God, she wasn't falling in love yet. It was too soon. She hardly knew the man. He wasn't even nice to her son!

"I don't think I'll get mugged on my way to the front door," she assured him, feeling more like herself.

"I know you won't if I walk you."

A gentleman. She wasn't sure whether that was a good thing or a hindrance. She *was* glad to see that he showed no annoyance when she hopped out of the car without waiting for him to open the door. He followed her without comment up the walk.

On the porch Rebecca tried the front door, and found it locked. "My keys are here somewhere," she said, opening her purse. In the two over-stuffed compartments, she found everything but the keys. She was about to delve further, when the door opened and a stream of light fell across Sam's face.

"Is that you, Mom?" The words were okay; it was the accusatory tone that made Rebecca wonder guiltily if her lipstick was smeared and whether Alan had heard the car pull into the driveway—how long ago?

"Of course it's me," she said. "You didn't have to wait up."

"I was just reading." Alan stared hard at Sam.

Sure he was. Just like she was reading the nights he was out and she sat waiting for him to be safely home, tensing if she heard a siren in the distance.

Sam nodded. "Alan."

"Mr. Ballard."

Rebecca prayed Sam couldn't interpret her son's voice the way she could. Alan was being scrupulously polite— and very snotty.

Rebecca gazed meaningfully at her son. "Well, let me say good-night to Sam." When Alan didn't move right away, she grimaced. "Scoot!"

He looked incredulous but, with obvious reluctance, withdrew into the living room.

Rebecca rolled her eyes and turned back to Sam. "I'm sorry. The perils of parenthood. Listen, are you sure you don't want that cup of coffee?"

"No, thank you." His gray eyes were hooded, his mouth unrevealing. He'd retreated again behind that imperturbable facade. She wondered if she had imagined how thoroughly it had cracked when he'd kissed her. "I'll let you go reassure your son."

"Ha! I wish I could pay him back for a few nights when he was two hours past his curfew."

The corner of Sam's mouth lifted ever so slightly. "There's always next time."

Would there *be* a next time? Rebecca schooled the part of her that wanted to ask when. "Right," she said. "Well, thank you, Sam. I enjoyed myself."

He didn't even look behind her to see where Alan was, just took a step forward across the doorjamb, lifted her chin and kissed her. Not long or passionately, but for a second she felt the sexual tension humming through him.

Then he said in a low, rough voice, "I did, too. I'll call."

Just like that, he was gone.

EXCEPT FOR THE BLUE EYES, Alan had gotten his looks from his father. Dad was getting a little soft around the middle, though, Alan noticed.

"Sorry I missed last week," Bruce Halstead said as he and Alan got into the shiny red pickup truck. "Things at work were hellish."

"It's okay," Alan replied. What else could he say? Excuses like that had worked on him the first year or so. Now he wondered who his dad was dating. She must be more interesting than he was.

That made Alan remember who his *mother* was dating, which gave him a funny feeling, as though a hole had just opened where his heart had been. He didn't know why having his mother date The Jerk bothered him more than his father seeing some woman he didn't like. It just did.

His father didn't start the engine right away. He rested his hands on the wheel and jovially asked, "Well, what shall we do today? Do you want to go throw the football around?"

"Sure," Alan answered. Once his dad had started the pickup, Alan continued, "I took my skis to get 'em tuned this week. If there's enough snow, maybe we could go skiing Thanksgiving weekend."

"I've been meaning to talk to you about that," his father said. "I've made some plans to be out of town for Thanksgiving. Can we make it up the next weekend?"

That hole where Alan's heart should have been yawned wider, and Alan said quickly, "Yeah, sure. I guess. Does Mom know?"

"I haven't mentioned it to her."

"What if she's busy?"

His father laughed. "You kidding? What would she be doing?"

"She's dating some guy."

There was a moment of silence. "Anybody I know?"

"Nah. He owns those rental stores. You know, White Horse? I clean the one in town when I work for Aunt Jess."

"He's got big bucks, huh?"

"I guess," Alan said unhappily. "He's a jerk."

His father didn't look very interested. Didn't it *bother* him that Mom might sleep with some guy, or even get married again?

"Maybe you just need to get to know him." His dad edged the pickup into a parking spot at the city playing field. "C'mon, let's grab that football."

The day was gray and chilly. Alan had worn a hooded sweatshirt and gloves with finger cutouts, but his father wasn't dressed as warmly.

They jogged out into the middle of the grassy playing field, then his dad cocked the football and said, "Run a two-three pattern. Let's see if this old arm can still put it out there."

Alan ran, cut and turned just in time to meet the ball, a perfect spiral that settled into his hands as neat as a girl's tits. That was one of his dad's sayings that Mom hadn't liked, Alan remembered.

The next time his father ran a pattern and he threw the ball, then they reversed again. There was a rhythm to it, a mindless beat that soothed Alan, let him forget about Ballard and about his father's plans for Thanksgiving. It was as though he were a child again, eight or nine, and he and his father were out here three or four times a week. Dad would talk about his football playing days, then show Alan how to hold the ball, how to flick his wrist for that spiral, how to cradle the ball against his chest so he couldn't be stripped of it.

Running and catching, throwing the ball so that it arced against the gray sky, Alan could almost forget the way things were. He could almost forget that his father had missed the past two visits, that he hadn't asked about the father/son banquet or what awards Alan had won. He could almost forget the glow in his mother's eyes and the way her hair had been messed up and her lipstick smeared when she'd come home the night before.

Almost, but not quite.

WHEN THE TELEPHONE rang, Alan yelled, "I'll get it."

Standing on a ladder in the living room, changing a light bulb, Rebecca thought, why not? The calls were all for her son, anyway. She felt like a living, breathing, answering machine most of the time. Alan had been holding out for call waiting, but so far Rebecca had resisted. *She* was the one who'd be interrupted every five minutes.

Finished, she had started down the ladder when Alan appeared in the doorway.

"Mom." His voice had changed. "It's for you."

"Is something wrong?" she asked, alarmed.

His mouth curled into a typical teenage sneer. "What could be wrong? My jerk of a boss is chasing my mother, that's all."

She said automatically, "Don't talk to me like that," but her tone lacked enough sternness. She was too happy to hear that the caller was Sam. It had been almost a week, and she had begun to question her own judgment. Had he really kissed her that way? Had his eyes darkened, his voice roughened, his hands caressed?

Now she passed Alan, who didn't move, and picked up the phone in the kitchen. "Hello?"

"Rebecca? This is Sam."

"Hi, how are you?" She could feel her son's gaze on her back, but she refused to let him intimidate her.

"Fine. You?"

"I'm just great. I was changing a light bulb and looking at all the dust on top of the moldings. I had to tear myself away when the phone rang."

He chuckled. "Listen, I was wondering..." Uncharacteristically, he hesitated. "You ever been to the Home Show at the King Dome?"

"The only thing I like better is the Flower and Garden Show," she said, meaning it.

"It starts tomorrow," Sam said. "We have a booth there. I wanted to see how things are going, check out the new tools. Any chance I could talk you into coming with me?"

Smiling, she said, "Sure. Go ahead."

There was a startled pause before Sam laughed again. "'Please' worked for me the last time."

"I'm a sucker for it. I'd love to go, Sam."

They arranged a time and agreed to have dinner in Seattle on the way home afterward. Rebecca hung up the telephone and turned to face Alan, who still stood silently in the doorway.

She raised her eyebrows. "I don't listen to your conversations."

"I can't believe you're going to see him again," he burst out.

Rebecca groped for a way to make him see her point of view. "Alan... He's an attractive man. I like what I've seen of him. Maybe he's not a good supervisor. I don't know. He didn't ask me to work for him."

"But—" Alan stopped.

"But what?"

"I don't like him!"

The wail made him sound young and vulnerable. She walked over, stood on tiptoe and kissed her son's rigid jaw. "I know. But, Alan, all I'm doing is going out with the man. It's not as though he's asked me to marry him. Right now, my dating Sam has nothing to do with you. Can you understand that?"

"No!" He slammed his fist against the door frame, swore and stormed out. The front door crashed shut behind him.

Rebecca watched him go, her buoyancy swamped by frustration and guilt. What was it about Sam that upset Alan so? Or was it really Sam who bothered him? Maybe he just hated the idea of his mother dating at all. More to the point, was she wrong to ignore his feelings?

Alan was the most important person in her life. Did she dare risk her relationship with her son just to see a man she really didn't know very well?

She knew the answer, even if she wasn't sure it was the right one. *Yes.* Sam made her feel like a woman again, not just a mother, a daughter and a breadwinner. She *needed* this. And if that was selfish, well, so be it. Didn't she have a right to be, once in a while?

CHAPTER FOUR

"ANYBODY EVER TELL YOU that you're a restful woman?"

"Restful?" The comment had come out of left field. Rebecca looked at Sam. "You're kidding."

He turned his attention from the freeway long enough for her to meet his eyes and see the faint twitch of his lips. "I don't kid."

She couldn't resist. "You're kidding."

This time his smile was full-blown and devastatingly sexy. "I might find it catching around you."

"Good," she said, before adding hopefully, "you really think I'm restful? Even if I talk all the time?"

"Sure." He looked over his shoulder before changing lanes. They were passing Northgate and the traffic was heavy, even though it was Saturday. "You're..." Uncharacteristically, he hesitated. "Content," he said finally. "That makes you undemanding."

Rebecca blinked. "I guess I am," she admitted. "Life isn't treating me too badly, even if my ex-husband is a jerk."

"If you were still married to him, that might be a problem."

"Umm," she agreed. "I worry about Alan, though. He *needs* his father, and Bruce can't seem to see that. When he has time, he shows up. When he doesn't, he makes excuses. Sometimes I wish Alan were a girl. Maybe his father wouldn't matter as much to him then. What do you think?"

Sam uttered a brief, almost harsh laugh. "I don't have kids, remember?"

"But you were one."

"I'm not so sure," he said cryptically.

Rebecca remembered wondering what had driven Sam at such a young age to be so ambitious. Escape from a miserable childhood?

"Do you have any sisters?" she asked.

"Two brothers."

She wanted to know more, but his expression was shuttered, and she had a feeling further questions weren't welcome. Well, surely sooner or later he would talk about his family and youth. How could he avoid it, when she was so close to her family that she seemed to talk about them constantly?

"Oh, well," she said. "If Alan were a girl, I'd have different problems. And really, he's a good kid. It's just that lately—" She stopped. Sam couldn't possibly be interested. After all, he'd known Alan for—how many months?—and had apparently never asked a single personal question.

"Never mind," she said. "Tell me, have you ever exhibited in the Home Show before?"

Sam shook his head. "Figured we'd give it a try once. See what effect it has on business."

"Will you be able to tell if it does?"

"Probably not statistically. But sometimes customers mention where they've heard of us." He shrugged and glanced over his shoulder as he changed lanes again. "I'll have a gut feeling about it."

"And here I thought you'd be all hardheaded calculations," Rebecca teased. "Do you tell your store managers you just have a feeling something will work?"

She had earned another crooked smile. "Hell, no. Why should I explain myself?"

Rebecca rolled her eyes. "Have you ever considered taking a seminar on interpersonal relationships and making employees feel good about themselves?"

He shot her a half amused, half irritated glance. "That touchy-feely crap isn't my style."

"Oh, I don't know, I think you touch and feel rather nicely," she said, straight-faced.

When he looked at her again, the amusement was still there. The irritation had shifted into something considerably more gratifying. Desire. "Thanks," he said. "I think."

"You're welcome," she assured him. "By the way, aren't you going to get off the freeway?"

"Damn," he muttered, and cut across two lanes of traffic to make the exit.

"Gee, you drive just like Alan," Rebecca observed, prying her fingers from the seat as the car slowed for a red light ahead. "Is it a masculine trait?"

"Maybe it's you."

"Because I drive you crazy?"

He was almost smiling. "Something like that."

A traffic cop directed them into the huge parking lot that surrounded the King Dome. The concrete monolith was home to the Seattle Seahawks, the professional football team. Rebecca let Sam concentrate on finding a parking place. He passed one empty spot, which he apparently considered too narrow. She supposed he didn't want to put his elegant gray Mercedes at risk, for which she couldn't blame him.

When he finally parked and locked up, they joined the stream of people heading into the Dome. Inside was color and noise. Rebecca smiled her thanks at a man handing out maps. "Where's your booth?" she asked Sam.

"We're number eighty-nine."

She scanned the map. "That looks like a good location. You ought to catch people before they're too tired."

Sam grunted. "Anything special you want to see?"

Rebecca smiled. "Everything. This qualifies as business for me, too, remember."

He quirked a brow. "I'd forgotten. I don't suppose you want to see the new tools."

"Or you the latest color in blinds." At his expression, she laughed. "Why don't we play leapfrog? You stop at the booths that interest you, then catch up with me. And vice versa."

He gave a brief nod. "You got it."

Actually, it was all they could do to keep track of each other. The aisles were jam-packed with crowds admiring the latest in hot tubs, bay windows and patio furniture. Glad she'd had the foresight to bring a shoulder bag, Rebecca took notes and collected pamphlets like mad. She loved the new line of pleated shades that looked like lace, and some wood valances that ranged from sleekly modern to country style with carvings of roses. Wood blinds were making a comeback, she noticed.

"Found anything interesting?" she asked Sam during a brief rendezvous.

He shrugged. "A couple of new sanders. And what do you think of a chimney vacuum with brushes? Would you clean your own chimney if you could rent the equipment?"

"Nope," she said cheerfully. "But that's not to say some people wouldn't. Did you see those wallpaper steamer removers? Now, I bet that'd go over big."

"I think most people slap one layer on top of the last."

"Unfortunately." She wrinkled her nose at him. "I guess steaming off wallpaper fits in the same category as cleaning your own chimney."

"There's my booth," he said. "If you want to go on, I'll catch up with you."

"Heck, no," Rebecca said. "I have every intention of admiring the latest in rental equipment. And I'm not alone," she added as they squeezed in.

A plump woman pushing a baby carriage was saying, "I didn't know you could rent a carpet stretcher. I'll bet we could have saved hundreds of dollars putting in our own carpet! Look, Pete, we could have rented a miter saw, too. I wonder if one of these stores is near us?" Her husband followed as she wandered over, still exclaiming, to pick up White Horse Rentals literature.

Rebecca poked Sam. "You're a hit."

"I am if she ever bothers to rent anything."

Rebecca pretended to study the tools on display while she eavesdropped on Sam's conversation with the employee manning his booth.

"How's it going?"

"Busy," the other man said just as tersely. He nodded at the glossy catalogs, which listed the equipment available and rental prices per day. "Our price lists are going faster than you expected. Hope our supply holds up."

"I'll make another trip down and bring more if you run low," Sam said. "Can you handle the morning shift tomorrow on your own?"

"Sure. One more body in here and I couldn't breathe, anyway."

"All right," Sam said. "Call if you need anything."

Rebecca joined them. "Hi, you look familiar. Don't you manage the store in White Horse?"

The tall, thin man smiled. "You bet. Hey, you have a son on the football team, don't you? My boy's a wide receiver. Chuck Heller."

"Of course!" Rebecca said in delight. "That was quite a catch he made against Snohomish. He almost pulled off a touchdown."

He shook his head. "Even another TD wouldn't have changed the end result. Snohomish was a powerhouse this year."

"Chuck's graduating, isn't he?"

"Yeah, got a scholarship to the University of Washington. What about your boy?"

"He has another year. He isn't sure where he wants to go then."

"Tough choice. Recruiters will be all over him."

"I'll tell him you said so." Rebecca smiled, conscious of Sam's silent presence behind her. "The booth looks great. You make me want to dive into half a dozen projects."

"We seem to be popular," he agreed. "Well, heck, enjoy the show."

"You, too."

Sam nodded curtly to the man, and he and Rebecca rejoined the flow of traffic. Without talking, they passed several booths that interested neither. Sneaking a look at Sam's frowning countenance, Rebecca asked, "Cat got your tongue?"

He barely glanced at her. "Nothing to say."

Now frowning herself, Rebecca dodged a toddler on a leash. Was Sam annoyed with her? But what on earth could she have done? Kept his manager chatting while potential customers waited?

Abruptly he said, "Your way takes longer than mine."

"What?" Rebecca stopped, and immediately somebody ran into her. Sam's large hand steadied her. "What are you talking about?"

"I figured you were giving me a lesson in how to give compliments."

"You're kidding." Rebecca rolled her eyes. "No, of course you're not. You never kid. Sam . . ."

"Forget it," he said brusquely. "Come on. We don't want to miss anything."

She dug in her heels. "I was being friendly. No more, no less."

"Then I'm out of line."

"Sam, I love to talk! Haven't you noticed? What's more, I say what I think." She held his gaze through sheer determination. "Alan would like it if you gave him a few compliments. He's a kid—he needs reassurance. I wouldn't dream of telling you how to run your business!"

His eyes were dark and steady. At last one corner of his mouth lifted, and his voice held a hint of humor. "You sure?"

"Well . . . If you asked for advice, maybe pleaded a little . . ."

He took her arm again and drew her into step with him. Her hip bumped his and she felt a delicious surge of warmth. Damn, he was sexy!

"Okay," Sam said, "then tell me what to do with a manager who can't do his job but whose family would be in a hell of a spot if I fired him."

Rebecca frowned with quick concern. "You make me glad I don't have any employees. Can you demote him to a job he *can* do?"

"Hell, I don't have anybody else who is up to managing, either. I'll worry about it when I do."

"I'm a big help."

"It's not your problem," he said dismissively.

The subject was obviously closed. Had he really wanted to talk about his problem, Rebecca wondered, or had that been Sam's way of letting her know she was out of her league?

And why was she spending so much time agonizing over what this man was thinking? If she did something that bugged him, he could say so. If he didn't like the way her mouth ran on, he wouldn't ask her out again. In the meantime, she was determined to quit reading shades of emotion into his every word.

"I want to stop at this wood refinishing place," she announced. "I've absolutely got to tackle my fireplace mantel, but with that carving it's going to be a horrible job. Who knows, maybe there's a brand-new miracle product."

"Good luck," he said. "I'll take a look at the lawn mowers."

Rebecca nodded and then plunged into conversation with a young woman who was the sales rep for a new line of stains and wood strippers. A few minutes later she stuffed their handout into her bag and turned to catch up with Sam. She spotted him in the distance. Head bent, he was listening to what the lawn-mower salesman was saying, and for just a moment Rebecca saw him as if he were a stranger. He had a presence that was impossible not to notice, an unsmiling, contained strength that scared Rebecca a little. The set of his broad shoulders and the hard planes of his face admitted no vulnerability. Did he feel compassion for those less capable? Was he the kind of man who would ever admit to needs of his own?

The crowd pushed her inexorably toward him. His expression was aloof, polite, and then he caught sight of her.

His smile warmed his face astonishingly, and Rebecca's heart skipped a beat. How could a woman resist a man who reacted like that to her?

And how could she explain that one to her son?

"Running out of steam?" Sam asked.

Rebecca firmly quelled her response. "I could go either way. Didn't you want to see more?"

Sam shrugged. "I glanced around when we were setting up. I don't like fighting a crowd."

"It's pretty stuffy," she agreed. "Well, if you're ready to wine and dine me . . ."

Only his eyes were smiling now. "And I said you weren't demanding."

She wrinkled her nose. "I didn't say it couldn't be at Burger King."

"Last I heard, they didn't serve wine." He deftly steered her toward the nearest exit.

"A little wine makes me dangerous," she reminded him.

The sidelong glance he threw her in response held more heat than she'd been near in years. "You tempt me," he said gruffly.

Good, she thought, but had the sense not to say it. After all, he might appreciate subtlety. Of course, if he did he'd quickly discover he'd come to the wrong woman.

And what a depressing thought that was.

FAST FOOD, her dinner wasn't. Sam took her to a tiny, out-of-the way Hungarian restaurant with goulash to die for. It reminded her of the homey little places in southern Europe where you could inspect the food cooking in the hot kitchen before you made your selection.

"Have you ever traveled?" she asked Sam.

He shook his head. "No time."

Rebecca cocked her head sternly and gestured with her spoon. "You're supposed to *make* time. It's required for good mental health, you know."

"Does my mental health seem poor to you?"

"Umm..." The red wine she sipped was causing her head to buzz pleasantly. "I think working until nine every night indicates you're slightly deranged. You're supposed to pay people to do that."

"You've never worked long hours?"

"All too often," she admitted. "But having a kid changes things. I need to have time for Alan, too."

Sam nodded. "Does he appreciate it?"

"Probably not," she answered honestly, "but he will when he's grown up. That's the theory, anyway." She wrinkled her nose. "Talk about delayed gratification."

A ghost of some powerful emotion flickered across Sam's face but disappeared before she could interpret it. "Would you like dessert?" he said impassively.

"Heavens, no!" She put her napkin beside her plate. "I've probably already gained another pound. But thank you, Sam. This was a wonderful dinner."

"I'm glad you liked it." He signaled for the check.

It was no surprise to Rebecca that the waiter quickly responded. She doubted that anyone ever ignored Sam Ballard.

During the drive home they talked desultorily, discussing nothing especially important, yet Rebecca had the impression Sam was a driven man. He saw a movie occasionally, admitted to reading only at bedtime, swam laps at the YMCA for recreation—and she'd bet those weren't leisurely ones.

"You'll drop dead of a heart attack at forty-five if you're not careful," she said, summing up her reflections.

In the dark car she couldn't see his expression, but he sounded wry. "That's what the swimming is supposed to prevent."

"Try relaxing. You need a hobby. Two weeks sailing in the San Juan Islands. Sunbathing at Maui." She ignored his muttered comment that he would just die of boredom. "Take the Orient Express. I don't know." She gestured extravagantly. "Collect comic books. Do *something* fun!"

"I *am* doing something fun. I took you to dinner."

"Combined with business."

Now he sounded surprised. "Did you mind?"

"Nope." Feeling bold and loving it, Rebecca reached over and took his hand, which had rested loosely on the steering wheel. She was heartened when he lifted her hand to his mouth and brushed it with a light kiss. Breathlessly she finished, "I can't think of anything I would have enjoyed more."

"Good." His voice was huskier than usual. "Though I can think of a thing or two."

Rebecca tried to sound provocative. It might have worked, if her squeaky voice hadn't given her away. "Like the Orient Express?"

"What do you think?" he said with a growl.

"I think I can hardly wait until you kiss me good-night."

"God, woman. You *will* have me driving like a teenager."

What was it she'd told herself about subtlety? Oh, well, she decided, cheered by his response. He didn't sound like a man who enjoyed the hunt and hated having a woman relinquishing her role as prey. Rebecca hadn't known that was how Bruce viewed a relationship between a man and a woman until far too late. She must have been shyer in those days, not confident enough to express her interest in him frankly. And by the time she *was* confident enough, her marriage had hit the skids. There were apparently lots of women out there who liked hearing teeth snapping at their heels.

When Sam steered the Mercedes into her driveway, he said flatly, "Your son's waiting up again."

Yellow light streamed from every window, including rooms Alan normally never entered. Rebecca sighed. "What was your first clue?"

"Is he trying to light your way home?"

"So I wouldn't get lost in the blizzard?" Damn it, what *was* Alan up to? Did he think Sam wouldn't kiss her if he felt too exposed?

Thank heavens, Sam sounded no more than thoughtful. "Maybe he's hunting for the shotgun."

Rebecca made no move to get out of the car. She didn't quite know how to ask, but she threw caution to the winds and plunged in. "How are you, uh, getting along at work? Is Alan being obnoxious?"

Sam laid an arm along the back of her seat. Rebecca could just feel his fingers brush her nape. Tingles tiptoed down her spine. "I didn't see him this week. I was busy at another store."

"Oh." Rebecca's mind felt cloudy, slow moving. Wine and sexual attraction had a way of doing that. "Not that I mean to imply that Alan would *be* obnoxious. Really, he's a good kid...."

"You keep saying that."

Sam caressed the back of her neck. His fingertips were warm, the skin a little rough, but his touch very gentle. Rebecca got goose bumps.

"I guess I've been waiting for you to argue," she said, her voice a wisp of its usual self.

Sam bent his head toward her. Huskily he asked, "Does he ever go anywhere?"

"Far, far away? Oh. You mean, like at night. Well, sometimes. There's his father.... And once in a while he stays with a buddy or one of his cousins. And there are always a few basketball tournaments. And..."

"Good."

Then Sam's mouth covered hers with passionate finality. If she had had a train of thought, he had just kicked it off the tracks. Lord, the man knew how to kiss! He was just gentle enough to render her defenseless, just demanding enough to send her blood pressure soaring. She forgot she even *had* a son about the time she heard Sam groan and he suddenly shifted his grip to better plunder her mouth. One of his big hands was under her arm, and his thumb made restless circles achingly close to her breast.

When she felt his teeth on her lower lip, Rebecca nipped him back. When his tongue slid sensuously into her mouth, her own fought back. She wriggled in an effort to get closer, let her head fall against his shoulder when his mouth traveled hotly along her jaw, down the vulnerable line of her throat. She wanted to rip her dress open, tear off her bra. Her nerve ends were screaming "Please!"

And damn the man, that's when he stopped. His mouth stilled against the soft skin at the base of her throat; he groaned again and lifted his head. "Unless you're feeling reckless," he said roughly, "it's probably time you go in and reassure that kid of yours."

The reminder of her son was less than welcome. She didn't want to be a mother right this second; she wanted to be a woman. She wanted to feel a man's weight above her, his mouth on her breasts, his hands everywhere.

Instead she had to face Alan's accusing gaze.

Sam released her. Sitting up, Rebecca groped for her purse and tried to regain her lost poise. "I, umm, had a nice time," she said. "The restaurant was wonderful, and the Home Show..."

"What about the kiss?" Sam asked.

Rebecca opened her car door before she let herself be reckless. "That was the best part," she said, and fled for safety. Assuming her house, which looked lit for an inquisition, could be called safety.

The slam of the driver's-side door told her Sam was right behind her. She could *feel* him behind her, with every one of those aroused nerve endings.

Gee, she thought, with the first spark of amusement she'd felt in a while, maybe she liked having a man nipping at her heels, after all!

On the doorstep, Sam grasped her upper arms and turned her to face him. "One for the road," he murmured, and kissed her hard. Then he was gone, leaving her to face the music.

JESS AND COMPANY were the first to arrive that Sunday. Rebecca was relieved to see that her sister's husband wasn't with her and her preteen daughters. Rebecca had never been able to put her finger on what she didn't like about Roy. The man had enough charm to thicken gravy, but somehow she'd never warmed to him. She'd seen her sister's increasing tension lately, which made Rebecca look with more disfavor on the husband she thought was at fault. Jess didn't talk about her marriage much, but Rebecca was pretty sure it was in trouble.

"Hey," Jess said as she hopped out of the red van that usually bulged with vacuum-cleaner attachments, long-handled window squeegees and the like. "I hear you're dating a hot prospect."

Rebecca strolled out to meet her sister and nieces. "Well, that depends whose viewpoint you're looking at him from."

"Yours is the only one that counts." Jess's short dark hair was a curly mop to match the ones she cleaned with. Her blue eyes sparkled now, which they hadn't much lately.

"Try that one on Alan," she said, and gave her sister a hug.

"Yeah, he's always threatening to quit on me if I don't rescue him from the dragon. Me, I wouldn't mind being trapped in a dungeon with a dragon who looks like that."

"How come you never mentioned what a hunk he is?" Rebecca asked before she hugged her two dark-haired nieces, one of whom was—shudder—getting breasts, a fact that made Rebecca raise her eyebrows as Stephanie slouched into the house.

"Did I see what I think I saw?"

"Yeah, but don't you dare mention it!" Jess whispered. "I *made* her wear something besides her usual oversize sweatshirt today. She's ready to *die* if anybody notices that her body has decided to do its thing. If Alan says a word..."

"I'll string him up myself," Rebecca promised. "I'm in the mood to do that, anyway."

"He's being a pain in the butt?"

"To put it mildly."

Jess shook her head. "Don't let him win. Remember how soon he'll be gone."

"I keep telling myself that." Rebecca glanced past her sister. "Oh, here's Lee and family. And Mom's with them."

Amid the general greetings, Jess and Rebecca became separated. Still, Rebecca cocked an ear when their mother asked, "Where are the girls? And Roy?"

"Steph and Sarah are inside," Jess said casually. Too casually, Rebecca decided. "Roy's still tinkering with that stupid transmission, and finally decided he was too dirty and grumpy to come."

Nobody commented, though the once a month Sunday dinners were sacred. No member of the family missed one without a damn good excuse. Working on a car didn't cut it.

But, then, nobody was sorry Roy *wasn't* here.

Joe, Rebecca's one unmarried brother, showed up soon after. He was the treetopper, a big man whose lazy charm and business acumen disguised the vulnerability beneath. He'd had a rough time in school, and Rebecca could still see the scars. She guessed they had something to do with why he had never married. He usually had a woman somewhere in the wings; he just never cared enough to actually marry one of them.

Rebecca had prepared several pans of lasagna for today. The only saving grace was that other family members brought the rest of the dinner. Lee's wife had made her famous blueberry pie, Joe had picked up French bread, straight from the bakery, Mom had whipped up a salad and vegetables and Jess had brought wine for the adults and lemonade for the kids.

Not having had kids of his own, Joe was the one to blow it with Stephanie. He strolled into the living room, took one look at his niece and let loose with a long, low whistle.

"Hey, sweetheart, you're going to be a knockout."

Stephanie hunched her shoulders, burst into tears and darted from the room.

Joe's mouth fell open. "What'd I say?"

Jess punched him in the arm. "Don't you remember being eleven? The kid doesn't want boobs, for crying out loud! Surely even boys don't like to be different from the rest of the crowd."

He grimaced. "Yeah, I remember being eleven. But all the girls will get boobs. Why not her?"

"Because all the girls haven't yet!"

Surprisingly, Alan spoke up. "I used to think up excuses so I didn't have to take showers after P.E., because I...well, because some of the guys were getting hair, and...well, some of us weren't."

Alarmed at the turn the conversation had taken, Jess looked over at nine-year-old Sarah, who glanced speculatively at her boy cousin. Lee's youngest, a thirteen-year-old girl, had lost her air of worldly wisdom and was listening avidly. Oblivious to his indelicacy, Joe said, "Jeez, I'd forgotten that. You, too, huh? I used to wish boys had a time of the month they could get out of gym."

"You mean, like have a period?" Sarah asked inquisitively.

Joe flushed. "Uh, yeah, something like that."

Just then Rebecca's mother came into the living room. "This doesn't strike me as a subject for children's ears," she said primly. "Jess, your daughter is sobbing her eyes out in Rebecca's bedroom. Alan, honestly, you ought to know better than to say things like that in front of a nine-year-old girl."

"Can I say them to Steph, so she knows it's not just her?"

"Certainly not!"

Out of the corner of her eye, Rebecca saw Jess nod vigorously at Alan and give him the thumbs-up. That was one conversation she wouldn't mind hearing, she thought. By the time Steph quit crying Alan would be so embarrassed, Stephanie would be lucky if she could figure out what her cousin was trying to tell her.

Shortly after dinner, Rebecca had a conversation of her own that she would have preferred to miss. The bulk of the cleanup was done. She and her mother were the only two left in the kitchen. She was drying pans and putting them away while her mother made coffee for those watching a Seahawks football game in the living room.

The older boys were planted in front of the TV, and the younger kids, including an unusually quiet Stephanie, had started a table-tennis tournament down in the basement.

Her mother turned off the coffee machine. "How are things, Rebecca? I've been worrying a little."

"Worrying?" Rebecca glanced over her shoulder. "You mean about business? It's been a little slow, but..."

"No, I meant Alan, and... oh, that man you're seeing. What's his name?"

"Sam, but I can't see what there is to worry about." Which was a blatant lie, but justified, she thought. "He's a perfectly nice man, and we've only had dinner twice." She flopped the dish towel over her shoulder and shrugged. "No big deal."

Her mother was an attractive woman. Her hair was short and stylish, russet brown in color and streaked with silver. She wore carefully applied makeup and gorgeous clothes that verged on being too dressy. Today's Pendleton wool slacks and blazer, with a teal-and-rust silk scarf knotted around her throat, were typical. Rebecca only hoped she looked as good at sixty-four.

"Just so you're sure." Her mother's hands fluttered. "Dating must be hard at your age. Everybody seems to be divorced these days. That can't help but leave scars."

"True," Rebecca agreed. "Though as it happens, Sam has never been married."

"Oh, dear. Do you know why?"

"I suspect because he's a workaholic." Rebecca put away the last pan. "You haven't been talking to Alan, have you? You know how irrational teenage boys can be."

"Alan?" Mrs. Hughes said innocently. "Has he been trying to call me?"

Rebecca hoped not, but all she said was, "Not as far as I know. I just thought he might be looking for someone to grumble to. He thinks his mother should remain as pure as the driven snow."

Big mistake. Her mother's back straightened. "Oh, Rebecca. You know it isn't safe these days..."

"Mom, give me a break!" Rebecca rolled her eyes. "I'm thirty-five, not sixteen. And no, I'm not sleeping with him. But if I start to, I have no intention of telling you." *So there,* she thought childishly.

Her mother sighed and pursed her lips. "Just be careful. I don't want to be a busybody—I hope you know that. But I love you, Rebecca. I'd hate to see you hurt again. You haven't had the best luck with men."

Translation: you don't have good judgment where men are concerned. Or was she reading something into her mother's words that wasn't there?

Rebecca banished her momentary irritation and smiled mischievously at her mother. "Oh, I don't know. I had a pretty decent dad, and I can't complain about Lee and Joe. What's more, as kids go, Alan's a winner, too."

Her mother relaxed and returned her smile. "True. I won't say another word. Instead you can tell me what you know about Roy. How rude of him not to come today."

"I don't know any more than you do." Rebecca hung the dish towel on the refrigerator door. "There. Done. Shall we serve the coffee?"

Her mother looked disappointed but acquiesced. As she carried a tray with sugar, cream and coffee cups into the living room, Rebecca wondered about the conversation. Was the whole family talking about her, just as they were about Jess? Why was her mother so suspicious of Sam?

Sure, she'd blown it when she'd chosen Bruce. That didn't mean her judgment was fatally flawed, did it?

If only Sam were a little more interested in Alan, she would feel a whole lot more confident. Trouble was, as a potential substitute for Alan's father, she'd have to rate him pretty low.

Which begged the question; which did she want—a man for herself, or a stepfather for her son?

Why, oh, why couldn't Sam want to be both?

CHAPTER FIVE

"THE BURKE MUSEUM has an exhibit of northwest Indian canoes." Bruce Halstead grinned sheepishly. "I remember when all you wanted to play was cowboys and Indians. Nah, it wasn't cowboys. Let me think." He frowned and snapped his fingers.

Slouched beside his father in the pickup and trying not to notice how closely they were tailing a transit bus, Alan said, "Pioneers. I wanted to go west on the Oregon Trail. Hey, cool. I haven't thought about that in years. Remember my coonskin cap?"

"Sure do," his dad said. "Wasn't that your uncle Joe's when he was a kid? And there was a plastic long rifle, too, I seem to recall."

"Yeah, and my favorite book in the whole world was Zane Grey's *The Last Trail*. Now that was some good stuff."

"Damn right." His father grinned again. "I still like Zane Grey. But give me a cowboy any day."

"No kidding." As if the gun rack in the back window of the cab and the hand-tooled cowboy boots his dad liked to wear weren't a clue. Not to mention the way he drove. Right now he'd found an opening, if you could call it that, and he stepped on the gas to go around the bus. Alan briefly closed his eyes. Jeez, was that how Mom saw his driving?

"Anyway, I was thinking you might like the exhibit."

"You want to take me?" Alan asked, surprised. He'd been to museums before but never with his father. Not that he remembered, anyway. Most weekends they just hung out at his dad's apartment, maybe watched a few games on the boob tube. Sometimes they tossed the ball around at the park or went to a movie. His father's taste ran to anything with Arnold Schwarzenegger in it, as long as he wasn't pretending to be a kindergarten teacher. The more gore, the better. Alan didn't mind that kind of stuff, though it wasn't his favorite. Whenever he told his mother what movie they'd seen, she would roll her eyes and mumble something about male hormones.

But Indian canoes?

"If you don't want to..."

"No, it sounds okay to me. Just not your style."

"Yeah, well, I've been thinking maybe we should do more together. I mean—" he didn't look at Alan, just beat his fingers in an uneasy tattoo on the sheepskin-covered steering wheel "—I know we both get caught up in our lives and don't always make time for each other. I've been feeling bad about it lately. What say we try a little harder?"

Alan stared straight ahead. The Edmonds-Mountlake Terrace freeway exit flashed past. Did his dad mean it? He hadn't exactly apologized for not seeing Alan more. Still, it couldn't have been easy coming out and admitting they didn't have the relationship they should. Alan could see how it had happened. How long had it been since Dad had left home? Four years? Maybe he didn't even feel like a father sometimes. He was this single guy who was good-looking enough and had enough bucks to appeal to women. And it wasn't as though Alan were a little kid anymore who really needed a daddy. He was okay on his own. But if his father really meant it, yeah, he'd like to see him more often.

"Sure," he said, trying to sound casual. "I know how it is. I'm pretty busy, too. Mom's always asking if I've moved out. She swears days go by that she doesn't see me."

That was a slight exaggeration. His mother was only teasing when she said that. But it was true that between football, basketball, school and his job, he didn't have too much time for just hanging around.

His dad grinned jauntily and held up a hand for a high-five. "Then Burke Museum, here we come!"

Actually, it turned out to be interesting. The exhibit was impressive, starting with a thirty-seven foot Kwakiutl sea-going canoe carved from one enormous cedar log. There were smaller ones from other northwest tribes, and tools used for carving, paddling and bailing the canoes. Alan read all the placards; he'd done a report in September on the Haida Indians of the Queen Charlotte Islands, so he'd seen pictures of their famous war canoes. These were neat enough, but one of the war canoes would have really been something to see.

"Did you know that the Indians always pulled their canoes up on the beach stern-first so they could launch faster in case they had to?" Alan asked. That was the kind of stuff that stuck in his mind; not really important information, but something that made you realize the Indians had been real, not just words in a history text.

His dad didn't seem to hear him.

"Hey, you seen enough? How about if we go find some lunch? The Rams are on at one. I'd like to catch that game."

Alan wouldn't have minded seeing the dinosaur skeleton, but he nodded. "Sure. Anything but Greek."

"Pizza?"

They took it to go and made a quick stop at 7-Eleven for a six-pack. Alan bit into the first hot, chewy piece of pepperoni pizza as his dad swore when the light on Forty-fifth turned red on him.

"You seeing anybody these days?" Alan asked.

"You haven't met Karen yet?"

Alan remembered his father's last girlfriend, a redhead who preferred movies with subtitles. Not exactly a match made in heaven. Her name had been…Melissa. Yeah, that was it.

"No, I don't think so," he said.

"Karen's a new bookkeeper in the office. She's built—" his hand swooped in a curvaceous line "—and she's a smart cookie, too. Real homebody. Divorced, but no kids. You'll like her. She wants to meet you."

What for? Alan almost asked. He wasn't exactly a major player in his father's life. It wasn't as if he were five years old and the woman would be stuck with him every other weekend for the next ten years. Assuming his dad ever got in the mood to remarry, that is. Somehow Alan couldn't see that. He thought Dad enjoyed being a swinging single again. His mom put it a little differently; she didn't criticize his father to Alan's face, but he had overheard her telling Aunt Jess that Dad was immature and irresponsible. "It's as though he's become a teenager all over again," she'd said.

Alan had wanted to storm into the room and argue, but something had held him back. Reluctant honesty, he guessed. He wasn't sure what made someone mature, but he knew that when he had a problem, he didn't go to his dad. It was his mother he *depended* on.

Had been able to depend on, until she'd met The Jerk.

He didn't want to talk about anything heavy anymore, so he didn't comment on Dad's girlfriend's desire to meet him. Instead he said, "Homecoming is this weekend. Any chance you can make it to the game? We're out of the playoffs, so this is it for the year."

"I'll try," his dad said, pulling into a parking spot behind his building, a big old house divided into apartments. "I won't promise, though. Karen's parents will be here from Chicago."

Alan grabbed the pizza box, while his father took the bag with the beer. "You still busy Thanksgiving weekend?"

"'Fraid so. But I'll tell you what. I'll come up and take you out to dinner the week before. What d'ya say?"

"You're on," Alan replied with a grin. A little voice in his head told him, *you've heard that one before,* but he ignored it.

After they watched the Rams wipe out their opponents, his father took him home. He had plans that evening, he said with a wink. Alan didn't really mind. That way he'd be home Sunday, the one day he had to hang around with his buddies. Besides, he didn't like the idea of his mother coming home from her date to an empty house.

"I'm having dinner with Sam again," she had said, sticking out her chin stubbornly and issuing a warning with her eyes.

"What about all those things you used to say?" He mimicked her. "He's got to be good with kids." Alan sneered. "Yeah. Right."

"Alan, I warn you. He's none of your business."

"I have to work with him."

"Are you trying to tell me that the fact that I've dated Sam has affected your relationship with him?"

"Damn straight it has," Alan said angrily. "At least before, he used to ignore me. Now he watches me all the time. It's like I'm on trial."

He remembered Wednesday that week. Cool as you please, The Jerk had looked up and nodded when he'd walked in. Alan had nodded back, even though he'd had an acid taste in his mouth. He'd made a point of moving the damn lawn tractors and sweeping under them, even though there wasn't anything to sweep. Then Alan had come around the corner to the office cubby and said, "I need to mop here tonight."

"Don't you usually do it Mondays?"

"Yeah, but I didn't get to it." *And what are you going to do about it?* Alan thought. *Fire me?*

The Jerk looked as if he were going to say something, then thought better of it. "All right," he replied coolly. "I need to check some inventory in back, anyway."

He reappeared just in time to let Alan out the front door at eight o'clock. Alan had started down the sidewalk, hands shoved in the pockets of his letter jacket, when Sam had said from behind him, "You did a good job tonight."

Alan stopped, then turned around. "What?"

"I said you did a good job."

He couldn't believe it. The way he'd busted his butt these past months, and *now* the guy said he'd done a good job. It didn't take a genius to figure out why.

He could hardly look at his boss without picturing him kissing his mother. Okay, she was pretty, and he guessed she was more interested in guys and sex than he'd imagined, but The Jerk? Alan had seen the way her lipstick was smeared, and how her cheeks were scratched from the shadow of his beard. But the idea of her letting him do anything else made Alan feel sick. One of these days she'd wake up and see what he was really like. If Alan could prevent her from doing something stupid in the meantime, she would thank him. He knew it.

So he was just as glad his father didn't want him to spend the night. While he waited for her to get home, maybe he'd call Grandma. She could talk to his mother, maybe convince her to quit seeing The Jerk. She seemed to worry about Mom. And Mom listened to her.

Feeling optimistic, Alan hopped out of his dad's pickup. "Hey, have a good time tonight," he said. "Call me when you have time."

His father gave him a thumbs-up. "Good luck with that game Friday if I don't talk to you before then. Give 'em hell."

With that his dad backed out of the driveway, honked the horn and squealed away from the curb. His mother would have been annoyed.

So what? he thought, listening to the silence of the house as he unlocked the front door. Maybe annoying her was the only way to get her attention these days.

Only he couldn't quite picture himself doing something dumb just to irritate his mother. Anyway, the last dumb thing he'd done had really backfired: he had introduced Mom to The Jerk. Look where that had gotten him.

No, if he wanted to keep her out of his boss's arms, he'd have to be creative. Calling Grandma was a good first step. After that, he'd do some deep thinking. He had a couple of hours before Mom arrived home. He'd come up with something.

"ALAN SPENDING the night with his father?" Sam asked. He tried not to sound hopeful. What was this, the third, maybe fourth date? It was a bit presumptuous to assume Rebecca would invite him in just because her son wasn't home.

Streetlights dimly illumined Rebecca's face as she said with what he wanted to interpret as regret, "No, not this weekend. Alan expected just to spend the day."

"Do they get along?" Sam asked. He was surprised to realize he actually felt a spark of curiosity about the boy and his father. Even something that was almost pity. He remembered himself at eight or nine, facing the fact that his father he was a brutal man who wanted obedience more than love from his sons.

"More or less," Rebecca answered, sounding a little doubtful. "Alan won't hear a word against Bruce, but he's not dumb. He's never once connived, the way kids do, to get Bruce and me back together. I really think he sees his father's flaws. He tries to accept them, act as though he doesn't mind when Bruce's carelessness about commitments leaves him in the lurch." She laughed. "Listen to me. I guess you can tell how I feel about my ex."

Wryly Sam said, "I won't ask if you're still in love with him."

"What a thought!"

Concentrating on the semi in front of him as they exited the freeway, Sam couldn't see her expression, but he could picture it. Nose scrunched up, she'd look like a kid confronted with a plate of brussels sprouts. That was one of the things he liked about her—the way her face mirrored every thought in her quick mind. No secrets there.

"Do you ever wonder why you made the decisions you did when you were eighteen or twenty?" Rebecca continued.

No. He'd seen one way out and taken it. But he didn't want to tell her that.

Fortunately Rebecca didn't wait for an answer.

"I must have been nuts. I *was* nuts. All teenagers are. Raging hormones. They absolutely erase common sense.

Bruce is attractive. Worse yet, he was a high-school jock. Quarterback of the football team. Pitcher on the baseball team. He was hot stuff. Every girl's heartthrob, and he wanted *me.*" She still sounded vaguely surprised.

"Hell, lady, of course he wanted you," Sam said. Two more turns and they'd be on her street. He wanted that goodnight kiss with a fierce desire awakened by the wistful wonder in her voice. "What I can't figure out," he said, "is why he quit wanting you. Or was it the other way around?"

"Maybe a little of both?" She sighed. "He started running around on me. But you know, I think it was my fault."

"Jerk," Sam muttered, and Rebecca chuckled, a delicious ripple of sound that was almost as good as fingernails trailing down his back.

"I don't mean it quite the way that sounded," she confided. "The truth was, I got more and more...assertive. Bruce called it bitchy. He did such a lousy job of handling our money, for example, I took it over. He hated having to ask me for money, so he'd just tear out checks from our checkbook and not write down how much they were for. When I said something, he got mad." She let out another sigh. "Well, you can imagine the rest. He wanted a cheerleader. I wasn't one even in high school."

"Thank God," Sam said. "Even in high school I hated those simpering looks and fluttering lashes. I always wondered what the girl was *really* thinking."

"What a lovely thing to say!" He could hear the smile in her voice. "A gentleman through and through. What's more, I think that's the longest speech I've ever heard you make!"

"Home sweet home." Sam turned the Mercedes into her driveway. The porch light was on, and a small lamp shone behind the lacy curtains in the bay window of the living room. There were no cars parked in front of the big white house, which meant no Alan. Sam set the brake and faced Rebecca.

As usual, she stated the obvious. "Alan doesn't seem to be home. I wonder..."

"Let's enjoy it while it lasts," Sam said, and reached for her. The illumination from the porch was enough for him to see her lips part as she swayed into his embrace. Jubilation surged through him and he bent his head to take her mouth with more force than usual. God, she tasted good. Sweet, hot, willing. Her neck was so smooth to his touch, her curly hair heavy and silky. He eased his other hand over her slender shoulder, his thumb tracing the line of her collarbone, down her arm, to her breast. The soft weight of it filled his hand, the peak pressing against his palm, and hunger clawed in his chest. He wanted her. He wanted—

Brilliant light flooded the car. Sam swore thickly and lifted his head, blinking against the glare of headlights from the vehicle that had pulled into the driveway right behind them.

"Your son has arrived," he growled.

Rebecca moaned and buried her face in her hands. "I'll kill him."

Gritting his teeth, Sam fought for self-control. Long practice meant he regained it quickly. "You know," he said almost conversationally, "Alan is beginning to get on my nerves."

"I wonder why." She straightened and turned her head to watch over her shoulder as her son's beater backed out of the driveway into its usual spot at the curb. A moment later the headlights went out and a car door slammed. Alan strolled up the driveway.

Sam rolled down his window.

"Jeez," Alan said cheerfully. "Sorry. Your car was dark. I didn't see you until I pulled in. I bet you thought I was a cop, gonna check your ID or something."

Sam let an uncomfortable silence build before he said impassively, "Funny, I didn't think that for a minute."

A choked sound came from Rebecca. Then she said, "Alan, would you mind letting me say good-night to Sam?"

"That's okay," Sam said. "I'll walk you to the door."

The situation was awkward, to say the least. Alan kept shooting daggers at Sam, who accepted the challenge by laying an arm around Rebecca's shoulders.

At the door Sam said easily, "Shall we have lunch this week? Say, Wednesday?" When she agreed, he said, "I'll stop by your store, then." He bent his head and kissed her, lingering just long enough to provoke the kid, but not long enough to incite open warfare. Then he nodded. "Good night, Rebecca. See you, Alan."

Rebecca said good-night in return, Alan muttered something under his breath.

Smiling, Sam retreated down the walk. There was a certain amount of entertainment value in Alan's efforts to prevent the inevitable.

And Sam had no doubt whatsoever what the next step in his relationship with Rebecca would be. A woman didn't kiss like that unless she meant it. Especially a woman as utterly lacking in duplicity as Rebecca.

Yes, *inevitable* was the right word. The question was, how would Alan handle it?

"DID YOU KNOW your son is mounting a campaign to make you dump Sam?" Jess asked cheerfully.

Rebecca's jaw dropped. "He's *what?*"

"You've got to promise not to tell him I told you," Jess said. "He'd hate me forever."

"Tell me."

"Promise?"

"Yes!" Rebecca snapped. Thank goodness no customers were around. They probably have thought she was yelling at a subcontractor. "Now, what'd he say?"

"He didn't actually say that much, just came by the office and wanted to talk about you. He asked if I was as worried about you as he was, tried to look surprised when I pleaded ignorance. He says Sam is ordering you around, and you just take it. He says that when he tries to complain about how Sam treats him at work, you always take Sam's side."

"Grrr."

"Yeah, well, I just thought you should know," Jess said blithely. "Bet you he's gone to Mom, too."

"Undoubtedly." Rebecca rolled her eyes. "I hope you set him straight."

"Well, I told him *I* like Sam, as much as I know about the man. And I reminded him that you're an adult, et cetera, et cetera. Not that my words of wisdom fell on fertile ground."

"What's with him?" Rebecca asked without really expecting an answer.

"Probably the same thing that's turning Steph into a weepy, defiant, boy-crazy monster who only looks like my daughter on the outside. Listen, I gotta go," Jess said. "Personally, I'm rooting for Sam."

Rebecca glanced up when the bell tinkled as the front door opened. "Speak of the devil."

"Gee, sounds like you're having a better lunch than my peanut butter and jelly."

"Thanks, Jess," Rebecca said, meaning it. "You know, if you ever want to talk..."

The insouciance in her sister's voice sounded forced this time. "Sure. Who else would I go to? Have fun, kiddo."

Thoughtfully, Rebecca hung up and stood to meet Sam. Despite her exasperation and frustration with her son, she felt a lift in her spirits just at the sight of the large, dark-haired man who'd walked in the door. "Hi. You're early."

He glanced at his watch. "I'll wait."

"I'm ready to throw in the towel." She smiled and happily accepted the brief kiss he gave her. "Just let me go tell Carol I'm leaving."

She came out of the back room to find him inspecting her display of ceramic tile. "What do you think?"

"You have a good selection," Sam said. "Do you install the tile?"

"Yes, or some people want to do it themselves. It's not a complicated job."

"We rent the tools."

"With a purchase, *we* loan them out free," Rebecca told him. "Sorry. I guess we're undercutting your business."

One of those unexpected smiles lightened his face. "What if I offer you a bribe?"

"Depends what it is," she said provocatively.

"Lunch?"

"Well, I won't make any promises...."

"Good enough."

On the way out to his car, Sam asked, "How would you feel about deli sandwiches we can take to the river park?"

"That sounds wonderful," Rebecca assured him.

The river wound its way right through town. Just above its banks, the city maintained soccer and baseball fields, as well as a playground and picnic area. At this time of year, the river was still low, though the rains had raised the water level some. Nobody was swimming today, but during the summer the beach was crowded and inner tubes were more popular than Michael Bolton.

She and Sam settled onto a bench high on the river bank, where they could look down on the green-brown channel. Two sea gulls, wanderers from Puget Sound just a few miles downstream, called discordantly from a perch on the bridge.

Rebecca was conscious of Sam's muscular thigh brushing hers as he shifted on the bench. In a funny way, she was more physically aware of him because she *wasn't* gazing straight at him as she would across a dinner table. Instead her peripheral vision and the reactions of her body kept her keyed to his every gesture.

He had left his sport coat in the car, and now he loosened his tie and rolled up his shirtsleeves. As he unwrapped his sandwich, Rebecca took a sidelong peek at his hands: fascinating, strong, square hands that were more expressive than his face.

They talked idly about work as they ate. Rebecca asked about the manager who wasn't doing his job.

"He means well," Sam said, tossing a piece of crust to a sea gull, which swooped to the rocks below to snatch it up. "Just doesn't know how to supervise. Can't say no when employees ask for favors, so then the ones who don't ask resent it. He's constantly shuffling the schedule to accommodate personal requests, and every so often he screws up and nobody covers a spot. I came in one morning at 9:30 and the place wasn't open." He shook his head. "The hell of it is, most employees don't make good managers. I have plenty of people to keep the equipment running, some decent clerks, but I end up doing too much managing."

From comments he'd made, Rebecca couldn't help wondering if that wasn't partly his fault; did he give his managers a chance to make mistakes and learn from them? She remembered his brief conversation with the White Horse manager at the Home Show. She hadn't sensed any friendliness, any confidence either way. But she could hardly criticize his management techniques. He'd shown he was touchy on the issue. Besides, she wasn't an expert herself.

"You're doing too much," she said, facing him now. "I wasn't kidding the other day when I said you'd end up with a coronary." She touched his hand. "Nobody should work until nine o'clock every night."

He raised a brow. "What do you suggest?"

"I don't know." Rebecca wadded up her sandwich wrapper. "Accepting less than perfection?"

"You think I expect perfection?" Sam snorted. "I wish I could. The minute you start hiring people to do a job, you have to let your standards slide."

"Now, wait a minute." Rebecca turned to face him. "I've found a couple of women who hang wallpaper every bit as well as I do. My brother Joe, the one who owns the treetopping business, has ten or twelve men working for him off and on, and he laughs sometimes and says he's damn glad he's the boss, because a couple of them can scale a tree a heck of a lot faster than he can. My other brother has a little more trouble finding good help—he owns the auto-body shop. Still, I can't believe you can't find competent employees. For goodness' sakes, Sam, are you always this negative?"

For a second she was afraid she'd offended him; heaven knows he wouldn't be the first person who didn't appreciate her outspokenness. His eyes were opaque, his face unreadable, but then a smile curled one corner of his mouth.

"You're right. I have some damn good employees. Just not enough of them. I suspect I spread myself too thin when I opened the last couple of stores."

"Is that when you started working such long hours?"

He looked away from her, gazed at a tree branch bobbing as the current carried it downstream. "More or less. I feel like the kid in that Dutch story, sticking my fingers in holes in the dam. If I'm at the Everett store, they have a crisis in Marysville. Too many complaints in Granite Falls, but when I shift employees the complaints keep coming. I don't know what the answer is."

"Close some stores?" Rebecca said tentatively.

"Not that simple. I have too big an investment in them." He grimaced. "I didn't mean to unload on you. Sorry."

"What are friends for?"

A smile lingered in his cool gray eyes. "Is that what we are?"

She reached out and took his hand. "I hope so. Partly, at least. I mean, there's no reason men and women can't be friends, is there? The couples I've known who've managed to stay married are the ones who actually seem to like each other. Have you noticed? Bruce and I didn't have a single hobby in common. Once you get over the sexual excitement, what's left?" Suddenly flustered, she added, "Not that I'm hinting at marriage or anything like that. It's just that I wanted you to know..."

Gently he covered her mouth with his hand. Smiling, he said, "You don't need to apologize. I agree with you. Liking goes further than lust. Not that lust doesn't have its place...."

Her heartbeat promptly speeded up. She couldn't look away from the gleam in his eyes. When his hand left her mouth to tilt her chin up, she met his kiss with parted lips.

The kiss was much too brief. And she would have protested, if she, too, hadn't been aware of the children's voices shrieking on the playground behind them, of the traffic rumbling over the bridge, of their exposed seat above the river.

Rebecca drew a deep breath and struggled for the composure that Sam had a gift for undercutting. Before she could begin a determined conversation, she heard the deep boom of a bass guitar. She turned her head to see a flashy red pickup brake at the top of the boat-launching ramp. Half a dozen teenage boys piled out and the music died a sudden death.

"Thank you, Lord," she murmured.

"Alan?" Sam asked.

"No, but two of his best friends." She raised her voice. "Hi, Carl. Hi, Evan."

"Hi, Mrs. Halstead," the two boys chorused.

With shoves and high-fives, the teenagers swaggered down to the beach.

Rebecca let out a puff of breath. "Boy, that was a close call. Alan would have died of humiliation if his mother had been caught necking in the park."

Sam's wicked grin made her insides do flip-flops. "I think necking is a little more...passionate than what we were doing. If you'd care for a demonstration..."

She tried to look sultry. "Sure, if you can find a deserted alley to park in."

"You're on." He closed his hand firmly over her elbow and lifted her to her feet.

Laughing, Rebecca let him hurry her to the car. Once inside, she made the mistake of glancing at her watch. "Oh, shoot!" she exclaimed. "I have to get back to work. Were you really serious about the necking? Can I take a rain check?"

Sam took her hand in his. "No, I wasn't serious," he said. "But, hell, yes, you can take a rain check."

"Oh, good," she said with satisfaction. "Which reminds me, are you busy this weekend? I've been thinking about getting started on a project at home."

He lifted a brow as he let go of her hand and started the car. "Not that mantel?"

Rebecca made a face at him. "Are you trying to make me feel guilty? No, not the mantel. I'm not brave enough to tackle it yet. Do you have any idea how hard it will be to get the old paint out of all those crannies?"

He shot her a glance she couldn't interpret before looking over his shoulder to watch for traffic as he backed out the car. "Yeah, I can imagine."

More uncertainly, Rebecca said, "What I have in mind is a rose arbor. Have you ever built anything like that?" Renewed enthusiasm overtaking her, she didn't wait for an answer. "It's probably dumb. Who has the time to sit and smell the roses, anyway? But I've always wanted an arbor, an old-fashioned kind that would go with the house. I saw one in a magazine that was just perfect. It almost looks like a gazebo, except it's simpler to build. Can't you imagine relaxing under a cascade of fragrant yellow and white roses?"

"I'm not much of a gardener," Sam said noncommittally.

She waved one hand. "I wish I were, but somehow my flower beds always have weeds, and the tulips poop out after a year or two, and I'm always forgetting when I should spray or fertilize and what likes manure and what doesn't—" She stopped for breath. "Obviously my desires outreach my abilities, or something like that. But I'm absolutely determined to have my arbor."

"What's stopping you?"

"Guilt," she said ruefully. "What else? In my heart I know the money ought to go elsewhere, like Alan's college fund. But the business has had a good year, so I figure this is the time. The thing is..." Rebecca bit her lip and hesitated.

"You need help."

"Well . . . yes."

Sam shook his head. "I wish I had the time, Rebecca, but this weekend I'm swamped. I'm sorry." Did he intend to sound as indifferent as he did? she wondered. "I'd hoped we could get together one evening, but I don't dare take a day."

"Oh." The one word sounded small, sad even to her ears. She hurried to add brightly, "That's okay. Maybe I can talk Alan into lending some muscle. It wouldn't kill him, do you think?"

"What I think is that he owes you a few," Sam said, sounding disinterested.

"I suppose so." She was silent until he pulled up in front of her store. "Thanks, Sam. I had fun, as usual."

"Don't forget that rain check."

"Sure." Her smile stayed steady. "Don't kill yourself at work."

"You can do your part to prevent it." He didn't seem aware of her perturbation. "Friday night?"

"Oh, dear. Alan has a football game. It's their last, too. Homecoming. Now, if your idea of a hot date is a thermos of cocoa and a hot dog from the concession stand..."

His brows drew together. "That isn't exactly what I had in mind."

Rebecca was on the verge of suggesting Saturday night, instead, when something stopped her. For the first time her vague uneasiness crystallized, and she had to wonder, did

Sam really want to be part of her life? Or did he feel nothing but physical attraction and casual liking?

There was only one way to find out.

She wasn't a good liar, but miraculously she sounded only slightly regretful as she said, "I'm afraid Saturday night is out for me."

A moment of silence followed. When she dared to look at Sam, she saw the frown still between his brows, but his eyes, as they searched her face, held a curious vulnerability.

"Well, hell," he said at last, running a hand through his hair. "I always liked a good football game."

Her sudden rush of relief made Rebecca realize how terrified she had been of his answer. "Wonderful!" she said jubilantly. She leaned over and kissed him on his scratchy jaw. "It starts at seven, but if we want decent seats we'll have to be early."

"I'll pick you up at six," he offered.

She almost felt a pang of guilt. She had always maintained that a relationship should be built on trust. But you had to have a basis for trust, didn't you?

And now she knew. Sam might not be eager to build a rose arbor or have fatherly talks with her son, but he was willing to take a first, tentative step into her real life.

What more could she ask?

CHAPTER SIX

REBECCA WIPED her hands on the dish towel as she smiled tentatively at her son. "Even if you have eaten, why don't you sit and keep me company?" She had just scrambled two eggs for herself, since Alan hadn't intended to be home for dinner.

From the kitchen doorway, Alan shrugged in an exaggerated teenage way that managed to convey a sneer. "If you want company, why don't you call The Jerk?"

Rebecca's eyes narrowed. "Why don't *you* call him by his name?"

"I don't say it to his face."

"Well, if you said it to offend *me,* you succeeded," she snapped, then was immediately sorry she had let him get a rise out of her.

She puffed out a breath and said in a more moderate tone, "I mean it. Will you keep me company? We haven't seen much of each other lately." And what little she had seen of him had been confrontational.

He stared right at her. "What's wrong, is he busy tonight?"

"Damn it, Alan, you're pushing me," she warned.

"Good."

The scene ended, as too many had lately, with Alan stomping out. Rebecca flung the dish towel to the floor as hard as she could and kicked it. A mature response, she thought mournfully. She couldn't remember ever being so angry at her son.

The eggs got cold while she brooded about how to handle Alan. She couldn't let him get away with talking to her like that. On the other hand, calling him on it would surely alienate him. Right now she needed to find a way to connect with him instead. She had to reassure him that Sam wasn't the threat Alan apparently found him. But how? Especially, when she and Alan hadn't had a civil conversation in two weeks?

She wasn't surprised to find herself picking up the telephone. Her mother had raised four children who had turned into reasonable adults. Maybe she would have a brilliant idea. At the very least, she was usually comforting.

"Hi, Mom," Rebecca said, when her mother answered. "How are you?"

"Just fine. I had lunch today with Janine, and she was telling me Lee's plans for expanding the auto-body shop. I do hope he isn't getting in over his head."

Rebecca curled her feet under her in the big easy chair by the phone in the living room. She forced herself not to look at the mantel, which always made her feel as if she should be working. "Has Lee *ever* gotten in over his head?" she asked, as she had so many times before. Her mother, a product of the Depression, always worried about every financial decision her children made, but since all four were successful, at least in a modest way, Rebecca could argue back each and every time with some confidence. Besides, of all of them, Lee, the eldest, was the least likely to be impulsive.

"Well," her mother said doubtfully, "I suppose not, but there's always a first time."

Rebecca reassured her that this was unlikely to be that first time and steered the conversation toward the subject she wanted to discuss.

"How are Lee's kids?" she began.

"Just fine. He and Janine are lucky they haven't had more trouble, as difficult as raising children is these days. Why, I'll bet Pete never even thought of trying drugs or anything like that."

Rebecca happened to know of a few incidents involving Pete, now twenty-one, that would have shocked Grandma, but she was content to leave her mother's illusions untouched.

"How is Alan?" her mother inquired.

"Did you read my mind?" Rebecca asked wryly.

"Well, he and I have talked a couple of times this week. You know, he's sincerely worried about you."

Rebecca snorted. "Alan is worried about *himself*. For heaven's sake, Mom, you know how self-centered teenagers are."

"Surely Alan is aware he'll be off to college soon. This man you're dating really doesn't have anything to do with him."

"You know that and I know that, but Alan doesn't," Rebecca insisted. "He seems to think Sam is replacing him in my affections. As far as I'm concerned, Alan is old enough to understand the difference between a mother's feeling for her child and her feeling for..." She stalled, unable to think of an appropriate word. Boyfriend? Ye gods, she was too old for that. Friend? That was a euphemism on a par with "passed away." Lover? Not quite, and too blunt, anyway.

Her mother supplied the word. "A man. Rebecca, has it occurred to you that he may be right? That this—" she paused infinitesimally, which somehow made the name sound disdainful ''—this Sam isn't the right kind of man for you?''

Bluntly Rebecca asked, "How would Alan know?"

"The two of you have always been close."

"Mom, we're talking apples and oranges. Alan might know what kind of parent I am. He has no concept of my needs as a woman."

Mrs. Hughes cleared her throat. "You're not letting those needs make you do something foolish, are you?"

Rebecca made herself take a deep breath before answering. Why on earth had she thought calling her mother would help? Because—of course—she always called her mother when something bothered her. And usually it helped, they were friends, not just mother and daughter. So why did she have the feeling she was being taken to task?

"No," she said through gritted teeth. "I hardly think having a few dates with a man constitutes foolishness."

"Wouldn't it be a good idea if you brought him to meet some of the family? He ought to know you do have family."

Some remnant of humor made Rebecca say, "With shotguns? Honestly, Mom. Introducing him to the family would make it look as if I expected a proposal any day!"

Her mother's silence spoke volumes. It also made Rebecca think. Wasn't that where she hoped her relationship with Sam would go? Why else did she care if he took an interest in Alan?

"Well, I'm sure you know best, dear," Mrs. Hughes said finally. "I'm just suggesting that you be cautious. Don't get carried away just because he's attractive." She managed to sound as if she doubted whether he was. "And try to be understanding of Alan's attitude. He loves you, you know."

Yes, she knew. Not the slightest bit comforted, Rebecca hung up a moment later. Why was it that they had ended up talking not about Alan, as Rebecca had intended, but about her? She hadn't even had a chance to tell her mother what a pill Alan had been! Did Mom really think his attitude was reasonable? Or did she think that only because she didn't know how atrociously he had behaved?

Rebecca sighed. Her anger at Alan had drained away, leaving behind depression. Maybe figuring out how to deal with her son wasn't really the point; what she needed to know was *why* he was so upset about her dating Sam.

She felt as though she were going in circles. Did Alan dislike Sam that much? Or was it the fact that she was dating at all that upset him? What if she'd gone out with that coach Alan liked so much, the one with the thick neck? Mightn't Alan have become jealous of him, too? Or was it the fact that she had ignored Alan's advice that rankled him so?

Maybe despite her best efforts she'd treated Alan too much like an adult, asking for advice and ideas, respecting his opinions as equal to hers. Perhaps he felt demoted to childhood at her insistence that her relationship with Sam was an adult privilege and therefore none of his business.

"Hell," she said softly.

All these years she had done her damnedest to be a good mother, and with a few dates she'd apparently lost her kid's trust. Now, short of saying goodbye to Sam, she didn't have the faintest idea what to do about it.

WHAT IN GOD'S NAME was he doing here? Sam wondered. He was forty years old. He hadn't seen a highschool football game in twenty-five of those years. Not since he'd played in one himself.

Funny, he hadn't thought about that in ages. He'd loved the game, and like every other teenage boy had had visions of playing in the NFL someday. In his sophomore year he had made the varsity team as a wide receiver on offense, in the secondary on defense.

That was also the year things had gone from bad to worse at home. He had been mowing lawns since he was about twelve; by fifteen he had a couple of other boys working for him. None of them worked as hard as he did, however, and while he'd been sweating his way through drills on the football field, his customers had dwindled, forcing him to choose between football and business. He had sworn then never to look back and second-guess himself, and he had kept that promise.

If he was tempted to break it tonight, it was the fault of Rebecca, who at the moment was slathering mustard on her hot dog while juggling a drink and a conversation with another woman and her teenage daughter. The girl was apparently a cheerleader, but at the moment she was on crutches. Rebecca was commiserating.

"You're going to sit on the sidelines, aren't you? Personally, I think you deserve a standing ovation every bit as much as the players do when they're injured. You ought to insist on a triumphant entry onto the field. What do you think?"

The girl blushed and giggled. "I hurt myself in practice, and it was just dumb. I mean, I was watching the boys work out instead of paying attention. We were making a pyramid and I got to be on top. When I slipped..."

Rebecca made a face. "I still think you're as noble as some guy who hurts his knee because he's volunteered to let a bunch of behemoths grind him into the grass. This sport doesn't really make much sense, does it?"

"They do wear pads." Sam felt compelled to point out.

"Yes, thank goodness, but that doesn't keep the boys from getting hurt." She smiled at the girl and her mother. "We'd better find our seats."

Sam spilled some pop on his sweater as they climbed over people on the shaky bleachers to their perch above the fifty-yard line. Rebecca, he saw as they settled onto the narrow, hard bench, had mustard on her chin. He reached over and wiped it off with a napkin before dabbing at his damp sweater.

"What's a little mustard between friends?" Rebecca said cheerfully, then leaned over to kiss him on the cheek.

Though the sky wasn't fully dark yet, the stadium lights were on. A roar rose from the crowd as the home team trotted onto the field. A second, if fainter, roar came from the other side of the field when the Arlington team poured out of the locker room. Sam was surprised to feel anticipation. There was something about the crisp air, the excited crowd, the bright banks of lights, the smell of hot dogs and popcorn, the referee's whistle and the thump of the ball as a kicker warmed up, that awakened pleasurable memories.

It didn't hurt having a sexy woman beside him bouncing happily as she craned her neck to watch the captains go onto the field for the coin flip. When someone called her name from higher in the bleachers, she turned to wave, and her full breast bumped Sam's arm. She smiled at him, then turned to see what was happening below on the sidelines.

Momentarily unnoticed, Sam watched her. What was it about her particular combination of features that he found so appealing? It wasn't just her wide blue eyes and perfectly straight, even elegant, nose. The few freckles on her cheeks and that softly rounded chin were almost childlike. Her mouth wasn't, though; it was sensual, and somehow very adult. Of course, her body had something to do with it. She wasn't quite overblown enough to be called voluptuous, but she definitely had a figure: tiny waist, full hips, breasts that would more than fill a man's hands. Even in the jeans and bulky sweater she had on tonight, her nicely rounded bottom had caught his attention as they'd clambered up the bleachers.

But then she smiled at him again, and Sam realized it wasn't her appearance that most attracted him. It was *her*. Serene one moment, deliciously flustered the next. Sometimes naive, sometimes unnervingly wise. Outspoken, warmhearted, quick to leap to her son's defense. Once you had Rebecca on your side, you could count on her, Sam thought. She was loyal, loving, smart, funny, and a damned good kisser.

None of which explained why he'd felt obligated to come tonight. But what the hell, he decided, rising to his feet with the rest of the crowd as the home team kicked off. There were worse fates than having to watch a football game.

Her son even turned out to be pretty good, which was lucky. From the minute Alan trotted onto the field, Rebecca was up and down like a yo-yo, yelling encouragement, gasping dramatically whenever the boy went down under a pile of bigger bodies, groaning when the referee called White Horse for holding.

Alan was the quarterback. For a junior in high school, he had a hell of an arm, not entirely under control yet, but the way he threw the ball had real potential. He was quick on his feet, too, managing to pick up yards instead of losing them several times when his offensive line broke down.

The game was a squeaker, tied up fourteen all at halftime. Rebecca collapsed back beside Sam as the team disappeared into the locker room. "Why did we come?" she asked. "I'm too old for this."

"It's just a game," Sam said.

She made a face. "A stupid game. Why did I have to be cursed with a son big enough to play it? Just think, if he were five-feet-six inches, he could run cross-country, instead."

"Yeah, but you'd spend hours watching him go around and around and around...."

She looked horrified. "I would, wouldn't I? At least this is exciting. Of course, I could have brought a book, the way I do to baseball games...."

"He plays baseball, too?"

"Yes, and talk about boring." Rebecca rolled her eyes. "But don't tell him I said so."

"Far be it from me."

She cocked her head and studied him. "You're a man."

"I hope so," he agreed gravely.

Rebecca punched him on the arm. "I wasn't done. Of course you're a man! What I was wondering is if you played football or baseball."

"Both," Sam admitted. "Only through my sophomore year."

"How come you quit?"

"Hey, I was a big-time entrepreneur," he said lightly. "Like you said, football's just a game. It got in the way."

Her unfathomable blue eyes searched his. "You must have been . . . different," she said at last. "Did your parents worry about you?"

Worry? He almost laughed. The day he'd announced that he wasn't going out for football, his father had beaten the hell out of him. Then his mother had worried about him, small use that was. In the insular little world of Sam's family, men played football; they didn't groom other people's lawns. However athletic and strong-willed he was, Sam hadn't been macho enough to satisfy his father, who had never recognized the desperation that had motivated Sam's choices. And why should he have? Then he would have had to acknowledge the cause of it. Himself.

"People didn't have the money to indulge kids the way they do now," Sam said. "Most of my buddies worked, too."

"True." Rebecca smiled. "You know, I'm still hungry."

"You're kidding."

"Isn't that my line?" Her mischievous smile was worth every uncomfortable moment on the old bleachers. "Nope, I'm not kidding. I'd love another hot dog, and maybe one of those cinnamon rolls. Don't they look good?"

Sam nodded at the neighbor to his right. "Not as good as the Irish coffee he has."

He settled for cocoa, though, while Rebecca put away the second hot dog and three-quarters of a giant cinnamon roll. Sam didn't mind the couple of bites she fed him. Nibbling the icing off her fingertips was a pleasure not entirely culinary. When her eyes met his afterward, he discovered he wasn't the only one whose imagination had added a spice besides cinnamon.

But the moment was lost when the two teams ran back onto the field and Rebecca rose to her feet, cheering lustily.

Sam felt a bittersweet pang in the region of his heart. It took him a second to identify it.

He would have liked somebody to care as much about him.

The realization was disconcerting. He was too old to be carrying around baggage from his childhood. He thought he *had* resolved his feelings for the family he'd written off. So why the hell did he feel jealous now?

He was brought sharply back to the present by Rebecca, who grabbed his arm. "Oh, my God—oh my God—oh my..."

Alan had been sacked, and was down for the count. Sam stood, too, and wrapped an arm around Rebecca. "He's probably just had the wind knocked out of him," he said, his gaze riveted on the boy, who lay on his own twenty-yard line, surrounded by coaches and trainers.

Rebecca buried her face in Sam's shoulder. "I can't look. Oh, my God, Sam..."

"He's moving his legs."

"He's not paralyzed?" She straightened, one hand covering her mouth. "I can't stand this sport."

"He's up," Sam said unnecessarily as the boy staggered to his feet, buoyed by the crowd's encouragement, and trotted off the field.

The kid who came on to take his place didn't look more than twelve. "They borrowing them from the junior high?" Sam muttered.

The man next to him shook his head. "He's a freshman. First game."

The new quarterback's voice squeaked as he gave the signal. When he received the snap, he retreated a couple of steps, his panic obvious even as he searched the field for somebody to dump the ball on.

"Oh, Lord," Rebecca said, "he's passing."

Sam groaned. The ball settled neatly into the hands of an Arlington linebacker, who looked around in surprise, tucked the ball under his arm and lumbered off toward the end zone. He made it, too, despite the futile and equally ponderous attempts of the White Horse offensive line to catch him.

Alan was on his feet, and even Rebecca didn't protest when the coach sent him back in for the next series of plays.

"They have to score," she said. "Alan was so sure they'd win tonight."

Tension built as Alan led the team down the field. Five minutes left, and the home team was down by six instead of seven, thanks to the hook the Arlington kicker had put on the last extra-point attempt.

Rebecca moaned, screamed, prayed. The team stalled on the fifteen-yard line. The third down play, a run up the middle, was suicidal.

"What the hell are they doing?" Sam asked in frustration. "They've got to go for it on the fourth."

They did go for it, but not the quarterback sneak that might have won them a safe first down. Instead Alan backed up with the ball, his arm cocked. Tacklers closed in, he dodged, all the while looking for an open receiver in the end zone.

Sam wasn't even aware that he was yelling, too, until the ball arced against the artificial lights and came down as pretty as a Christmas package, right into the outstretched hands of a receiver, who caught it midair, then landed with both feet inside the end zone before falling out of bounds.

After the tumult, Rebecca said, "That was Chuck Heller. Your manager's son. The one who's going to the University of Washington."

"The kid's good," Sam said, surprised.

"Tell his father so."

"Alan played a hell of a game, too," he admitted.

This time her smile reminded him of a Cheshire cat. "Tell him so, too," she suggested.

Sam retreated into silence as the crowd grew noisy again for the easy extra point and then the kickoff. He liked to think that he gave people their due. Rebecca didn't seem to agree. And maybe she was right. Maybe he didn't offer compliments as often as he should. Damn it, was it wrong for him to expect a decent performance on the job?

Nevertheless he had to admit to himself that it was easier to chew somebody out than acknowledge something done right. Hell, maybe he had more of his father in him than he wanted to acknowledge. He couldn't remember his father ever once saying the simple words "Good job."

Maybe they'd stuck in his throat, the way they now did in Sam's.

Sam emerged from his reverie to find that the defense had held. The offense took to the field again. After each snap, Alan dropped to one knee and the remaining seconds ticked off.

"Yes!" Rebecca said with satisfaction when the buzzer sounded. She and Sam waited their turns to file down the steep bleacher stairs. "Now, wasn't that fun?" she asked.

Fun? Sam glanced at the field, where the winning team was being smothered by leaping, yelling, crazy high-school kids. The football helmets bobbed among the sea of fans. Sam couldn't even spot Alan.

"Yeah," he said slowly. "It wasn't bad."

"It wasn't bad?" Rebecca snorted and poked him in the back. "Sam Ballard, I know darn well you can do better than that."

He grinned and swung her from one row of the bleachers down to the next. She arrived breathless and smiling. "I'll work on it," he said. "Maybe I can practice on you."

"Okay," Rebecca said as they reached the bottom of the bleachers and the exiting crowd hemmed them in. "I'm game."

He bent his head so nobody else could hear him. "You're cute when your nose is bright red."

"Buddy, that won't get you far."

"Would you like to come back to my place?" he asked abruptly.

There was a curious moment of stillness amid the hubbub, and the simple invitation seemed to hang in the air. He was asking more, and she knew it.

At Rebecca's hesitation, Sam swallowed his disappointment and said, "It's late. I shouldn't have suggested it."

Complicated emotions showed on her face, but the hand she tucked into the crook of his arm was trusting. "I don't know about that," she said for his ears alone. "I would have started to worry about my sex appeal if you hadn't suggested it pretty soon."

"Lady," he murmured in her ear, "I was ready to drag you home by the hair the minute you walked into my store."

"My, my." Her eyes laughed up at him. "And I questioned whether you were a man."

"Care for some proof?" he asked roughly.

Her voice was as sweet as the icing on the cinnamon roll. "Why, I believe that would be a good idea. Just to be sure, you understand."

"Is this a yes to my proposition?"

Her smile had disappeared and her eyes were full of trepidation, but her answer was steady. "Yes."

"Good, then let's get the hell out of here." Her hand clasped firmly under his arm, he began to weave through the mob, skirting the sidelines.

Unfortunately their route brought them face-to-face with Alan, who was triumphantly swinging a pretty blond cheerleader into a dance while his friends applauded.

Alan froze when he saw Sam. The others were still talking, laughing, unaware of the tension between Rebecca's son and the man who kept her tucked to his side.

Sam knew the words he had to say, but they stuck in his throat like dry bread.

He forced them out, anyway. "You did a hell of a job, Alan. You deserved to win this one."

The kid was just young enough to flush and shuffle his feet. He didn't want to be gracious, but Rebecca had taught her son well. "Uh, thanks," he mumbled.

Silence would have descended if Rebecca hadn't jumped in. "You scared the daylights out of me! What were you doing, taking a nap out there in the middle of the game? Next time, will you walk off the field first?"

The boy grinned and blushed again. "Right, Mom." His gaze shifted to Sam. "I think maybe I'll skip the dance...."

"Go," Rebecca said firmly. "You deserve to celebrate. Besides, didn't you ask Kelly?"

"Yeah, but..."

"No but. Have fun."

"Are you going home now?" he asked stubbornly.

"Nope." She smiled. "Drive carefully."

Sam nodded and steered Rebecca away. He was well aware that Alan watched them until they were swallowed by the crowd.

REBECCA CHATTERED all the way to north Everett, where Sam lived. She knew darn well she wasn't fooling anyone, least of all herself, into believing she was cool and collected. What she was, was terrified. But she couldn't seem to shut her mouth.

"Dunn Lumber is having a sale this week," she told Sam, who listened politely. Maybe. Who knows, he might have tuned her out fifteen minutes ago. She rattled on anyway. "So if I can borrow one of my brother's pickups, I'll go get the stuff to build my arbor. Alan was busy this weekend, like you, and there's certainly no rush. I just

want to be sure it's done by February so I can plant bare
root roses when they're available. Plants are cheapest when
they're bare root, you know. Besides, there's a bigger selection. I haven't decided which ones to buy yet. I'm hoping I run into a knowledgeable nurseryman—or should I
say nurseryperson? That sounds awkward, doesn't it?
That's the trouble with our language. It's sexist, and
there's no practical way to fix it—''

"We're here," Sam interjected. He reached up to press
a button that opened one door of a large, detached garage.

Rebecca had only a vague impression of the house,
which she confirmed when they emerged from the garage.
Handsome and old, which came as a surprise. "I thought
you lived in a condo," she said, puzzled.

"I do." Sam locked the side door to the garage behind
them. "This place was remodeled into four condomini-
ums. I have the ground floor."

"It's gorgeous," she said, gazing at the building, which
must have been built around the turn of the century, when
turrets and deep front porches were commonplace in
houses—if you happened to be a railroad or lumber baron.
"How did you find a plum like this?"

"I looked around a lot before I bought it," Sam said.
He took her arm and guided her to a back door that led
through a screened-in, second porch.

"The condo?"

"The building."

"You mean . . . you own this whole thing?" She felt
dumb. She had realized he must be well-to-do, but not *how*
well-to-do. He must have paid half a million for this place,
though he was probably recouping the investment in out-
rageous rentals on the other three condos.

"Mmm-hmm." Sam turned on lights, revealing a kitchen that belonged in *Home* magazine: sea-green Italian tile, custom-made maple cabinets, a cavernous brick fireplace and a butcher-block island.

"It's beautiful," Rebecca said, turning slowly. "I didn't picture you—" she stopped.

He raised an eyebrow. "Picture me what?"

"Well, you didn't seem all that interested in old houses or gardens or anything like that. I just thought...maybe you had a modern condo or something. But this...it's spectacular." She knew she sounded as stupefied as she felt. "You could probably give me plenty of advice. Although my house will never look like this, no matter what I do to it."

Sam shrugged. His tone was indifferent. "I'm the last one you should ask for advice. I didn't do the work. I bought the place, hired a contractor and moved in when he was done."

Rebecca stared at him. "Don't you *like* old houses?"

He shrugged again. "I can go either way. I thought I could do well on this place, and so far it's worked out."

It finally sank in: he didn't care about this beautiful old house one way or the other. It had been convenient, and a good investment. He'd probably insisted the remodeling stay consistent with the age of the house only because that would increase its value. He had a house she would kill for, and it plainly left him cold.

She felt as if she were standing there with a complete stranger.

Still, a stranger who smiled in a way that stirred her blood, even as she struggled to remember why she'd thought accepting his invitation was a good idea.

"Sam, I'm not sure..."

An eyebrow arched again. "Aren't you?"

"I'm scared," she said bluntly.

He wrapped his hands around her upper arms, then released her. The smile gone, he frowned down at her. "Scared of me?"

"No." She bit her lip and looked away from Sam's intense gaze. "Of myself, maybe? I don't know. I just... Well, things weren't as loose when I was a teenager as they are now. I married Bruce awfully young. Since my divorce, I've dated a bit, but..."

The frown made his face harsh. "You're trying to tell me you've never slept with anybody but your husband, is that it?"

She nodded, her cheeks hot. Great. The woman Sam thought he knew was outspoken, bold, even brash—thoroughly adult. Now came the hidden side. She was probably more naive than her sixteen-year-old son!

Sam's voice softened as he gently lifted her chin so she had to look at him. "What are you afraid of? That you won't know what to do?"

Put that way, she sounded like a ninny. Thirty-five years old, and she felt sexually inadequate.

What could she do but nod?

"Sweetheart..."

Was he laughing at her? She studied him suspiciously.

"The way you kiss me, I don't think we'll have any trouble in bed."

"I've had more practice at kissing!" she retorted.

Sam bent his head so that his mouth hovered just above hers. His voice was a sensuous rumble. "Look at it this way. Practice will eventually make for perfect sex, too."

Rebecca opened her mouth to argue. *Practice* sounded so cold-blooded. She wanted to be swept away. She wanted fireworks and bells ringing. Damn it, she wanted perfect the first time! But, for once in her life, she didn't get a word out. Sam's kiss saw to that.

CHAPTER SEVEN

SHE HAD SENSED the passion and the heat behind Sam's cool facade before. But then it had been held in check. This time his passion was raw. He didn't coax, he demanded. If she had imagined him waiting patiently for her, she'd been wrong. There was nothing patient about the man whose mouth staked a claim she couldn't deny.

Her nervousness became a hazy thing, soon supplanted by a sexual hunger as urgent as Sam's. The way his tongue slid into her mouth reminded her body of an age-old rhythm it ached to dance to again. Feeling the groan in his chest, the slam of his heartbeat, knowing she and she alone had cracked his iron composure, were as good as an aphrodisiac.

She wound her arms around his neck and slid her fingers into his hair. He pulled her up to his body so fiercely his belt buckle hurt, and she became excruciatingly aware of his arousal. No, *patient* wasn't the word to describe him.

Then he abruptly swept her up into his arms, like Scarlett in *Gone With the Wind*. Rebecca gasped and he swallowed the small sound with another kiss as passionate as the last. She held on tightly. Somewhere in their progress through the house he turned sideways and shouldered a door open. Until he lowered her to the quilted softness of a bed, Rebecca had paid no attention to where they were.

Sam lifted his mouth from hers and braced himself above her. His eyes were almost black, so stormy had the gray become. He asked hoarsely, "Still scared?"

If he wanted a lie, he had come to the wrong woman. "Petrified," she whispered. Her palms loved the rough texture of his shaven jaw.

"Do you want to stop?"

The fact that he had asked despite his obvious desire told her plenty about the kind of man he was. She managed a tremulous smile. Her heart was pounding harder than it had when she'd thought Alan was hurt. "No," she said huskily. "Don't stop."

Sam made a rough sound of satisfaction and pulled her to a sitting position. She lifted her arms obligingly so he could peel off first her sweater, then the turtleneck that was beneath. Thank the Lord she'd worn a pretty, lacy bra tonight and not one of her everyday ones. Poor Sam would be disillusioned enough to discover what a thirty-five-year-old mother really looked like under the all-important veneer. Of course, the bra wouldn't save her from the brutal truth. Suddenly she wished desperately that she had her twenty-year-old body back.

"I don't know if I can do this," she announced, hunching her back.

He brushed his thumbs over her nipples, still disguised by the bra. Her embarrassingly obvious reaction seemed to delight him. "Why?" he asked, amusement beneath the rough desire. He calmly released the catch of her bra.

"Do you suppose we can turn the light off?" Rebecca asked hopefully.

"Over my dead body," he murmured as her breasts spilled into his hands and he bent his head to kiss their pale curves. He looked up and grinned. "And I'm a long ways from dead right now."

"That's obvious," she agreed wryly. Almost of their own volition, her hands slid under his shirt to caress the solid, warm wall of his chest. His muscles rippled beneath her touch, and some of her self-consciousness abated. She just wouldn't look at herself. Not that she looked so bad, but she definitely had a few bulges she would rather disown. Maybe Sam wouldn't notice them. Or maybe he had some, too.

If so, she couldn't find them. He tugged the shirt over his head, allowing her a glimpse of sleek muscles and shoulders broad enough to shelter her from the rain. Then he let her feel his weight as he kissed her with thorough sensuality.

She'd forgotten how good it felt when bare skin met bare skin. When her breasts were flattened by a man's chest. She wriggled experimentally, made a soft sound of pleasure at the result. He groaned and moved his mouth down her neck, trailing delicious sensation over her collarbone to her full breasts. The touch of tongue to nipple brought a fresh shock of pleasure. Rebecca arched her back and Sam drew her nipple into his mouth, suckling gently.

Heat seemed to flow through her veins, pooling between her thighs. She pushed up against his leg, which lay between hers. Sam laughed huskily and reached for the zipper of her jeans while he kissed her breasts in turn again. She began quite urgently to wish the rest of their clothes gone, light or no light. When she ran her fingernails down his back, Sam groaned again and rolled over, so that she lay sprawled on top of him.

Achingly aware of the hard ridge pressing against her belly, Rebecca rose to sit astride him and moved her hips in a way calculated to drive him to despair. Sam cupped her breasts in his hands and gazed up at her with a look of such hot desire, he raised her temperature another notch.

"Still not sure you can go through with it?" he asked roughly.

"I'm not sure I could stop," she admitted.

"I know damn well I don't want to," he said. "If you'll lift up a little, I can get your jeans off."

Rebecca obliged, although the whole matter took longer than it should have because she was unbuttoning the fly of his jeans at the same time. He finally growled in frustration and rolled her off him, disposing of their last stitches of clothing with careless haste.

Then he lay on his side, raised on one elbow and looked her naked body up and down with hooded eyes. Rebecca flushed. "Now you can see what I mean about those five pounds. Or maybe it's ten. Someone my age can't afford—"

"Any woman your age would kill for a body like yours," he interrupted.

"Do you mean that?" Rebecca asked anxiously.

Sam gave her a wolfish smile. "*I*'d kill for your body. In a manner of speaking."

"Oh." Rebecca answered his smile with one that undoubtedly made her appear wanton. Whatever that was. "I'm glad," she said softly. "You can have it, you know."

"I intend to," he said in a raw voice that did exquisite things to her nerve endings. "Immediately."

He didn't quite mean that, although she would have been ready for him. Instead he seemed to take a certain pleasure in making her wait as he kissed and stroked and teased. She did her best to pay him back in kind, reveling in the way his muscles tightened under her hand, the rough sounds he made in the back of his throat, the desperation she saw on his face.

When, after taking a moment to protect them both, he wrapped her legs around his waist and began to ease his way inside her, he was controlling himself by the thinnest thread. His teeth were gritted, his eyes glazed and sweat made his shoulders slick. Rebecca hung on for dear life. She had forgotten this, too—the sensation of being filled, the enormous satisfaction at her ability to accommodate a man she loved. But there was more, and she wanted it, too. She wanted it as she couldn't remember ever wanting anything from a man in her life.

He pulled back as slowly as he had entered her. Did he think she'd break? She tightened her muscles around him and lifted her hips in an instinctive effort to stop him.

"Am I hurting you?" he asked through clenched teeth.

"No," she gasped. "Oh, no."

"Good," he murmured against her mouth, before he kissed her and surged more deeply.

Her body was on the verge of shattering. She tried to put off her climax. This felt so good. Too good. She kissed him back, frantically pulling him harder, deeper. She was mindless, all sensation, all need.

Sam's thrusts were increasingly urgent, out of control. He pressed intoxicating kisses over her cheek and neck, a counterpoint to the explosive rhythm she both wanted and fought.

"No, no," she whispered, then cried out as her bones seemed to dissolve. But her long shudders were met by his as she pulled him with her into the storm.

They lay quietly for a long while afterward. Rebecca was reluctant to start thinking again. For once in her life, she let go of worries, of should-haves and shouldn'ts. She just enjoyed the weight of a man pressing her down, the utter relaxation that was as sweet in its way as the more intoxicating pleasure of lovemaking. She moved her hands lazily over the damp, muscled expanse of Sam's back and kissed his shoulder and the sleek skin at the base of his throat.

He lifted his head and smiled crookedly. "Weren't sure you knew what to do, huh?"

Rebecca laughed and hugged him. "You've given me back my confidence. Although maybe it was your expertise that carried us. What do you think?"

The amusement in his eyes faded and left something unnameable that chased Rebecca's laughter away. "I think," he said huskily, "that you're a beautiful, sexy woman who could make any man think he'd died and gone to heaven. Even one as undeserving as I am."

She felt as if he'd grabbed her heart and given it a squeeze. "Thank you," she whispered. "But you are *not* undeserving. You're the nicest man I know. And believe me, I'm at an age to appreciate nice."

The gray eyes that searched her face were the furthest thing from cold right now. "Nice, huh? Is that the best you can come up with?"

"How about if I tell you I heard bells ringing? I think there might have been a few fireworks, too."

"A few?" His eyebrow rose devilishly. "Shall we see if we can improve on that? After all..."

"Practice makes perfect?"

"Mmm-hmm." He bent his head to kiss her breast.

Rebecca pretended to ponder for a moment, although a delicious sensation of warmth was already stirring in her belly. "Well," she said thoughtfully, "I suppose I ought to give you a chance."

"Fair enough." His teeth closed gently on her nipple. He flicked his tongue over it, then lifted his head to smile wickedly. "Although it wouldn't hurt if you contributed some of your own...expertise."

Rebecca ran her foot over his muscular calf. "No," she said gravely. "I don't suppose it would."

After all, she decided some time later, being swept away was all very well. But doing half the sweeping was even more fun.

ALAN WAS SURPRISED when his father called Tuesday to invite him to spend that weekend. "It'll give you a chance to meet Karen," he said.

Alan couldn't have cared less if he met Karen, who might be the hottest thing around at the moment, but would be forgotten in two months. But he remembered his and Dad's talk about trying harder to be part of each other's lives. Maybe this Karen would be okay.

Still, he hesitated, torn. He knew what his mother would be doing at home with him gone. But he also knew that if he turned down this weekend, he might not see his dad for another month or more. At last he said, "Sure. You gonna pick me up, or shall I drive myself?"

"What's your mom think about that?"

"She wouldn't mind," Alan said, pretending to sound surprised. Actually, he wasn't sure what Mom would say. She hadn't let him drive into Seattle by himself yet. But there had to be a first time, right? And she was tiptoeing around him these days, which made it likelier that she would agree. She'd probably give a mile in the hope he would come back with an inch of approval about her and Sam. Well, that was tough luck. He wasn't going to lie about how he felt, not if it meant having The Jerk around all the time.

He had a sudden image of Sam saying "You did a hell of a job, Alan," but he slammed a door shut on the memory. The Jerk had just wanted to impress his mother, that's all.

"Well, okay," his father was saying. "Can't say I hate saving the trip up there. Bet you're going to be glad to leave that little burg in the dust."

"No kiddin'," Alan agreed, but he had to slam another door on the empty feeling that always accompanied thoughts about leaving home. He was too old to get homesick! Not that he was afraid of missing home. No, what really scared him was the idea that nobody would miss *him*.

He waited until after dinner that evening to mention his father's invitation. The meal had been peaceful, since both he and his mother had skirted the subject that would have ensured an argument. His mom was picking up the dirty dishes when he said, "Dad asked me to spend this weekend with him. He has some new girlfriend he wants me to meet."

She paused halfway to the sink. "Girlfriend?"

"Yeah." He looked at her back, wondering whether she was jealous at the idea. Didn't she still feel *something* for his dad? "Karen somebody or other. I don't know what he expects me to do. Give her the gold medal for achievement?"

"Don't be snotty," Rebecca said automatically, resuming the washing-up. "It's possible she has no more interest in meeting you than you do in meeting her."

"Yeah, I guess so," he admitted. It was probably true that she wasn't looking forward to it, whatever his dad said. In an ultracasual voice, he added, "Dad wants me to drive myself."

"Oh, Alan." His mother deposited the dirty dishes in the sink and turned to face him, a frown crinkling her brow. "There's so much traffic down there. You haven't been driving all that long...."

"Come on, Mom," he begged. "All my friends drive wherever they want. You even let me go to the Tacoma Dome when Evan was driving. How come you trust him and not me?"

She made a face. "Did I say I trusted him? *Trust* is not a word I'd use in connection with a teenage boy."

"Oh, great," he said sarcastically. "I'm such a screw-up, right?"

She came across the kitchen and kissed him on top of his head, whisking away before he could protest. "Alan, you know perfectly well I was teasing you. As for this weekend..." She paused, then capitulated. "All right."

"Hey, cool." He leaped up and gave her a fast hug. "Uh, what are you going to do this weekend?"

She wiped the table, not meeting his eyes. "For starters, see if I can borrow Joe's pickup to buy that lumber. Although I've obviously lost your labor. Maybe after school next week?"

"Basketball practice starts," he reminded her.

"Oh, hell," she muttered, then sighed. "Maybe Sam..."

Alan ignored her quick glance. He didn't want to talk about The Jerk. If he did, he'd just get mad again. He already dreaded seeing the guy the following night at work.

"I've got to do some homework," he said hurriedly.

"Okay, okay. Scat!"

He scatted while the going was good, even though he wasn't all that eager to work on calculus. For once he felt good, though, and he wanted to keep it that way.

His good feeling evaporated Friday afternoon after school when he walked in the back entrance at his mother's business. He wanted to remind her he was leaving; he figured he'd throw some stuff in his duffel bag and get going. It was a little early, but maybe he could hang around the university district for an hour or so before he went to his father's.

A woman was browsing through wallpaper books at the big table in the rear. A little boy was coloring in the kids' corner. Alan's mother was at her desk, her back to him. She was on the telephone. She must not have heard him come in, because she kept talking.

"How does spaghetti sound?"

Spaghetti? Suddenly feeling cold, Alan stopped in his tracks.

She laughed and twirled the phone cord. "Oh, six, six-thirty. Somewhere in there." She paused again. "I'll look forward to seeing you, Sam." Then she hung up the phone and turned in her chair. The soft smile that hovered on her lips burned itself into Alan's brain.

At the sight of him, her eyes widened and her smile vanished. "Alan!"

"Making plans for the weekend?" he said nastily.

She lifted her chin. "As a matter of fact, I am."

"I suppose you're going to have a romantic couple of days building a rose arbor."

Her eyes narrowed. "Not that it's any of your business, but Sam is working this weekend. He's coming to dinner tomorrow night, and that is *all*. End of conversation."

"Yeah, well, have fun." Alan turned on his heel. "I'm gone."

She called after him, but he kept moving. At home he threw stuff in his bag, hardly thinking about what he would need. He kept seeing his mother's dreamy smile. It made him sick.

WANDERING THROUGH the university district should have been fun. He was old enough to blend in now, which was a good feeling. The University Bookstore was one of his favorite hangouts, and there were lots of places to eat cheap. Today, though, he didn't buy a single book and he couldn't remember later what he'd eaten. He was too busy imagining himself saying stuff to Mom that he didn't quite dare in real life. Like, *Why won't you listen to me?*

Funny, because he remembered the way Mom used to hug him when she whispered in his ear "It's you and me against the world, kiddo." Feeling as if she needed him had almost made up for Dad moving out. He'd known that was coming; his parents had hardly talked to each other for months before his mom had worked up the guts to throw Dad out. Alan hadn't wanted it to happen; he kept telling himself they'd talk things through somehow, that Dad would tell Mom he really loved her and promise not to see other women. Not that Alan was supposed to know about the other women, but he'd overheard fights. He'd heard Mom scream, "How do you think it makes me feel?"

He wanted to ask her the same thing now. He knew all about there being different kinds of love. Just because she'd fallen in love with someone didn't mean she loved Alan any less. He was ready for her to remarry, provided the guy was someone like Coach James whom Alan could respect. But for his mother to ignore completely how he felt, to choose a jerk who was already making Alan's life miserable... Well, how was he supposed to feel? Like welcoming him with open arms?

When he got to his father's, a woman answered the door. She was prettier than he'd expected, and younger, too. She sure wasn't old enough to be his mother, which made him uncomfortable. His dad called, "Who is it?" and then came into the living room to find out. He wrapped his arm around the woman, and she cuddled up to him. Grinning, he said, "Hey, Alan. Meet Karen. Karen, this is my boy."

She smiled and held out her hand. Alan shook it, feeling clumsy and self-conscious. Everything about her seemed wrong for a stepmother, from her waist-length red hair and the freckles over her small nose to the thin ribbed shirt that let Alan see what his father had meant when he'd said she was built.

"Alan," she said sweetly. "How nice to meet you. Bruce talks about you all the time, you know."

He glanced at his father, but he was beaming at Karen. "Uh, yeah?" Alan said. Brilliant, he thought.

"I was just making cookies," Karen announced. She batted her eyelashes at Dad. "Bruce's favorite. Raisin-oatmeal."

Alan hated raisins, but he didn't say anything. He let his father put his duffel bag in the spare bedroom, then followed Dad and Karen into the kitchen.

There he started to reach for a beer in the fridge, but Dad said, "Hey, better save that until you're older. I bought some cola for you. That's what Karen likes, too."

Alan's mouth almost dropped open. *Older?* What was that all about? His father never let him get drunk or anything, but he hadn't objected to a beer or two, either.

Cheerfully Karen said, "I keep trying to give up caffeine, but I have to admit I like it. You, too, huh?"

"Not especially," Alan replied ungraciously. "I don't have any problem with it."

"Have a cookie?" she invited.

"No, thanks." There was an awkward silence. Alan sat down at the table without anything to drink. His father's eyes met Karen's.

Then Bruce said in a hearty, fake sounding voice, "Well, tell me all about the game. Did you run up those stats?"

Dad hadn't cared enough to ask when he'd called earlier in the week. So why the big interest now?

Alan shrugged. "We won. I guess I had an okay game."

"I'll bet it was better than okay. Hell, you inherited the old arm from me. It's got to be better than okay!"

"I wish I'd seen you play," Karen told his dad. She bent to take a sheet of cookies out of the oven, and the snug black leggings she wore outlined a nice view. Alan looked away uncomfortably.

"I should have taken you to see Alan play," Dad said. "Next best thing, right?"

Alan guessed he was supposed to laugh. He felt stupid and blockish just sitting here feeling like an outsider. The little looks they were giving each other, his father's "this is my boy" routine, her sweet smiles—they were enough to make him wish he were home, even if The Jerk was there, too.

"You should have seen the pass Alan made against Snohomish," his father went on. "Dropped back under pressure, dodged a couple of tackles..." He pretended to feint, using the beer as a mock ball. "And then he threw a bomb, just as pretty as it could be, right into his receiver's hands. That's when I knew he had the talent to make the NFL." He shook his head. "I wish my own father had encouraged me to go on with the game."

Dad hadn't even played college ball. Alan had seen his high-school stats. They weren't bad, but they weren't good enough to attract college recruiters, either. Nobody had offered a scholarship, and from what Mom had said, Dad wasn't really interested in college, anyway. Now he was making it sound as though he'd been on the verge of this fantastic career, and all he'd missed was a push from his father. That was a bunch of bull, which made Alan embarrassed for Dad.

And Alan didn't like the way he implied he was there at every game of his son's, either. Actually, Alan hadn't played all that well against Snohomish. But it happened to be the only game his father had made this year.

Jeez, Alan thought. Dad was in a tie with The Jerk.

"Well, what do you want to do this weekend?" Dad asked. "We'll let you pick. Movie, theater, you name it."

They both gazed expectantly at him.

Theater?

His incredulity must have shown, because Karen laughed. "Your dad and I are educating each other. He takes me to the ballet—I go to a tractor-pull with him. Makes life interesting."

Now Alan knew where the museum idea had come from. Somehow that made him mad. These days, everything seemed to make him mad, and he didn't understand why. No, that wasn't true. He did understand. Sort of. Things were changing, and he didn't like it. Parents weren't supposed to change!

Especially not when it was too late. He remembered his father refusing to go see *Cats* when the Broadway play had come to Seattle, and how much that had upset his mother. And he wondered whether it would have made a difference to his father if Mom had looked at him with that soft smile Alan couldn't forget.

"I don't really care what we do," he said. "Just a movie would be okay."

They looked at each other again, over his head. Then Karen said brightly, "Let's do something more exciting than that. I've been so looking forward to meeting you."

Feeling graceless, he shrugged.

She pretended not to notice. "I have three tickets to the symphony. I talked Bruce into giving it a shot. What do you say?"

What could he say? *I want to go home?* He had to remind himself that probably right now—or was it tomor-

row night?—his mother was fixing a spaghetti dinner for
The Jerk. He didn't want to know what they were going to
do afterward. He'd been trying to keep them apart, but
deep in his heart he had known from the beginning how
hopeless that was. So going home wouldn't serve any pur-
pose. He was stuck there with his father and Karen, who
was too young and too nice. Who was changing his father.

Alan hated it.

"Sure," he said. "The symphony's okay with me."

"AND SO LEE IS expanding his auto body shop," Rebecca
told Sam. "He's going to start doing detailing and interior work, too. Sort of like me going from wallpaper to
window coverings, I guess. Mom thinks he's walking out
onto a limb, but Lee's smarter than that." She paused.
"More garlic bread?"

"No, thanks." Sam took a sip of wine and smiled
faintly. "You're a good cook. And I like the candlelight."

She'd turned off the lights in the dining room. The warm
yellow flicker of candlelight carved shadows beneath
Sam's strong cheekbones and left darkness lingering in
corners of the high-ceilinged room. Rebecca knew the
gesture was ridiculously romantic, maybe enough to make
Sam nervous, but on the other hand, she *wanted* the dinner to be romantic. Besides, she hadn't refinished the
molding in here, not to mention stripping the wallpaper
from the plastered walls, so the harsh light of electricity
made the room less than appealing. And eating in the
kitchen, as she and Alan did, hadn't seemed right, either.

"Oh, good," she said. When there was a moment's
pause, she reverted to their earlier conversation. "You've
expanded your business a whole bunch of times. Is it
scary? Or does it get less nerve-racking?"

"Scary? I wouldn't put it that strongly," he said with an easy shrug. "If you've done your planning, there shouldn't be too many surprises."

Rebecca made a face at him. "Why doesn't it surprise me that you'd say that?"

"You don't believe in planning?"

"Well, of course I do. Up to a point. But I *like* surprises. Aren't you ever..." She waved her hands. "Extemporaneous? Spontaneous? Hey, they rhyme."

His eyes smiled, though his mouth hadn't even twitched. "Sure I am. I didn't plan to invite my janitor's mother out for pizza."

"Oh. Well, that's true." She decided to forgive him. "I'm sorry, I seem to go on and on about my family, and you haven't met a one of them." Rebecca drew a deep breath. "Have I mentioned that my whole family gets together once a month for Sunday dinner?" She'd been trying all evening to slip this in naturally. "Next week's dinner will be at Lee's—you know, the one with the body shop. It's pretty informal. Any chance you'd like to come? At least then you'd have faces to stick with names."

She congratulated herself that she'd sounded appropriately casual. Sam would never guess that, in the eyes of her family, accepting an invitation to Sunday dinner was next best thing to proposing.

She was grateful that he didn't know that, because he turned out not to be interested. Looking no more than politely regretful, he said, "I wouldn't want to intrude on a family occasion. I'm afraid I'll be out of town next weekend, anyway," he said.

His expression was a wall that stopped Rebecca from pressing him. "I'm sorry," she said, hiding her disappointment. "Maybe another time. I think you'd like my brothers and sister. Wait a minute. You already know Jess, don't you?''

''We've met. She sends me a bill once a month.''

''You never say anything about your family. Do they live around here?'' Rebecca asked curiously.

''Seattle.''

Rebecca waited for him to expand on the flat answer. When he didn't, she said, ''Didn't you mention brothers? Do they have kids?''

Sam met her gaze unemotionally. ''So my mother says. I've never met them.''

Aghast, she repeated, ''Never met them?''

''We're not close. I haven't seen my parents in ten years. My mother writes. Once in a while she calls.''

He sounded so...matter-of-fact. Rebecca set down her fork and stared at him. ''Do you...do you hate them?''

His voice still impassive, Sam said, ''They're water under the bridge. I was angry when I left home. I've gotten over that, but I'm not interested in spending Thanksgiving with them, either.''

''Not even with your brothers?''

''Good God, I hardly even know them.''

Rebecca tried to imagine the utter loneliness of life without any family at all. How would it feel not to have people you could always turn to? People who loved you no matter what? Her mind balked at picturing a life so devoid of something she considered essential.

She wanted to know what Sam's childhood was like, what his parents had done to make him so angry that he had never wanted to see them again. But for once, she knew better than to probe. Sam was not a man who talked easily about himself. If he wanted to tell her more, surely he realized she would be happy to listen.

She must not have disguised her shock, because Sam said abruptly, "Not all families are like yours, you know."

"I don't want to sound as if I think we're perfect," Rebecca said, troubled. "I mean, the fact that we all live here in the same town leads to problems. We can't hide anything from one another. Sometimes I wish my mother didn't know every single thing I do. I swear we have a grapevine faster than the speed of light. But it's nice knowing that...well, that they all care. Don't you ever miss your family?"

"You don't miss what you've never had," Sam pointed out.

"Well, I suppose..."

"Now, what you *have* had is a different story." His gaze warmed as it lingered on her mouth before meeting hers again. "You can get to missing that."

Rebecca was pretty sure they weren't talking about family anymore. When he looked at her that way, as if she were infinitely desirable, she couldn't say she minded the change of subject.

"Of course, there's that saying about familiarity breeding contempt. Or do I mean boredom?" she wondered aloud.

"Oh, I seriously doubt I'll get bored. What about you?" Her gaze was locked to his. "I... rarely get bored."

"I'm glad to hear it." Sam set his wineglass down decisively. "You sure Alan won't be home tonight?"

"He isn't supposed to be." Rebecca threw caution to the winds. "Are you asking in the hope you can throw me over your shoulder and carry me upstairs? Because if so, I could put the inside bolts on. Then, at least if Alan tries to surprise us, he can't get in without my unlocking the door for him."

"I take it you're all for being tossed over my shoulder?"

"Well, that sounds sort of undignified." If deliciously primitive, she decided. "But being carried off to bed *was* fun," she concluded simply.

Sam's laugh was half groan. "Lady, you have a way of turning me on like a light switch. I don't know how you do it."

Recklessly she swallowed the last drops of ruby wine. The warmth as they glided down her throat seemed to keep traveling, heating her blood. "I wasn't trying. Not exactly."

"That's what gets me." He pushed his chair back, scraping the legs on the wood floor, then stood and circled the table so that he stood behind her. Gently he began to massage her shoulders and neck. It should have been relaxing, but somehow it wasn't. His touch was warm, deft. Listening to his husky voice, not being able to see him, was curiously erotic. Sliding one hand up the smooth skin of her neck, Sam went on, "You say the damnedest things. Women are rarely so... direct."

Rebecca tilted her head back and closed her eyes, luxuriating in the feel of his hands. He took the pins out of her hair and ran his fingers through it.

"I just... don't always think," she admitted breathlessly. "I commit horrible social blunders. I've been known to hideously embarrass my son."

"I'm past being embarrassed," Sam said in that same gravelly voice. "I like honesty."

"I'm...glad," she murmured, just before he bent to kiss her neck. At the sharp nip he gave her, a shiver went down her spine. She knew he had felt her tremble, because he laughed huskily and came around the chair to pull her into his arms. She went eagerly, meeting his mouth with equal passion. What was it about this man, whom she couldn't pretend to understand, who sometimes frustrated her? Why him? Intoxicated by his touch and his kiss, she couldn't begin to answer her questions rationally.

He bent suddenly and swung her up into his arms. Rebecca grabbed him. "You don't have to...."

"I know a hint when I hear one." His eyes glowed with fire. "Besides, I thought it was fun, too."

She had just enough composure left to tease. "So you do have fun once in a while."

With Rebecca in his arms. he strode across the dining room toward the entry hall and stairs. "Thanks to you. You have the strangest effect on me."

"Strange?" She ran her lips lovingly over his scratchy jaw, down to the more vulnerable skin of his neck. "I thought this effect was considered normal."

A thread of humor made his voice even deeper. "Depends on which effect you're talking about."

He paused at the foot of the stairs to kiss her again. In the utter silence of the house, the sharp ring of the phone was an alien sound that startled them both. Sam lifted his head. "Tell me you don't need to get that."

"I don't need to get that," she said. "That's what answering machines are for."

Hers had already kicked in. It was always strange hearing her own voice. Just as Sam started up the stairs, the machine beeped and Rebecca's mother began to talk.

"Hi, it's Mom. You haven't called for a day or two, so I just thought I'd say hello. How's Alan adjusting to that man?"

Oh, Lord, Rebecca thought in horror. Mom, *shut up.*

But her mother's voice, unusually penetrating, continued. "I shouldn't say any more about the whole subject, because you know what I think. But you're making Alan very unhappy, and I wonder if a few dates are worth it. Surely you can find a nice man who would be interested in Alan, too."

They had almost reached the top of the stairs. Cheeks flaming, Rebecca sneaked a look at Sam's face. His mouth was set in a grim line.

"So just stop and think, will you, dear? Well, enough of being nosy. Call when you have a few minutes. I'll talk to you later." Silence followed, then the answering machine clicked off.

At the head of the staircase, Sam lowered Rebecca to her feet. Gripping her upper arms, he held her with his eyes in a challenge she couldn't ignore. "So," he said flatly. "Do you want to stop and think?"

Tension crackled between them, but Rebecca refused to let her gaze waver. "No," she said baldly. "If I'd wanted to stop and think, I'd have done it a long time ago. Now I just want to... feel."

The muscles in his jaw clenched as he stared her down. She didn't retreat, just waited.

"I don't seem to be popular with your family," he said at last.

"Jess likes you."

He wasn't impressed. "Because my checks are never late."

For the first time, Rebecca let her gaze drop from his. She examined the top button of his shirt while she said awkwardly, "My mother is a worrier. She loves her grandkids. She's just being... protective."

Still sounding angry—and she couldn't blame him—Sam said, "Do you feel the need to be protected?"

Rebecca sensed that she was on the edge of a chasm, but she didn't hesitate. "No," she whispered. "Not from you."

"Then to hell with your family," he growled, and swept her into his arms.

CHAPTER EIGHT

REBECCA GAVE Sam the grand tour the next morning, firmly squelching her worry that she might be boring him—whatever he'd said to the contrary the night before. As far as she was concerned, friendship—or love—meant listening to the other person, caring about his or her concerns. She happily listened when Sam talked about work, so he could darn well listen to her plans. She wanted *somebody* to listen, since Alan sure wasn't interested in a rose arbor, and every time she brought up the subject with her mother, she fussed about money and whether Rebecca's budget could handle it.

"Let's take our coffee outside," Rebecca suggested after Sam had strolled through the house with her, making appropriate noises whenever she paused.

Sam lifted a brow but followed her.

Rebecca opened the French doors that led off the back parlor, a replacement for the sliding glass door that had been one of several ill-conceived efforts to update the house in the 1950s and 1960s. That same summer Alan had pickaxed the concrete patio and helped her lay a small brick one more in keeping with the eighty-five-year-old house's ambience.

The sun was warm on Rebecca's face, although the air felt crisp and the leaves were changing to fiery red and orange and yellow on the Japanese maples and dogwoods and cherries she had planted the first year after she and

Bruce had bought the house. So long ago, she thought with a pang. How old had Alan been? Eight? Nine?

"You do the work back here yourself?" Sam asked, glancing around. Narrow beds of perennials outlined the rectangular yard, while a circle of old-fashioned pink roses surrounded a birdbath and were in turn outlined by a low hedge of glossy green boxwood in the center of the lawn.

"Mmm-hmm," Rebecca confirmed. "Really, I like gardening better than working on the house, even though I've always loved old houses. Maybe it's because of my job. Stripping wallpaper or molding feels too much like work now. The trouble with gardening is finding the time and money. I can spend a hundred bucks at a nursery in the blink of an eye. If I started my own perennials from seed I could save money, but that only works so-so when you don't have a greenhouse, or at least a cool place like a garage with windows. I've tried taking cuttings from roses—see, that pale-pink climber over there is one I grew from a cutting. But finding the rose you want to take a cutting from is the trick. I don't know that many other people who like to garden."

"Aren't there garden clubs?"

"Yeah, but I don't have time to join clubs." Rebecca took a sip of coffee, then tucked her free hand under Sam's arm. "Come on," she said eagerly. "Let me show you where I want the arbor." Glancing down at her with amusement, Sam let himself be tugged forward. Gravel crunched underfoot as they followed the path that bisected the yard. Rebecca had hopes of replacing it someday with brick, which was so much warmer in color and had the feeling of permanence she liked.

"Over here," she said, leading him to a sunny corner that was partially screened from the house by a venerable lilac she guessed was as old as the house itself. "See, from here to here—" she paced off the space "—with a white rose on this side and a pale-yellow one here. I think I've settled on Madame Alfred Carrière and Alister Stella Grey. Don't they sound romantic? I love the names of old roses, even if I massacre them. I don't speak French at all. Do you?"

Sam shook his head, a faint smile playing around his mouth. "Did you know you're sloshing coffee all over?"

"I am?" Rebecca wrinkled her nose. She had apparently been gesturing enthusiastically—of course with the hand that held the coffee cup. "Oh, well." She dumped the rest in a flower bed. "Do you suppose a little caffeine will give these daylilies a growth spurt?"

"You never know."

"Have you ever built anything like this?" Rebecca asked.

"Afraid not," Sam said. "I've spent too many years renting tools to other people to be an expert on using them." He stepped forward and lifted her chin with one hand. "I hate to say it, but I'd better be going. I'm expected at the Lake Stevens store today."

"Do you work every Sunday?" Rebecca asked plaintively.

He kissed her lightly. "Damn near."

"Sam, you need some recreation. Like a nice long vacation."

"You planning to throw it all over and come with me?"

"Don't I wish," she said with a sigh. "Alan would disown me."

Sam grunted. "He has to learn to accept the fact that you're an adult who has the right to a life of her own."

Her eye brows rose. "Are you seriously suggesting a vacation?"

"Unfortunately, no." Sam grimaced. "I don't dare drop the ball these days. I'd probably be bankrupt by the time I got home."

Rebecca poked him in the stomach. "Now, that's a slight exaggeration. Admit it. Nothing terrible would happen if you disappeared for a couple of weeks."

Sam smiled crookedly. "That's one of the things I like about you. You're an optimist."

She imagined her arbor arching overhead and said thoughtfully, "Maybe that's why you're not interested in gardening."

He waited.

"Because you're a pessimist. You'd never believe a skinny sapling could ever be an honest-to-God tree, or that those wizened roots you stick in the ground in November could grow into peonies with flowers so big they're decadent. Gardening requires faith. And isn't faith really optimism?"

Sam studied her inscrutably. "God knows," he murmured.

Rebecca had to laugh. "Okay, okay, I'll shut up. *And* walk you out to your car."

"At least I don't have to pack." He glanced down at his rumpled shirt and khaki pants. "Though I wish I'd brought a razor."

"Oh, I don't know." Rebecca tucked her hand in the crook of his arm again and deliberately bumped him with her hip. "I sort of like the morning-after look." She smiled up at him. "It's rough and tough and dangerous."

"Try itchy."

"See? A pessimist."

They strolled contentedly through the gate at the side of the house and turned the corner to the front. Rebecca leaned over to pluck some dying blooms from a hot-pink aster that showed splendidly against the blue lace-cap hydrangea behind it. She straightened in time to see Sam turn his head sharply toward the street.

"I should have made a quicker getaway," he muttered.

"What?" Then she, too, recognized the engine sound of a car turning the corner. "Oh, dear."

"Dear?" Sam repeated sardonically. "Depends on your point of view."

The car screeched to a stop beside the curb. Alan climbed out, stared at Sam's car in the driveway, then gave his car door a vicious slam. He started slowly toward the house, not yet seeing them.

Rebecca girded herself for battle and stepped forward. "Alan."

He stopped, his gaze moving right past her to the dark man behind her. "Mom . . . Mr. Ballard."

The insolence she'd expected to hear in his voice wasn't there. Nothing was. He looked tired, too, she thought, frowning.

"Is everything all right? You're home so early."

A shrug. "I just got bored."

"Oh. Well." She smiled placatingly, even if she wasn't sure she needed to. "Let me walk Sam to his car and then I'll be in. You can tell me all about it."

"There's nothing to tell." He must have seen her skepticism, because his gaze shied away from hers. "Uh, sure."

She was surprised to hear Sam's deep voice. "See you Wednesday, Alan."

He gave a jerky nod. "Yeah, see you," he mumbled, then kept going, taking the front steps in one leap and disappearing inside the house.

Rebecca and Sam crossed the springy lawn to the driveway and Sam's Mercedes. Sam bent his head to brush his mouth over hers. For an instant his lips firmed and he deepened the kiss, as though he were tempted to reenact some of the previous last night's splendor, but then he broke the contact and stepped back. "Lunch this week?"

"If you have the time," Rebecca agreed. She smiled. "Don't work too hard."

Humor showed in Sam's eyes. "Wouldn't think of it."

"Tut-tut. Lying isn't good for your soul."

"Even little white ones?"

The words that popped out of her mouth startled her. "That's what Bruce used to say."

Sam's eyes sharpened. "About what?"

"Why he lied to me. After all, if he'd told me the real reason he was late getting home from work, it would have hurt my feelings." She gave herself a mental shake. "Good heavens, I don't know what made me think of that."

Sam leaned back against the car and crossed his arms. "Making a few parallels?"

"Never." She braced her hands against his chest and stood on tiptoe to kiss him lightly. "White lies aren't your style. Something tells me you're more likely to be brutally honest."

"Is that a compliment?" he asked wryly.

"Believe it or not," Rebecca said, half-surprised herself, "I think it is."

"Then on that note, I'll tactfully say goodbye," Sam said humorously.

His second kiss left her lips tingling. Rebecca stood in the driveway and watched his car disappear. The Mercedes was well out of sight before she turned reluctantly to go into the house.

She half expected to see curtains flutter as she went up the walk, but they remained still. Inside she followed the sound of clanking pans and found Alan in the kitchen, opening a can of soup, a not-unusual sight for a teenage boy who'd passed six feet without stopping.

"Your dad doesn't feed you breakfast?"

Alan turned on the burner. "They were having some kind of fancy omelet. I didn't feel like hanging around."

Rebecca's brows rose. So far Bruce had been discreet enough not to have a woman over when Alan visited. Was that changing?

"'They'?" she queried.

He dumped some water in the pan, not looking at her. "Yeah, like I told you, he's got this new girlfriend. Karen. I don't know if they're living together, but they acted like it."

Rebecca sat down, her gaze never leaving Alan. "Do you like her?"

"She didn't give me a chance not to. I mean, she's pretty and always smiling and trying to make it seem like I'm as important as Dad is. I don't know whether it was an act or not."

"And your father?" Rebecca asked slowly.

For the first time, she heard bitterness in her son's voice. "He can hardly take his eyes off her."

Softly she said, "I'm sorry."

She saw him draw a deep breath before he reached for a bowl in the cupboard. "What's to be sorry about? It's his business."

"But you came home early." She prayed Alan wouldn't close up on her now. She could hardly believe he was talking to her again.

"They were going to church. Can you believe it?"

"Well, you've been known to sit in a pew on Sunday morning."

"Yeah, but Dad?"

She picked her way carefully. "He must like her very much."

Alan's words were a cry of pain. "But he never even mentioned her until a few weeks ago!"

Rebecca stood and went to his side. She didn't quite dare wrap her arms around him. "You know, the way he feels about her and the way he feels about you are—"

He interrupted, mimicking her voice, "Two different things. I know, I know. It's just..." His almost adult mask crumpled, revealing the bewildered face of the twelve-year-old he'd been when his father had left. "I hardly ever see him. Why couldn't we just have done stuff together without her?"

"Maybe he wanted you to get to know her. I mean, if he's thinking of remarrying..."

Alan looked at her, really looked at her, for the first time since he'd arrived home. "You know why he wanted me there?" he asked.

Wordlessly she shook her head.

"He wanted to impress her with what a great father he is," Alan said starkly. "I could tell. It was all for show."

"Oh, honey." She held out her hand, but he ignored it.

"And then I come home and find The Jerk still here. He spent the night, didn't he?"

Rebecca let her hand drop. "You don't expect me to answer that."

"Why not? Are you trying to sneak around?"

"I just don't think my sex life is any of your business," she said stiffly.

"You're just like Dad," Alan sneered. "All you care about is—"

"No!" In a burst of anger Rebecca slapped her hand down on the countertop so hard the bowl jumped. "If you don't know better than that," she snapped, "I've wasted the past sixteen years."

Her son backed up a step, his expression alarmed. Even so, he argued. "Then how come you're spending so much time with—"

Rebecca stabbed him in the stomach with her finger. "Don't say it. I'm warning you!"

"With . . . Mr. Ballard?"

Rebecca tried to get a grip on herself. "Because I like him," she explained. "Because he's an attractive man and I *do* have sexual feelings, believe it or not. Because I *might* even want to remarry someday. I can't spend my life being nothing but a mother, even though I love you dearly. Can't you understand that?"

When he didn't answer immediately, Rebecca's heart sank. Had she done such a poor job of raising her son that he had no sense of security in her love? Did he really believe she would abandon him in a second for the first man who expressed an interest in her?

Alan hung his head and mumbled an answer she didn't quite catch.

"What did you say?"

He squirmed, then spoke so quickly it was obvious he was trying to get confession time over with. "Yeah. I guess I do understand."

"So then, what's the big deal?" she demanded.

He squirmed some more. "I knew you wouldn't leave me or anything, not the way Dad did, but sometimes I thought . . ." He foundered.

She took pity on him. "You thought if your own father could quit loving you, maybe your mother could, too."

Alan looked up, startled. "How did you know?"

"It doesn't take much imagination." She gave him a tremulous smile. "First of all, I don't believe your father has quit loving you. He may not be reliable, but that doesn't mean he doesn't care. Second . . . Kiddo, he and I are different people. I will *never* stop loving you, even if you do something horrible, like . . . like murder or flunking out of school or . . ."

"Putting a gouge in the living-room floor?"

She stared at him. "Are you trying to tell me . . . ?"

He grinned irrepressibly. "Just kidding. Gotcha!"

"Rat!" Rebecca began to laugh. She held her arms wide. "Can I have just one hug?"

"Yeah, okay." He submitted to an embrace so tight her arms ached. When he stepped back, she saw the moisture in his eyes before he quickly averted his face. "Jeez, I forgot to turn on the soup."

Rebecca tried to sound normal. "Well, you're in luck. I, the supermom, will heat it for you. I'll even throw in a piece of homemade blueberry pie."

"Cool." Alan had himself together enough to look sheepishly at her. "I guess I've been kind of a jerk lately, haven't I?"

Her voice was dry. "I might even say 'The Jerk.'"

Alan winced.

"However, I'll let it go this once. *Just* this once. Message received?"

"Yeah." He thought about it. "That doesn't mean I have to *like* Mr. Ballard, does it?"

"Alan!"

"Just kidding. Kind of." All his troubles apparently forgotten, he headed for the telephone. Over his shoulder, he said offhandedly, "Hey, I think I'll call and see if Geoff wants to shoot some hoops down at the school this afternoon. Yell when the soup's done, okay?"

Rebecca rolled her eyes heavenward. "And he wonders why I need some romance and excitement in my life?"

REBECCA TIPTOED around Alan during the next few days. She didn't kid herself that one talk had solved all their problems. The fact was, she was still dating a man he didn't like—and one who had no apparent interest in her son. Which might be just as well. She shuddered to think how Alan would respond if Sam made a clumsy 'fatherly' approach to him.

She couldn't decide whether or not to make an attempt to promote some kind of relationship between them. Maybe she should have Sam over to dinner when Alan was home. On the other hand, she could just see herself carrying the entire conversational ball while Sam communicated with an occasional lifted eyebrow and Alan sulked. Maybe dinner wasn't such a good idea.

Sam called Monday to suggest they have lunch on Wednesday. Alan answered the phone and handed it to her without editorial comment, which was an improvement. He also hung around the kitchen while she talked, which made her self-conscious. But when she hung up and he still didn't comment, she decided not to make an issue out of it. She'd just have to get used to conducting a romance right under the nose of a teenager.

She made a point of calling her mother back and suggesting, as tactfully as she could, that she *not* leave messages concerning Sam.

Rebecca didn't have the nerve to tell her mother that he'd heard every word she'd said that night—after all, Rebecca could hardly admit she'd been home and hadn't answered the phone because Sam was carrying her up the stairs to her bedroom. She did, however, point out that Sam might be with her when she checked her messages.

"But surely your telephone messages are private," her mother protested. "You don't listen to them in front of casual acquaintances, do you?"

"In the first place, Sam is not a casual acquaintance," Rebecca said as evenly as she could. "In the second place, yes, I probably would. Why not? I have very few deep dark secrets. Besides, I couldn't stand not to check my messages just because I have someone with me. What if Alan needed me to pick him up?"

"Well, that's true," her mother conceded. "I suppose it *would* be embarrassing if Sam heard what I said."

"Yes, it would," Rebecca agreed sweetly.

Suddenly her mother chuckled. Had it been anybody else, Rebecca would have said she'd giggled. "Oh, dear," Mrs. Hughes said. "It just struck me as funny. I don't know why."

Rebecca remembered Sam's expression, and it struck her as funny, too. She collapsed into a chair laughing.

"I never thought of being overheard hours later," her mother said between giggles. "Talk about modern problems!"

Rebecca felt cleansed by the time she hung up. She had missed the regular talks with her mother. It was her own fault if she'd reacted like a teenager whose mother disapproved of a friend, instead of an adult who could stand up for her decisions.

She quit feeling so charitable when her mother dropped by the store on Wednesday, just before lunch. Rebecca glanced surreptitiously at the clock and the front door. Ten minutes to twelve. No sign of Sam yet. Giving her mother a distracted smile, she finished ringing up a sale for some wallpaper that had come in that morning.

"Have a good day," she told the customer, then said, "hi, Mom. Are you out shopping?" *Tell me this is a coincidence,* she prayed.

"Oh, I've seen so little of you lately," her mother said vaguely, "I was just in the mood for a chat. You're never very busy around lunchtime, are you?"

"No, but I'm afraid I have a lunch date today."

Her mother's surprise looked feigned. "Oh? Anybody I know?"

"Sam," Rebecca said levelly. She glanced again at the clock. "In fact, he should be here any time. Why don't you and I have lunch tomorrow? You're right, it's been a while."

"Oh, what a good idea," her mother said. She wandered over to the tile display. "Is this a new line? How pretty."

"Yes, it is." Rebecca started feeling panicky. Would Sam think she'd set him up to meet her mother? "Can I walk you out to your car so I can start locking up?"

"Oh, but I'd love to meet him. Don't you think it's time? Why don't you invite him for Sunday?"

"I did, but he's busy." Or not interested in meeting her family, Rebecca wasn't sure which. "I'll suggest it again next month."

"What a beautiful shade of peach." Her mother stroked a large tile with the design of an iris cut into it. "I wonder if food would get stuck in there?"

"The idea is to use just a few interspersed with plain peach. Or maybe a row on the backsplash." Rebecca glanced longingly at the front door. "Mom..."

"How are things going with Alan?"

"Better," Rebecca admitted. "Mom..."

"Oh, is this him?"

Damn. Sam was indeed opening the front door.

"He's very handsome," Rebecca's mother whispered. She abandoned the tile display and came to Rebecca's side, where she waited with a polite smile fixed on her lips.

Unhappily resigned to the inevitable, Rebecca called, "Hi, Sam, I'm back here."

She tried to see him through her mother's eyes as he came toward them down the main aisle, past mounds of carpet samples and the accordion files of vinyl flooring. He was a large man, she realized afresh, even intimidating. His unsmiling mouth was firm, his gray eyes heavy lidded and unrevealing. A short haircut had subdued his dark wavy hair, while today his white shirt and slacks were crisp, a civilized veneer over the powerful body beneath.

Large, handsome and not very friendly was her objective assessment. That is, until his eyes warmed with a smile that softened the hard line of his mouth.

"Rebecca."

Her toes almost curled. "Hi, Sam." She hesitated infinitesimally. "Sam, I'd like you to meet my mother."

"Margaret Hughes," her mother announced, holding out her hand. "How nice to meet you at last. I've heard so much about you."

Eyes wary, he inclined his head and shook her hand. "It's a pleasure to meet you."

"What a lucky chance that I stopped by," Mrs. Hughes continued chattily. "Rebecca has been positively mysterious where you're concerned. We've all been dying to meet you."

He listened politely.

"Of course, Alan's mentioned that you're his boss at the rental store. I understand you're the owner?"

"Yes, I am."

"Do you live here in White Horse?"

"No, in Everett."

"Oh, was that where you started the chain?"

Rebecca rolled her eyes.

"Yes, as a matter of fact it was," Sam said.

Before her mother could continue the inquisition, Rebecca broke in. "Mom, if you'll excuse us, we'd better get going. I have to be back by one."

"Of course." Without sparing Rebecca a glance, Mrs. Hughes smiled at Sam with the kind of charm that made her hard to resist. "Sam, we'd all love to have a chance to get to know you. Rebecca's family is very close. Is there any chance you can join us Sunday for dinner? It's not formal at all—our gatherings are quite relaxed, I promise. But we'd all feel so much better if we knew the man Rebecca is dating. Not that I mean to scare you!" She chuckled. "But Rebecca's brothers are still just a little protective."

Sam slanted a look at Rebecca that she couldn't interpret. She would have liked to crawl under her desk and hide. Protective! As if Lee and Joe cared whom she was dating! But she couldn't quite bring herself to confront her mother in front of Sam.

The silence lasted just long enough to become uncomfortable. Then Sam said stiffly, "Thank you. I'll look forward to it."

"Oh, good." Mrs. Hughes patted Rebecca's arm. Her wink wasn't meant for Sam's eyes. "Then I'll be on my way. Until Sunday!" she said gaily, and hurried out of the store.

Rebecca waited until the front door had closed behind her mother before groaning. "God, I'm sorry, Sam. I don't know what got into her. No, I can guess. Alan. She's determined to find out whether you're fit to associate with her grandson. Forget me. All that stuff about my brothers was absolute nonsense. They are much too busy to worry about who I'm dating. I know you had plans this weekend, so I'll just make your excuses Sunday. I absolutely refuse to let my mother put you on the spot!" At

Sam's cool, unreadable gaze, her flustered speech came to a halt.

"No, she's right to be concerned," he said simply. "I'll come Sunday."

"But..."

"Don't worry about it. Now, let's go have lunch."

As she collected her purse and let Carol, who worked for Browder's Flooring, know that she was leaving, Rebecca was a mass of conflicting emotions. How dared her mother just "happen" to be at the store and insist Sam present himself for inspection as if Rebecca were a sheltered sixteen-year-old?

Yet her motives were understandable, and she *had* succeeded. Rebecca did want Sam to meet her family and for them to get to know him. If he'd been making excuses just because he was uncomfortable with the idea of her large, close family, surely he'd discover Sunday that they were perfectly nice people.

The conclusion Rebecca came to was that she'd give her mother hell for taking matters into her own hands—but the results Rebecca couldn't complain about.

Except for one thing. She sneaked a look at Sam as he held open the door for her. His expression was aloof, his cool gray eyes distant. She had a horrible feeling he felt pressured—and could she blame him?

She let out a small sigh. Sunday would be the litmus test. Sam would finally have to face the fact that her family were part and parcel of her. Either he could live with that or he couldn't.

Wasn't it better to find out now?

COMING HAD BEEN a big mistake. The moment Rebecca ushered Sam into the living room at her brother's house that Sunday, Sam knew he should have accepted her offer to make his excuses.

Not that he'd expected to enjoy himself. This afternoon was slated as an inspection, there was no getting around it. He'd spent the past several days irritated with himself for agreeing. Why the hell had he let himself be bulldozed?

He knew the answer: Rebecca. Damn it, she wanted him to meet her family, to like them. And he wanted to please her, even if he was far from certain he was willing to go the last mile: commitment and marriage.

Despite his irritation, he'd figured this one occasion wouldn't kill him. He would be civil, refrain from putting his elbows on the table and answer as few questions as possible. Duty done, he would leave as soon as he could.

What he'd blocked out was that this was a family. Curious about him, sure, but also talking, laughing, gossiping, teasing, quarreling. Teenagers were everywhere, starting with the driveway, where a basketball hoop hung above the garage. Sam and Rebecca had had to cross the grass to avoid the intense game of one-on-one being played there.

Inside the modest rambler, there were people everywhere. The rich aroma of a turkey in the oven wafted from the kitchen. Rebecca added her covered bowl to others on the counter, then tugged him behind her into the living room.

"Hi, everybody," she called, and was answered by a chorus of hellos. An NFL game blasted from the TV; a man with a beer in one hand was bellowing at the incompetent refs, while Alan and another boy seemed to be trying to explain the basic elements of the game to a girl in a baggy sweatshirt and leggings.

A family. A gathering like a million others, even if the faces were ones he hadn't seen before. Norman Rockwell could have painted this family to represent all the others.

Including Sam's.

His muscles tightened and he felt like a Vietnam vet in the middle of a fireworks display. Trapped, knowing his reaction was irrational but unable to quell it. He wanted to shake off Rebecca's small, determined hand and make a run for it.

Too late. Mrs. Hughes advanced like an enemy tank. "Rebecca!" Mother and daughter hugged each other with seeming warmth, then the mother held out her hand to Sam.

"How nice to see you again. I'm so glad you could come."

More likely, she was glad he was obedient. He shook her hand. "Thank you."

At a momentary lull in the football game, Mrs. Hughes raised her voice. "Everybody! Meet Sam Ballard, Rebecca's guest."

Hell. A barrage of stares assessed him. He was conscious of Rebecca to one side, smiling, and of Alan's expressionless gaze. Sam stood there with his hands dangling helplessly at his sides; he felt like a ten-year-old required to give a presentation in front of the class.

No, worse. He felt like a ten-year-old at home, where another family gathering pretended that everything was all right, that they were just another happy family who loved being together.

Rebecca's family began to parade by Sam. First her sister, Jess, with the Little Orphan Annie hairdo and mischievous blue eyes.

"Hey, how'd my big sister nail my best customer?" Jess asked.

Sam was saved from having to answer by Rebecca's retort. "You met him first."

Little sister made a face. "Must have been my wedding ring that put him off."

An older man with sandy hair, a hearty manner and the family's blue eyes introduced himself as Lee, the bodyshop owner. Another man with an easy smile and a certain amount of sympathy in his eyes was Joe. Teenage girls and boys followed, plus a younger girl who studied him for an unnervingly long moment out of huge blue eyes. Then came Roy, the football fan, who slapped him on the back on the way to the kitchen for another beer. Yet another woman, with no family resemblance, whom Rebecca introduced as Lee's wife.

Sam felt numb. He accepted a beer from Lee, whose beefy hands were grease stained and marked by welding burns. Seeing one of those hands wrapped around a bottle of beer, Sam had a disorienting sensation of déjà vu. His father's hands looked just like that. It surprised him how easily he remembered them so many years later.

But, then, he'd known his father's hands well. Matt Ballard had been a man with a hot temper and no inclination to hold it. If he didn't like the way one of his sons looked at him, he backhanded the boy. When at sixteen years of age Sam had put a dent in the bumper of the family car, his father had broken his nose with his fist and cracked three ribs with the toe of his boot. A wide, thick belt hung by the back door for minor infractions and was a constant reminder of how their family was ruled by fear.

The part that made Sam most bitter was that as adults his two brothers had apparently forgiven their father. "Hell, that was just Dad," his brother would say tolerantly on the rare occasions when Sam called one of them. "He's mellowed." And then Sam would hear about how

NO RISK, NO OBLIGATION TO BUY...NOW OR EVER!

GUARANTEED

PLAY "ROLL A DOUBLE" AND GET AS MANY AS FIVE FREE GIFTS!

HERE'S HOW TO PLAY:

1. Peel off label from front cover. Place it in space provided at right. With a coin, carefully scratch off the silver dice. This makes you eligible to receive two or more free books, and possibly another gift, depending on what is revealed beneath the scratch-off area.

2. Send back this card and you'll receive brand-new Harlequin Superromance® novels. These books have a cover price of $3.50 each, but they are yours to keep absolutely free.

3. There's no catch. You're under no obligation to buy anything. We charge nothing – ZERO – for your first shipment. And you don't have to make any minimum number of purchases – not even one!

4. The fact is thousands of readers enjoy receiving books by mail from the Harlequin Reader Service® before they're available in stores. They like the convenience of home delivery and they love our discount prices!

5. We hope that after receiving your free books you'll want to remain a subscriber. But the choice is yours – to continue or cancel, anytime at all! So why not take us up on our invitation, with no risk of any kind. You'll be glad you did!

THE HARLEQUIN READER SERVICE®: HERE'S HOW IT WORKS

Accepting free books puts you under no obligation to buy anything. You may keep the books and gift and return the shipping statement marked "cancel." If you do not cancel, about a month later we will send you 4 additional novels, and bill you just $2.71 each plus 25¢ delivery and applicable sales tax, if any.* That's the complete price, and – compared to cover prices of $3.50 each – quite a bargain! You may cancel at any time, but if you choose to continue, every month we'll send you 4 more books, which you may either purchase at the discount price...or return at our expense and cancel your subscription.

*Terms and prices subject to change without notice. Sales tax applicable in N.Y.

they had gone to the ball game with Dad, brought their wives and children over for holidays and for Sunday dinners. Just like this one.

He did his damnedest to withdraw from the chaos. How the hell did they stand all the noise? For a refuge he chose the group around the TV set, though he didn't like Roy, the beer guzzler who resented every call the referees made against the Seahawks and said so loudly. Roy was given to snapping at the kids whenever he thought they were too noisy. Sam wondered why somebody hadn't told *him* to shut up so they could watch the game.

Even there he wasn't left alone. First the nine-year-old wandered over.

"You're Aunt Becca's friend, aren't you?"

He agreed that he was.

"She's my favorite aunt. Well, I like Aunt Janine, too. You must really like Aunt Becca."

A preteen girl just getting breasts leaned over the back of the couch. "Why else do you think he's here?" she asked rudely.

The younger one stuck out her tongue. The big sister— cousin?—ignored her and turned to Sam.

"Aunt Becca's cool, isn't she?"

"Yeah," he said. His head was beginning to ache with the tension he felt. He looked across the room at Rebecca. *Rescue me, damn it.* But she smiled and waved before resuming her conversation with one of her brothers.

Jess came and plopped on the couch next to him. "You guys giving him a hard time?" she demanded, sternly eyeing the girls.

"We were only talking," said the little one.

"Just so they weren't giving you the third degree," she told Sam. When the older girl sniffed and whirled away,

Jess laughed. "She's mine. I hear it'll get even worse when she turns thirteen. You have any sisters?"

"No, brothers."

"Does your family live around here?"

"Seattle," he said.

Fortunately she wasn't all that interested.

"Mostly I think I'm lucky to have family right here in town." She cast an odd glance at her husband, who in disgust had just thrown the remote control down on the couch. "Roy might not agree," she added ruefully.

But, then, Roy was no prize, Sam thought. He didn't comment. She did. In fact, she turned out to be almost as chatty as Rebecca. Only he wasn't as interested in what she had to say.

Eventually amiable Joe took her place. He was more interested in Sam's answers than his sister had been. Sam's headache gripped him with fingers of pain as he waited expressionlessly for each question. He was determined to see this through, but that didn't mean he had to like it.

He didn't know whether to be relieved or apprehensive when Jess announced dinner.

Roy scowled. "Hell! There's still ten minutes to go. I'm bringing my plate in here."

Sam thought he saw a shadow cross Jess's piquant face, but she gave a forced smile. "Nobody will drag you away from the game," she promised. "Sam, are you so devoted to the Seahawks you can't stand to join us at the table?"

Sam stood. "No, I'm not much of a fan."

Roy shot him an incredulous glance. "You don't watch football?"

"I don't usually have time," Sam said, his gaze cool.

Rebecca met him at the arched opening to the dining room. "Hi," she said softly. "Surviving?"

He didn't have a chance to answer. Her mother effortlessly parted him from Rebecca.

"Why don't you sit here beside me?" Mrs. Hughes suggested. "We'll finally have a chance to talk."

Great. Sam braced himself for the continuation of the ordeal. The adults gradually took their places at the table, while kids trooped in and out filling plates.

Heads were bowed as Lee said grace, then serving bowls made the rounds. Sam had barely loaded his plate, when Mrs. Hughes pinned him with a steely smile.

"Does your family live around here, Sam?"

"Seattle."

"How nice to have them close. Has Rebecca had a chance to meet them yet?"

"I'm afraid not."

"Family is so important, don't you think?"

"I'm not close to mine." Thank God, he thought.

She patted his arm. "I'm so sorry. I hope we can show you what you've been missing."

Sam inclined his head. He wondered if these people really liked one another as well as they pretended to. Or was the obvious tension between Roy and Jess only the tip of the iceberg?

"I suppose Rebecca has told you about her marriage." Mrs. Hughes shook her head sadly. "I'm afraid I never cared much for Bruce."

Poor Bruce.

"We've been so fortunate in Janine, Lee's wife. She's always fit right in. Why, I hardly remember she's not my daughter."

Not a word about Roy. Presumably he *didn't* fit right in. Sam felt grudging sympathy for that viewpoint, even as his irritation grew. Why did Rebecca put up with this crap? Would she have the guts to ignore her mother's gently worded advice on whom she ought to associate with? Was Jess having to pay for her foolishness in bringing a man into the family who didn't quite "fit in"?

"I understand Alan works for you," the matriarch continued serenely. "I do hope my grandson does a good job."

"Alan's fine," he said shortly.

"I know it's hard for him to adjust to his mother dating again. Children never like to think of their parents as anything but, do they?" She chuckled. "Gracious! I wouldn't dare remarry. I can just imagine how stunned they would all be!"

Sam inclined his head again.

"Well," Lee said from across the table. "Rebecca hasn't told us much about you. Did you grow up around here, Sam?"

Proud of his self-control, Sam politely endured another round of grilling. Other conversations swirled around him. When he looked down the table at Rebecca, he saw her laughing at something Joe had said and teasing him back, her nose crinkled in that way Sam found so endearingly sexy. She didn't even glance Sam's way.

She had tossed him to the wolves with a vengeance.

Apparently satisfied, Lee finally turned to Rebecca and said something innocuous about the meal. Sam took a few more bites he didn't taste.

On his other side Janine offered him a basket of warm biscuits. "So," she said cheerily, "do you have family in the area, Sam?"

CHAPTER NINE

IN RETROSPECT Rebecca realized how difficult the afternoon must have been for Sam. At the time she'd anxiously watched as he'd become more and more aloof, his grim expression a challenge fewer members of her family were willing to accept.

As far as Rebecca was concerned, the dinner was a disaster. Sam clearly hadn't liked her family, and she seriously doubted that any of them had liked him. How could they, when he'd spoken in monosyllables?

He drove her home afterward in almost complete silence. Rebecca, who chattered through nearly all of life's little crises, from childbirth on down, couldn't think of a thing to talk about.

In her driveway, she said brightly, "I'll, umm, speak to you later?"

Sam nodded, frowning. "I'm sorry," he apologized, sounding grudging. "I'm no social animal."

"It's okay," Rebecca said quickly. She was already sliding out. "I know how overbearing my family can be en masse."

"I'll walk you up."

"Oh, you don't have to—"

But he was out of the car and moving to her side.

More silence.

"Don't you ever get together with fewer of you at a time?" Sam asked abruptly.

"Well, sure, but these Sunday dinners have become kind of a tradition. If Joe ever starts a family or any of the rest of us have more kids, we may have to do something drastic, like rent a hall. In the meantime, it's sort of fun and..." Rebecca bit her lip. "I'm the one who should be sorry," she said quietly. "I know you must have gotten the third degree."

"You could say that."

Her key out of her purse, she turned to face Sam on the front porch. "Just forget it, okay?"

He searched her face with curious intensity. "Maybe," he said gruffly. "But don't you forget this." He grasped her upper arms, holding her still as his mouth captured hers in a punishing, exhilarating kiss. No tenderness, no coaxing, just a blunt reminder of the shocking, breathtaking passion they had shared.

When he released her, Rebecca staggered. He didn't notice, so quickly had he turned away. A lump in her throat, she made her way to the porch swing and sagged onto it.

She almost saluted as she watched his car disappear down the street. Then she sighed. Well. His message had come through loud and clear. In fact, despite her perturbation, she had been ridiculously receptive.

Trouble was, that still left her with a problem. Did sexual compatibility balance the undoubted disapproval of her family?

"DAMN." Alan slammed the phone back in its cradle.

Rebecca looked up from the grocery coupon she was carefully cutting out of the Sunday-morning paper, which still sat unread on the coffee table. "What's wrong?"

Alan shrugged. "It's just Dad. He's never home."

"What do you mean, 'never'? You saw him last weekend."

"Since then. He hasn't answered his phone all week. I wonder what the deal is."

Bruce just being himself, Rebecca thought cynically, but she had long ago learned to suppress such remarks. "Maybe he's out of town."

"Well, why didn't he tell me?" Alan demanded.

"Has he ever reported his movements to you?"

Alan threw himself into a chair with all the grace of a horse deciding to roll on its back. "No," he said reluctantly. "But . . ."

"Are you worried about him?"

He frowned. "No, I guess not."

"Well, try again this evening. Presumably he has to work tomorrow, unless he took a vacation."

"Yeah, with Karen," he said gloomily.

"Hey, you were the one who cut your visit short, remember?"

"They kept kissing in front of me."

She almost laughed at his complete disgust. "I'm glad to know you have the good taste not to neck in the halls at school."

His lip curled. *"Neck?"*

"Yeah. You know, make out, smooch, mmm . . ."

He rolled his eyes. "I figured it out, Mom."

"Well, do you?"

"What?"

"Neck?"

"None of your business!"

She smiled unrepentantly. "Then give your dad a break."

He brooded for a few minutes while she continued cutting out coupons. "Don't you mind?" he said at last. "I mean, Dad with a girlfriend and everything?"

"No," Rebecca said without the slightest hesitation. "Do you know it's been four years now since we separated?" He nodded, and she continued, "Sometimes he seems like a stranger to me. I can't remember what it felt like to kiss him. I feel . . . detached. Do you know what I mean?"

Alan nodded again. "How come you bother with those coupons? Wow, twenty-five cents. Big deal."

"Because I'm basically stingy."

"Oh." He fidgeted. Rebecca waited for him to work up the nerve to say whatever he had in mind. "I heard Aunt Janine and Grandma out in the kitchen today talking about Sam," he finally managed.

Carefully Rebecca put down the scissors. "I should give you a lecture about eavesdropping."

Alan didn't seem to hear her. "He's really not that bad. They didn't give him a chance."

Rebecca looked down at her hands. "No, but he didn't give them a chance, either."

"He's been okay to me, considering."

"Yes, he has," Rebecca agreed. It was one of the few things that gave her hope. "You might mention that to Grandma when you're talking to her. I have a feeling you did point out a few other things to her earlier."

He flushed. "I was just bitching. You know?"

"Yeah, I know." She smiled at him. "I love you."

He grinned, looking like a little kid for a minute. "You're okay, too, Mom."

"Why, thank you." She hoped he didn't notice the dampness in her eyes. "I'm overcome." Rebecca cleared her throat. "How would you feel about my inviting Sam to dinner some evening this week?"

Alan looked alarmed. "When I'm home?"

She nodded.

"Do you have to?"

"No." She waited.

"Oh, jeez." He stood up. "Okay, I guess. But you do the talking."

She made a face at him. "That's rarely a problem."

"I gotta do some homework," Alan announced, and departed.

Was she crazy? Rebecca wondered. Probably, she decided, but knew she had no real choice. Today had scared her. It had made her wonder if Sam was dreadfully wrong for her. She *had* to find out, before it was too late. Before she admitted, even to herself, that she loved him.

THE INEVITABLE CHAT with her mother still caught Rebecca unprepared. Guiltily aware she had been neglectful, she'd suggested they have lunch on Tuesday. Over sandwiches at the deli down the street from her business, they talked about everything under the sun *but* Sam. They laughed over a funny incident at Tulalip Bingo, her mother advised her on how to handle an overdue account belonging to an old family friend and they worried together about Jess and Roy. This was the mother she was used to, the friend to whom she could say anything.

Over coffee and cheesecake, she did. "I shudder to ask, but what's the consensus on Sam?"

Her mother took a sip of coffee, looked her in the eye and said, "That he's a boor."

Shocked by the blunt answer, Rebecca slowly set down her fork. "Wait a minute. That's a little unfair. Surely it was obvious that Sam's just a reserved man. He wasn't rude!''

"No?" Mrs. Hughes's delicate eyebrows rose. "If you mean he didn't come right out and say anything unpleasant, that's true. In my book, however, it's equally rude to appear utterly uninterested in everybody around you. Surely good manners alone should have compelled him to make a pretense."

Hot anger burned Rebecca's throat. "Just like good manners compelled *you* to put him on the spot so he *had* to come?"

"I most certainly did not!" Her mother's nostrils flared and she sat regally straight in the overpadded booth. "Suggesting that a man who has been dating my daughter for some time make the effort to meet her family does not seem unreasonable to me. Wouldn't you worry if Alan dated a girl he didn't want you to meet?"

"Yes!" Rebecca snapped. "But he's a teenager. I'm an adult."

"Sam may be one, too, but he didn't act like one."

"You mean you didn't like his manners."

"Give me more credit than that." Although she didn't back down a whit, the lines that aged her face were suddenly more apparent. "If you have nothing in mind but a sexual interlude, maybe he's fine. I don't know— I'd rather not know. If you're imagining that Sam Ballard is husband material, I think you're dreaming. A man interested in marrying a woman is also interested in her family."

Sickening fear mixed with Rebecca's anger. "Obviously this is a discussion we'd better end." She grabbed her purse and the check the waitress had left on the table. "I shouldn't have asked what you thought of him. More to the point, I should have talked Sam out of coming Sunday. Now, if you'll excuse me, I have to get back to work."

"Rebecca . . ." Her mother reached out a hand.

However horrifying this anger between them was, Rebecca could not, would not, respond to any overture. "I'll talk to you later," she said coldly, and turned away.

She couldn't remember ever feeling so alienated from her mother. She vaguely recalled an argument about Bruce when Rebecca had announced her intention to marry him. Oh, God, why had she set herself up for this again? She already felt guilty. She had asked her mother a question; her mother had answered.

Yeah, well, there were answers and there were answers. This one had been harsh, Rebecca reminded herself. A final judgment. Had her mother expected her merely to nod like a good little girl?

Perhaps it was fortunate that her afternoon was busy, since this let her cool off before she had time to really think about her mother's criticisms. Several women wanted help finding wallpaper, and Rebecca booked an appointment to hang paper for another customer whose order had just come in.

"If it were a nice square, blank room, I'd try it myself," the woman said. "But a bathroom... How on earth do you get it behind the toilet?"

Rebecca smiled reassuringly. "Practice, and the right tools."

"Better you than me."

Finally, an eternity later, she went home. A glance at her watch reminded her that Alan wouldn't be back from basketball practice for another hour. Wearily Rebecca went into the kitchen and put on hot water for a cup of tea.

There was a certain irony to that, she thought. Her mother was the tea drinker in her family. The coziness, the comforting quality of tea were forever associated in Rebecca's mind with her mother.

Okay, forget comfort, Rebecca told herself. *Be honest.*

Was her mother right? Had she been blinding herself to Sam's faults? Did his interest in her extend no further than her bedroom?

It was hard to be totally honest, she found. She wanted so much to believe that Sam was falling in love with her, just as she was with him. She wanted to believe that he, too, was thinking about the future, figuring out how they could adjust their complicated lives to fit each other's needs.

But did she have a single piece of evidence to suggest that he *was* falling for her?

"No," she said, almost whispering. Yet her voice echoed in the silent, high-ceilinged kitchen. She suddenly felt very alone, even a little scared. Had she jeopardized her heart and her relationship with her son and her family for a dead-end affair with a man who hadn't made even a pretense of sharing his past or future with her?

When she thought back, all Rebecca could remember was superficiality, sweetness and light. Had they ever once had a dead-serious conversation, the kind where they talked about what they wanted out of life, what they needed from each other, where this relationship was going?

No.

Rebecca steeped her tea, letting it become dark and almost bitter. That was how she felt.

She had accepted Sam's reserve, assumed that expressing emotions was difficult for him. In her own chatty way, she had told him everything about her he needed to know. She'd kept telling herself that he would reciprocate someday, when he knew her better, when he was more comfortable, when the time was right.

Would the time ever be right?

She had to talk to him, force the issue. She had to *know*. She needed to say, *Why didn't you try harder to get along with my family? Do you care so little that it wasn't worth the effort?*

Well, she'd left a message yesterday on his answering machine, asking him to dinner Friday evening. He hadn't replied yet, but unless Sunday had totally turned him off, she assumed he would agree. Unless, of course, he made an excuse when he found out she intended for Alan to be there.

Sam didn't call that evening. Instead he dropped by her store at noon the next day. Rebecca was figuring out dimensions for valances ordered by a friend of her mother, when she heard footsteps and looked up.

Sam was strolling toward her, hands shoved in his pockets, tie discarded and his white shirt unbuttoned at the neck. One of those faint, impossibly sexy smiles curved his mouth, though his eyes were guarded. "Any chance you're free for lunch?" he asked.

Her gaze dropped from his. "Umm, sure. Give me a second."

She'd hoped to marshal her thoughts, make lists, memorize a speech. She didn't want to sound antagonistic, accusing, only matter-of-fact, presenting her point of view. Right now her point of view felt muddled and inarticulate. She was tempted to put the confrontation off, to enjoy lunch with the most attractive man who had ever looked twice at her. Maybe *he* would bring up the subject, she thought hopefully, with a true coward's sense of optimism.

She grabbed her purse and said goodbye to Carol, then let Sam usher her out into the unseasonable sunshine. It was November, and her roses were still blooming. The first frost had yet to strike, although the hues of autumn were all around.

"How about that new Mexican restaurant?" Sam asked casually, holding open the passenger door of his car for her.

Rebecca had the length of time it took him to circle the car and get in behind the wheel to think. To bring herself up short.

She had to *know*. She'd procrastinated long enough.

Trying to sound equally casual, she said, "Would you mind if we got sandwiches from the deli again to take to the river park? There's something I'd like to discuss with you."

His eyes narrowed, but he inclined his head. "Why not?"

Rebecca's nervousness built as they drove to the deli, stood in line, made their choices, then went back to the car. There was no way on earth she could withstand her tension in silence.

And what else could she talk about besides her family?

"Alan's first basketball game is tomorrow night," she told Sam. "He's a guard. Huge as he seems to me, he claims not to be big enough to play forward, at least not when he gets to college. He's quick, though, so he might actually get recruited for both sports. I'd rather see him play basketball, just because basketball players don't seem to get hurt the way football players do. I shudder to think of three-hundred-pound behemoths driving him into the ground. But he loves being a quarterback, and...well, it's his choice. Unfortunately."

"He's good," Sam said dispassionately.

"Did you really think so?" She waited hopefully for reassurance. As though it mattered right this second.

"Mmm-hmm." Sam parked the car in the nearly empty lot by the playground. "If you can get the bag, I'll bring the drinks."

"Oh, sure." She waited while he locked up. When they fell into step, she opened her mouth to continue the chatter that was a safety net for her—and discovered abruptly that she couldn't think of a single thing to say. She was terrified at the risk she was about to take.

They had the bluff above the river to themselves. They sat down and Sam opened the bag, handing Rebecca her sandwich and accepting a can of pop from her.

Silence reigned as they unwrapped sandwiches. Sam sat gazing out at the green-brown river that flowed, low and sluggish, between the high banks. In profile his face was strong and unapproachable, without the softening effect of the humor that often showed in his eyes.

"Well?" he said.

Oh, Lord, she thought. The moment of truth.

Rebecca groped for the right thing to say, for that speech she had intended to memorize. Nothing came. Her chest felt tight, and she had no appetite for her sandwich. Just to occupy her hands, she slowly wrapped it again.

Sam glanced from the sandwich to her face. An eyebrow twitched. She silently begged him to say something, anything, but, of course, filling the silence wasn't his way.

In the end she blurted, "How do you feel about me?" She was infuriated by the betraying squeak of her voice.

He scrutinized her. "Isn't that obvious?"

"No," she said straight out. "I thought it was, but Sunday I got to thinking. I make assumptions. I've probably made some big ones where you're concerned."

"Let me guess," he said slowly, a spark of anger in his eyes. "It's your mother who got you thinking."

"Does it matter?"

"Damn right it does." The muscles in his jaw tightened. "How old are you?"

"Thirty-five."

"Past letting your mother critique your friends, don't you think?"

Rebecca's chin came up. "Did I say she did?"

He was scowling now. "I heard a sample of it, remember?"

The infamous phone message. She'd forgotten. "All my mother wanted was to meet you. Alan has had a hard time adjusting to the fact that I was dating. Is that so unreasonable?"

His voice was harsh. "Sounds like your mother's the one who isn't adjusting."

That did it. Rebecca's nervousness vanished in a rush of anger. "Just because you live in a vacuum doesn't mean the rest of us should! I love my family, and they love me."

Sam laughed mirthlessly. "Yeah, right, the Brady Bunch."

"What's that supposed to mean?" she demanded.

"That it's pretty obvious your brother-in-law doesn't think things are so rosy. And what about your ex-husband? He didn't rate high with Mom, did he? Are you going to tell me that didn't influence you?"

"What, you think I drove my husband into the arms of other women?" she snapped.

"I think most men are capable of acts of childish rebellion."

Rebecca stared at his hard, angry face, scarcely able to believe she had heard him right. She felt . . . violated. Sick to her stomach. Defensive.

"Have I driven you to rebellion?" she asked levelly.

"No." Sam moved his shoulders as though trying to relax tense muscles. His voice softened. "Rebecca, I'm not trying to be an SOB. I...like you. You know damn well I'm attracted to you. But I see you letting your mother run your life. I'm too old to submit myself to a girl's parents for approval, for God's sake. That's what was happening Sunday, don't kid yourself."

"That's not true," Rebecca protested weakly. It *was* true in her mother's eyes, if not hers. No, she was still kidding herself. She *had* sought her family's approval, been anxious that Sam make a good impression. She'd wanted them to like Sam, as they hadn't liked Bruce.

"Bull," he said bluntly. "Question is, are you going to put up with it?"

Feeling like a coward, Rebecca avoided his gaze and turned to look at the river. "Are you suggesting that I totally disregard my family's opinion? What about my son? Doesn't he count, either?"

"Alan's not the issue here, is he?" Sam made a move as though to touch her, then drew back his hand. "We've been spending time together, even though Alan's done his damnedest to stop us. But you take me to meet your mother, and next thing you want to know what my intentions are. That's what you're asking, isn't it?"

Without really seeing, Rebecca watched a branch drift downriver. She shook her head. "No. I wanted to know why you hated Sunday so much, and—" she hesitated "—why you didn't even *try*."

"Damn it, Rebecca, I'm not much good with people." He sounded awkward. "I wouldn't know how to start, even if I wanted to impress a crowd with my sterling qualities."

"But you didn't try," she said again.

"How do you know?"

Startled, she turned her head. His face was impassive, but there was something vulnerable in his eyes that made her wonder. "But...they're all such nice people," she said, perplexed.

"They didn't look that way from the outside. They looked damn cold."

Rebecca opened her mouth, closed it. Was it true? Had the eyes that to her seemed warm, curious, friendly, to Sam appeared coldly inquisitional? Had they looked that way to Bruce, too? To Roy?

She felt strangely disoriented, as though the earth under her feet had shifted ever so slightly.

"Has this discussion gotten us anywhere?" Sam asked.

"I don't know. I have to think."

Sam watched her but didn't comment.

"Will you take me back to work now?" Rebecca asked.

He nodded. For once Rebecca was grateful for his silence. As it was, the five minute drive back to the main street was strained. Rebecca had no idea where they stood. Sam had said some harsh things; he would undoubtedly view her accusation that he hadn't even tried to get along with her family in the same light. Would he call her again? Was she supposed to call him once she'd done some thinking? Her state of uncertainty made her feel as if she were fifteen again. In high school she could have sent her girlfriend over to ask one of his friends how he felt about her, thus saving herself from a painful rejection if he no longer wanted to see her. In the real, grown-up world, it wasn't so easy.

In front of Browder's, Sam made no move to get out. Both hands were wrapped around the steering wheel; he looked straight ahead through the windshield. Rebecca reached for the door handle, but was startled by his voice, rougher than usual.

"I don't want to lose you."

"Maybe not," she said sadly. "But you're not sure you really want me, either, are you?"

"That's not quite fair."

"No. I'm sorry." She opened the door. "I guess we both have some thinking to do. Goodbye, Sam."

If he answered, she didn't hear him.

THE PHONE RANG just as Alan was heading out the door Wednesday evening for work. His mother was off showing samples of blinds to some woman who wanted to redo her living room. He almost kept going, then hesitated, even though he didn't want to take a chance on being late. He still hadn't reached his dad; as far as Alan could tell, he hadn't been home for the past ten days. Maybe he was calling.

Swearing, Alan turned back toward the kitchen. By the time he got there, the answering machine was doing its thing. He'd just listen to hear who it was. Then if the call was important, he could pick the phone up.

"Alan, it's Dad," the disembodied voice announced. Alan made a move toward the phone, but his hand froze just above the receiver at his father's next words: "Karen and I got married last week. It was kind of impulsive I wish you could have been there. We just flew down to Reno and did it, then stayed for a honeymoon. I know you liked Karen, and she thought you were the greatest. Come on down in a week or so and we'll celebrate. What do you say? Listen, give me a call when you can." Click.

Alan groped for a chair and sank into it. Married? His dad had gotten married without even telling him first?

The answering machine rewound and its red light started blinking. Alan pushed the Play button. The message began again. "Alan, it's Dad. Karen and I got married last week."

Alan violently punched the button again, cutting off his father's voice. Jesus. Married. He'd never thought Dad wanted to marry again. And to some woman he barely knew? Two or three months ago he'd been seeing what's-her-name.

His mostly blank gaze came to rest on the kitchen clock. "Oh, no," he groaned, jumping up. He was going to be late. Sure as shooting, this was the night Sam would be sitting there staring at his watch.

He speeded on the way, slammed to a stop in the small parking lot. Finally, at 6:10, he hurtled in the front door of White Horse Rentals.

He knew right away that Sam was in a bad mood. Scowling, his boss looked up from where he sat behind the counter.

"You're late."

Alan had been trying not to think. "The phone rang just as I was leaving," he said. "It was my—" He stopped abruptly. As if The Jerk cared.

Sam's expression changed. "Is something wrong?"

"Nah." He stood there like an idiot, his hands shoved in the pockets of his letter jacket. He should get to work. Why was he glued to the floor?

Sam stood up and circled the counter. "Who was it?"

He sounded as if he expected an answer. Now.

"My dad." Alan didn't mean to say any more but somehow words kept spilling out. "He got married. Last weekend. I didn't know he was going to. I mean, I've barely met the woman. Karen. Her name's Karen. She's, I don't know, maybe twenty-five or something. Like halfway between Dad and me. How am I supposed to think of her as a stepmother?''

Sam leaned against the counter, watching Alan intently. "You don't see him that often, do you?''

"No, but..." Suddenly he was angry. Kick-a-hole-in-the-wall angry. "It won't be the same. We always did stuff together. Sometimes, anyway." Bitterness crept in. "He could hardly make it to my ball games, even though he liked to talk big about how talented I am. Do you know, he only came to *one* football game this year?''

Sam nodded.

"So I guess it shouldn't make any different, but..." Alan's face crumpled and he blinked hard to keep from crying. "He's different. It's like I don't even know him anymore.''

"You're lucky to have your mother.''

Two weeks ago Alan would have said something snotty. Tonight he took a deep breath. "Yeah. I know I am. Well." He shrugged awkwardly. "I'd better get to work. I'm sorry I'm late.''

"Forget it. Some things are more important than a job. Any job.''

"Yeah, well, thanks." To his surprise, Alan realized that he felt better. Less angry, as though just saying the words had drawn some of the raw, ugly emotion out of him. He was glad Sam hadn't given him that pep talk about how his father really loved him, and how having a new wife wouldn't affect how he felt about Alan. Yeah, right, he thought. Easy for grown-ups to say.

The next couple of hours passed without another word. Alan scrubbed and dusted and mopped with a detachment that surprised him. Twice he glanced up to see Sam watching him, but not critically. He couldn't tell what Sam was thinking.

Alan intended to make a point of staying fifteen minutes over to make up for being late, but at ten to eight, Sam said, "Time to pack it up."

"But I haven't been here two hours."

"I want to go home," Sam said. "I might as well close up, instead of leaving you to do it."

"Well, sure." A few minutes later, as Sam held open the door for him, Alan said, "Thanks. I'll, uh, see you."

"Good night, Alan," Sam said simply.

Then, to Alan's surprise, Sam actually smiled.

REBECCA LAY in wait for her son. When he walked in the front door at eight o'clock on the dot and called a hello, she stood up. "Hi, I'm in here."

He appeared in the doorway.

"How was work?"

Alan gave her an odd look. "It was okay. Sam let me leave early."

"He did?" Brilliant. What was Alan supposed to say—no, he didn't?

"He wanted to close up."

"Oh." She smiled nervously. "How are the two of you getting along these days?"

"Better," Alan said with a shrug. "When is he coming to dinner?"

Rebecca sat down and reached for the TV guide. As if she cared what was on. She said offhandedly, "Oh. I'd almost forgotten. I did ask, but we've had ... a disagreement. I don't know how things stand."

"What's that supposed to mean?"

"I don't know if he still wants to come, that's what. Does it matter? Am I interfering with your social calendar?"

"So he doesn't want to come."

"I don't know!" She glared up at Alan, who loomed above her. He looked back at her as if she were an idiot.

"How can you not know?"

Trouble was, she felt like an idiot. "Because," she said with exaggerated patience, "he left a phone message saying Friday night was fine. Then we had lunch and our...disagreement. Now I have absolutely no idea whether he's still planning to come Friday night or not. Does that answer your question?"

Alan sighed loudly. "Jeez, Mom. Way to go."

Rebecca threw the TV guide as hard as she could across the room. It struck the wall and fell to the floor, the pages fanned open. Her burst of temper made her feel better enough to say mildly, "Can we drop the subject?"

"Sure, only... Are you going to fix a fancy dinner Friday or what?"

"You planning to put Coach James on standby?"

"Nah." Looking depressed, Alan dropped into a chair. "He never called to ask you out anyway, did he?"

She shook her head.

"I guess you were right," he said gloomily. "He is too young for you."

"What, do I look especially old right now?"

"It's not you." His face twisted. "It's Dad. He left a message tonight."

Rebecca blinked at the dizzying change of subject. "And?"

"He got married." Alan looked up at her with the same bewildered, beseeching expression he'd worn the day she'd to explain why his father had moved out. "To Karen. The one I told you about."

"Oh, Alan." She touched his hand, surprised at her indifference to the news. "You liked her, didn't you?"

"I guess she's okay. But . . . he did it without even telling me."

Rebecca threaded her fingers through her son's. He returned her clasp, his hand so much larger that it engulfed hers. Gently she asked, "Would you have liked it any better if he *had* told you?"

"I don't know." He gave it some thought. "Maybe not. The thing is, she's too young for him."

It was almost funny. If Rebecca hadn't had such a lousy week, she might have laughed. "Years aren't what count, you know. Despite what I said. Some people are emotionally mature at a young age. Some never are."

"And Dad isn't. Is that what you're saying?"

She'd expected hostility. What she got was understanding. "I'm just saying that maybe your dad and this Karen meet somewhere in the middle. Maybe they are right for each other."

"Yeah." His brow was crinkled and he seemed to be looking at something she couldn't see. "Yeah. Maybe."

CHAPTER TEN

GUESS WHO'S COMING to dinner?

Making a face, Rebecca shoved the biscuits in the oven and kicked the oven door shut. Maybe she should have let Alan put somebody on standby. At least then all of this wouldn't go to waste.

From behind her, Alan asked, "What time did you tell him to come?"

"Six?" she said hesitantly.

"You mean you don't know for sure?"

Rebecca tried to sound confident. "I'm pretty sure."

"Way to go, Mom," Alan said for at least the second time in as many days.

She couldn't even chew him out. He was right.

Involuntarily her gaze went to the clock—5:58. In about three minutes, she would know how it felt to be stood up.

"Well," she said brightly, "at least we'll have a good dinner. It's no big deal if Sam doesn't show. I can't imagine that he will when we left things so up in the air. After all, he works most evenings." She managed a laugh. "Why am I telling you that?"

He just looked at her. She quit talking. She wasn't fooling him. And she had just discovered that being stood up in front of your own kid was the depth of humiliation.

The doorbell rang. Rebecca's pulse jumped, then resumed double-time. She discovered one more thing: she was just as nervous about Sam's arrival as she had been at the possibility that he wouldn't come.

Alan stood up from his spectator's seat at the kitchen table. "Hey, cool. Maybe he's here, after all."

"You go answer it," Rebecca said to his disappearing back. "No, why don't you let me get it?" she added to the empty kitchen.

She heard a rumble of masculine voices, then her son reappeared followed by Sam. Her heart contracted, and Rebecca realized how much she had hoped.

Or had she feared? After all, he could have taken the decision on their future out of her hands. Maybe the coward in her had hoped he would do that.

Her self-analysis took only a split second, during which she watched Sam approach. He was dressed casually, but the khaki pants made her conscious of his lean hips and long legs. Rolled-up shirtsleeves hit her weakest spot; she loved the sight of a man's strong, tanned forearms. She glanced nervously up at his face. He looked contained, his eyes hooded, his mouth a firm line that revealed nothing.

He was nearly in front of her before she saw beyond the mask he wore in self-defense. Perhaps it was his voice that gave him away. Gruffly he said, "Were we still on for tonight?"

"You bet," Rebecca answered, doing her damnedest to sound as though she'd never doubted for a moment that he would come. Behind Sam, her son rolled his eyes. Rebecca glared at him. Looking hastily back at Sam, she said more truthfully, "Well, I'd hoped so, anyway. Otherwise Alan and I were going to be eating cashew chicken for the next week."

Some indefinable tension went out of Sam's bearing, and he smiled crookedly. "If Alan is like most teenage boys, he could put a week's worth of food away in one sitting."

Rebecca smiled back tentatively. "Were you like that?"

"I was a jock," Sam said. "Nothing like a good workout to give you an appetite."

"That's what I keep telling her," Alan agreed. "Is dinner almost ready, Mom?"

Sam glanced at her son, and Rebecca blinked, feeling as if she'd been released from a spell. Somehow she always forgot the effect Sam had on her. He'd made her feel like a lovesick teenager, with all the joy and misery that implied. No, things weren't quite as bad as they had been at sixteen. At least now she had confidence in her sexuality, in the effect she had on Sam.

Some of her nervousness abated as dinner progressed. Alan was clearly making an effort, which was all you could ask of a teenage boy. He said please and thank-you, didn't reach across the table for seconds and occasionally even had something to say. Rebecca carefully steered the conversation into safe channels; not a word about her family crossed her lips. They talked about high school and college sports, the recruiters who were already nosing around Alan, Sam's business, her business and the ominous noise her car made when she braked.

"Has Alan taken a look?" Sam asked, glancing with raised eyebrows at her son.

"I don't know much about cars," Alan admitted. "Dad didn't really teach me anything before—" He broke off.

"Bruce used to say he'd teach Alan everything he knew once he was old enough to be useful," Rebecca said. She made a face. "He can't be doing much of that kind of work anymore, or he'd have picked up his tools. One of these days we should sell them all so I can actually get the car in the garage."

"What tools do you have?" Sam asked.

"Umm..." She looked at Alan. "There's some kind of saw—I wish I knew how to use it."

"It's a table saw," Alan explained. "There's all sorts of other stuff, too. A circular saw and a jigsaw and a drill. You know. Then wrenches and the things for the car."

"And neither of you know how to use any of it?" Sam looked incredulous.

"Well, it's not quite that bad," Rebecca said. "I mean, I can use the jigsaw and drill and hammer and level. We don't do too badly when we put our minds to it, do we, Alan?"

"Nah." Alan kept his head down as he moved food around his plate. "I wish I knew how to use the table saw, though."

"Want a lesson?"

Rebecca would have sworn that Sam was as surprised by the offer as Alan was.

"You mean, you'd show me how?" Alan said, looking up. Rebecca poked him under the table with her foot, and he flushed. "Thanks. I mean, sure, if you really mean..." He wound to a flustered stop.

"I don't mind," Sam said. "Got any scraps of wood lying around?"

"The garage is full of those, too," Rebecca said. "And Lord knows what else. Why don't you guys go play around out there while I clean up?"

"That doesn't sound fair," Sam said.

"Who said life's fair?" She sighed melodramatically. "A woman's lot..."

"Jeez, Mom, it's not like you even have to wash the dishes."

"I was kidding. Truly. Can't you tell by now?"

"You kid even when you mean it."

"Does she?" Sam murmured. "How do you tell the difference?"

Alan grimaced. "I guess."

Sam surprised them both by laughing again. His face changed so when amusement softened the hard lines, when his gray eyes glinted. Rebecca's heart constricted. Sam so rarely let his emotions show through that she felt honored when he did, as though a crack in his impassive facade were a display of trust on his part.

A smile still lingered around his eyes when he and Alan headed out the kitchen door toward the detached garage, which Rebecca had hardly looked at in months. It had been Bruce's preserve. And though she was hardly proud of that now, she had yet to overcome the sexual stereotype. She ventured far enough into the dusty, cobwebbed garage to grab her hoe and shovel, occasionally thought about cleaning it out so she could park the car there in winter—and always threw up her hands. Who had time for such jobs?

Her thoughts turned to Alan. Why hadn't she known he wished he knew how to use his father's tools? It wouldn't have taken a genius to guess. She'd tried so hard not to push him into being a replacement for Bruce. Her son wasn't ready to be "the man of the family"—a saying she detested—and she wasn't going to make him feel guilty about it.

Well, guess what? she thought ruefully. He felt guilty, anyway. Or inadequate, at least.

She took her time clearing the table and loading the dishwasher. She didn't want to interrupt Sam and Alan. If a little male bonding was going on, far be it from her to interject herself. Although she wouldn't mind knowing how to use the table saw, too. Of course, if Alan knew how and she didn't, he might feel proud enough to want to help her build the arbor. Now, wasn't that devious? she marveled.

ALAN WATCHED as Sam examined the saw. Then they hunted out some extra blades and cleaned them up. Even though Alan wanted to do some cutting, he didn't mind that Sam spent a lot of time talking about safety and accuracy.

"This manual's pretty clear," he said, having thumbed through it. "The trick to using a saw like this is following the instructions to the letter. You don't need skill—you need patience. Check yourself. Use a square to find out whether the saw and the rip fence are aligned. Make some gauges of your own." He glanced at Alan to be sure he was listening, then went on. "Now, this is a general-purpose blade. Think about what blade would be best for each project. If you're cutting plywood, for example, you want one more like this—" he chose a different one from the workbench "—because it makes a smoother cut. No matter what you're using, remember that the blade teeth get clogged with sawdust. Clean 'em regularly and keep them lightly oiled so they don't rust." He shook his head over the blade in the saw, which was streaked with gritty patches of rust. "Take care of your tools. Otherwise, they won't work right for you."

"Is that why everything that comes back to the rental store is cleaned up? I always thought..." Feeling dumb, Alan didn't finish.

"That's why," Sam agreed. "What did you think?"

"That...well, it was for looks."

A hint of humor in Sam's eyes offset his grave tone. "Keeping the floor clean is for looks. With the tools, it's for function."

A flush crept up Alan's neck, but he nodded.

"Now..." Sam glanced around. "How about that piece of plywood over there?"

Sam showed Alan where to stand, how to feed the wood into the saw without losing a hand. How to miter and rip cut and bevel. "There's more you can do," he said. "Dadoing and coving. You can even cut a circle. But let's start simple." He let Alan make some cuts, standing behind him and steadying his hand a couple of times.

Alan's self-consciousness disappeared in the face of Sam's patience. He was almost as big as the older man, but not as . . . solid. Yeah, that was it, he thought, sneaking a look at Sam. It wasn't just physical, though. Everything about Sam was solid. He was the kind of guy you could depend on. For the first time, Alan could see why his mother liked him.

Even giving instructions Sam didn't waste words. Everything was to the point and definite. Alan bet he never said anything he didn't mean.

Which was why he felt good when Sam told him, "You're doing fine."

By the time his mother stuck her head in the door and asked, "Hey, can a mere woman observe?" Alan knew he would never again think of Sam as The Jerk. And he hoped desperately that Sam didn't know that's how he'd thought of him before.

He almost felt jealous when Sam glanced at his mother with a certain warmth in his eyes and said, "I didn't know you were 'mere.'" Except then Sam looked to see if Alan had set up the next cut and nodded at him. "Okay, Alan, what are you going to do first?"

"Clean the blade."

Sam smiled, just the least tilt of his mouth, and said approvingly, "Good."

Alan hardly even understood why the one word loosened some knot inside him.

WELL, SO MUCH FOR her belief that Sam wasn't willing to make an effort, Rebecca thought that night long after he had gone home. A man interested in nothing but her body wouldn't have spent more than an hour giving her son a lesson in woodworking. Especially since Sam didn't seem all that interested in woodworking for its own sake. No, he was being kind to Alan, plain and simple.

And Alan had been receptive—miracle of miracles. Rebecca had the feeling Sam had an advocate in her house now.

Sam had suggested lunch again, and Rebecca had agreed quickly, ignoring the flutter of panic in her chest.

Where did that leave her now? Ready to take a leap of faith that included ignoring her mother's opinion?

Was Sam right that a woman her age shouldn't even *consider* her mother's opinion?

As she lay in bed hoping for sleep, Rebecca felt mildly schizophrenic, so firmly did two separate voices in her head wage their battle.

What's wrong with being friends with your mother? she argued.

Nothing. But you don't quit seeing a man because one of your friends doesn't like him. You don't decide how much of your income you should save because a friend thinks you should be thriftier.

I ask advice from my friends.

What friends? Between your mother and your sister, you don't have time for any other friends.

They care about me.

Sure they do. But do you really want to spend the rest of your life justifying your every thought and decision to your mother?

She doesn't ask me to justify anything.

No?

I'm the one who needs somebody to talk to. I ask for her advice.

With a friend, that would be reciprocal.

Mom does talk to me about her own worries.

Does she listen to your advice?

I think so.

What about Jess? Does she tell you her problems?

No.

End of discussion, Rebecca declared firmly. She flopped onto her stomach and wadded the pillow up into a squishy ball.

Drum rolls. And the winner is . . .

She kicked the covers off and flipped over, onto her back. The window was a rectangle of faint light from the streetlamps. Otherwise the room was dark, except for the illuminated numerals on her clock radio—1:30. Thank God she could sleep in tomorrow.

And the winner is . . .

Sam had asked questions she wasn't sure she could answer. Maybe he wasn't the issue anymore. Maybe he wasn't the one keeping her awake.

What had suddenly become central was her relationship with her family, especially her mother. Was it time for her to find out for herself what it felt like to be on her own? Sam or no Sam, would she ever be totally confident that her life was the way she wanted it to be if she didn't try being more independent?

Or had Sam introduced doubts to serve his own interests?

Well, maybe he had, she thought tiredly, but whatever his motive, the doubts were there now, fluttering like pale-gray moths that had slept the day away. Now they were beating at the window, wanting in. Awake and desperate.

"Damn you, Sam Ballard," Rebecca said aloud. "I *liked* my life. I don't need this."

She crawled out of bed, went into the bathroom and switched on the light, blinking at the sudden brightness. Her face looked pale in the mirror. She ran her fingers through her hair and studied herself. She wasn't getting any younger, that was for sure. If she let him go, would she ever again have a chance at the kind of happiness Sam had awakened in her?

She was thirty-five years old, and she'd never felt this way before. She'd married Bruce out of a teenage infatuation that hadn't lasted when real life had reared its ugly head.

What she felt now was different. The infatuation was there, that bubbling excitement caused by physical attraction. But the other components of the mix were scarier. She felt... tenderness. Protectiveness. Vulnerability. A willingness to share even the hurtful parts of life. She wanted to punch Sam's father, give his mother a shake. She wanted to convince Sam that he could trust her, even if he'd never before been able to trust the people who mattered. She wanted him to love her and love her son, and want to protect them and share the hurtful parts of their lives, too.

Maybe that was answer enough. Rebecca searched her face in the mirror.

"Okay, Sam," she said, her own gaze grave, "We'll try it your way."

THE ONE TIME Rebecca wanted desperately to sleep in, and Alan chose that morning to get up at 7:30. Of course he tried to be quiet, but what teenage boy knew what the word meant? He tiptoed past her bedroom door in his size-eleven high-tops, then thudded down the stairs two at a time. In the kitchen he dropped something, swore, called "Sorry, Mom," then banged a few cupboards. Rebecca gave up and headed for the shower. She stayed there until the hot water ran out.

She'd had a cup of coffee, thank heavens, before the phone rang. She would have cheerfully ignored it. Alan, naturally, picked up the receiver.

"Hey, Grandma... Yeah, sure Mom's here. For you, Mom," he said unnecessarily.

Rebecca looked wistfully at the cereal box and took the receiver. Her mother's first words were calculated to make Rebecca feel even guiltier than she already did.

"Rebecca, I want to apologize for what I said about Sam. I didn't care for the man, but I should have been more tactful."

"I did ask," Rebecca reminded her.

"That doesn't excuse me." Uncharacteristically, her mother hesitated. "I suppose I've been ... well, a little jealous because he's taken so much of your time. To be honest, I've missed you this past month."

Tears prickled beneath Rebecca's eyelids. "Oh, Mom."

"Will you forgive me?"

"Of course I will!" Now the tears threatened to overflow.

"I thought maybe the two of us could do something together this weekend. Maybe go shopping? It would be fun. We haven't done anything like that in ages."

Rebecca bit her lip so hard she tasted blood. The temptation was enormous. Say yes, go, recapture the closeness she had valued for most of her life. Try to persuade her mother to see Sam as she did; gossip about Jess and Roy, discuss for the tenth time whether Lee could really afford to expand his business. Return to the safe, contented fold.

Or find out, once and for all, what life was like outside it.

Her voice was scratchy. "Mom, can I take a rain check? I have plans this weekend."

Her mother sounded disappointed but philosophical. "Oh, what?"

She opened her mouth to lie. "I..." Some part of her balked. "Mom, I..." Not another word would come.

"Rebecca?"

It had to be said, however difficult. She closed her eyes, swallowed and began, "Mom, I don't want to hurt you, but I'm really feeling the need for some... distance. I almost told Sam I couldn't see him again, just because you disapproved of him. I need to trust my instincts. I'm so used to coming to you for advice, I'm not sure I know how to trust myself. Do you understand?"

"No. No, I'm afraid I don't."

"Mom, I love you. This is something I have to do for myself."

Her mother said icily, "I can see his hand in this."

"Sam has nothing to do with it."

"He has everything to do with it! Rebecca, can't you see that?"

She wanted to be angry so that this would be easier. Unfortunately she was hardly ever lucky enough to have things the easy way. "No. He's a... catalyst. That's all."

"If you'd rather not talk about him when we're together..."

"Mom," she said desperately, "I'm not cutting off ties. I just think maybe I need some time. Please try to understand."

Her mother's voice was resonant with pain. "How can I?"

The next sound Rebecca heard was the quiet click of the phone being hung up.

PREDICTABLY, not an hour had passed before the phone rang. Rebecca barely got a hello out before her sister said, "What's this I hear from Mom? I kept telling her she must have misunderstood."

"Jess..."

"I mean, it's ridiculous. The two of you are so buddy-buddy. Do you know I've always been a bit jealous? I'm sure Mom loves me, but sometimes I've wished... Well, what am I going on and on about? The point is, she's gotten it into her head that—"

Rebecca tried again. "Jess..."

"That you don't want to see her. Do you think maybe you could call her?"

"Jess."

"What?"

"I did tell her that I wanted a little more space. I'm sure you realize that she dislikes Sam. She told me so at some length. I just got to thinking about it and realized that at my age my mother's opinion shouldn't be so important. She doesn't understand. I hope you do."

Rebecca was getting used to the silence that followed most of what she said into the telephone. At least her sister's response was somewhat different.

"Yeah, I understand." Her tone was wry. "She doesn't make any secret of how she feels about Roy."

"Don't you sometimes want just to shut her out?"

"It would hurt her feelings."

"What about *our* feelings?" It was a cry from Rebecca's heart.

"I guess I don't put my feelings first."

"So you think I'm selfish?"

"I didn't say that," Jess retorted. "I just want you to think about what really counts. Mom's been there for you for thirty-five years. How long have you known Sam?"

Anger finally flared. "Damn it, Jess, you're missing the point. I took a long look at myself and realized I'd never made a significant decision in my life without consulting Mom and Dad. It's time *I* took responsibility."

Another of those silences opened into an uncrossable gulf. "What about the rest of us?" Jess asked at last. "Would you rather not hear your little sister's advice, either?"

"I'd like it better if my conversations with you were a two-way street," Rebecca said evenly.

"What's that supposed to mean?"

"That I've always confided my troubles to you. When's the last time you told me yours?"

"What makes you think I have any?"

"God, Jess, do you think we're blind?"

"Maybe I'm just not ready to talk about it."

"Well, maybe I don't feel like talking about Sam, either."

"Then we don't have much to say to each other, do we?" Jess snapped. "Give me a call when you wake up, why don't you." Slam.

Rebecca was left with dead silence in her ear and a suspicion that she'd behaved childishly. Why hadn't she stuck her tongue out while she was at it? She and Jess had been such good friends. And her sister had been a lifesaver in the stormy, uncertain days after Bruce had left. Now Rebecca had paid her back with resentment.

She slowly hung up the telephone, then poured herself a third cup of coffee, deliberately not adding any sugar. The bitterness of the brew suited the way she felt.

When ten minutes later the phone rang again, she picked it up and didn't even wait to hear a voice. "Hi, Lee," she said tartly. "Or is it Joe?"

ALAN WAS ONLY vaguely aware of his mother's dark mood; he was too preoccupied with his own. He should have called his father by now with congratulations he didn't feel. He'd picked up the phone ten times or more and put it back down.

Partly he was just mad. It hurt that his dad had gone and gotten married without even telling him first. But he was also afraid he'd humiliate himself by showing how he felt. He wanted to sound casual and not very interested, say things like, "Hey, how was the wedding? Great honeymoon? Yeah, well, I'm busy for the next couple of weeks, but I'll see you soon."

Trouble was, he didn't think he could pull it off.

And he was afraid that his *not* calling gave away how he really felt.

His dad left two more messages. Finally, inevitably, he caught Alan when he picked up the phone on the second ring, expecting to hear from one of his buddies.

"Dad." He thought fast. "Oh, wow, I've tried calling a couple of times. But when you weren't there, I didn't want to just leave a message. You know."

"You didn't mind my springing this on you? You know I would have liked to have had you at the wedding, but I figured your mother wouldn't let you come to Reno with us, so I didn't even ask. And since we combined the wedding and honeymoon . . . Anyway, it's done. What do you think?"

Glad his father couldn't see him, Alan said, "It's great, Dad. I hope you guys are really happy and everything."

"Karen has been worrying about your reaction."

"She isn't marrying me."

"Well, in a manner of speaking she is. Hey, if my boy doesn't like her, we've got a problem."

Then why didn't you ask me first? Alan thought, but he said, instead, "I liked her. What's not to like?"

"She's a jewel, isn't she? I'm a lucky guy."

Alan wanted to ask what was so wrong with Mom, but he put a lid on it.

They went back and forth a couple of times, with Alan pretending everything was just fine. He was so busy coming up with a quick excuse in case his father wanted him to come to Seattle that weekend that he didn't pay much attention when his father asked, "Don't you have a basketball game Thursday night? Is it at home?"

"Yeah, we're playing Stanwood. It's our opener."

"What say Karen and I come on up to watch you? I'm looking forward to seeing that jump shot of yours."

Sure. He just had to see that jump shot, when he couldn't be bothered to make most of Alan's games in the past two years. Grudgingly Alan replied, "Sure, that'd be okay." But then he paused, as though suddenly remembering something. "Or maybe you should come another time. You know that guy Mom's dating, Sam? Well, he was at a bunch of my football games, and I know he's planning on Thursday."

"That's okay. I don't mind meeting him."

"You don't?" he repeated dumbly.

"Why should I?"

It hit Alan hard—the knowledge that things really were dead between Mom and Dad. It wasn't that Alan had ever thought they would remarry. But they *had* been married. How could you not care at all about somebody who'd been your wife?

"I don't know," he mumbled. "I just thought... Never mind."

"See you Thursday, then," his father said cheerfully.

"Yeah. See ya." Alan slowly replaced the receiver. He felt sick.

Why had he said that about Sam? Now if Sam wasn't there Thursday night, Alan's father would ask Mom about him. Mom's mouth ran about ten feet ahead of her brain. Alan could just hear her. *Sam? Oh, he only came to one football game. Alan said he expected him to be here tonight? I wonder why. As far as I know, Sam isn't interested in basketball.* Or Alan. She wouldn't say that, but Alan knew it, and she'd be thinking it.

Dad wasn't stupid. He would know why Alan had said that.

"Great," Alan said out loud. "Now you're stuck between a rock and a hard place."

Should he tell Mom what he'd done, ask her to cover for him? Maybe she'd even invite Sam. He *had* come to that one game; maybe she could talk him into this one.

But she would want to know why Alan had lied. No, she wouldn't even have to ask—she would guess. He didn't want her to find out how much Dad's remarriage still bothered him. Jeez, he was sixteen. Too old to be jealous of his father's new wife.

By Wednesday evening, Alan still hadn't done anything about his problem. He'd mentioned once to his mother that Dad was planning to come to the game with his new wife. Mom had just looked surprised and said, "Oh?

That's nice, Alan. I know you miss having him around more often.''

Yeah. Right.

After that, he'd started wondering what Sam would say if he asked him to come to the game. He could do it casually, as if it weren't any big deal. He'd even practiced in front of the bathroom mirror, until his mother's voice had come through the closed door. ''Are you talking to me, Alan?''

''No.'' He'd quickly turned on the cold water faucet and yelled over the noise it made, ''I just bumped my knee.''

Sam's Mercedes was parked out in front of the rental store when Alan arrived at six o'clock. Alan knocked on the front door and waited for Sam to let him in. When, through the glass, he saw the older man get up from the counter and walk toward him, his heartbeat speeded up. He felt the way he did before a game: jumpy, a little scared.

Sam turned the lock and pushed the door open. '''Evening, Alan.''

''Uh, hi, Mr. Ballard.''

''Somebody spilled oil in back. Would you dump a bag of sand on it, then sweep it up?''

''Yeah, sure.'' Alan watched Sam circle the counter. He looked tired, even a bit older. Sitting back down, he rolled his head as though his neck were stiff, then picked up his pen.

After a moment during which Alan didn't move, Sam glanced up and eyed Alan appraisingly. ''Yes?''

Alan shifted his weight from foot to foot. He tried to remember how he'd practiced this. ''I have my first basketball game tomorrow night,'' he said, too fast. ''I was wondering if you'd come. I mean, if you're busy or something . . .''

''What time is the game?''

"Seven."

Sam shook his head. "I have a late-afternoon meeting in south Seattle. I don't see any way I could get back before eight or so. Maybe another time."

"Oh." Alan stood there like a dummy. He forced himself to add, "That's okay."

When he still didn't move, Sam lifted an eyebrow. "Is it important?"

Alan stared down at his feet, memorizing how many eyelets his high-tops had. "It's just that..." He shrugged uncomfortably. "I told my dad you were coming." He waited for Sam to ask why.

The silence seemed interminable.

Then Sam said quietly, "I've done things like that."

Alan looked up. "Really?"

"My father and I had problems." His voice was unemotional. "I never wanted him to know how much it hurt."

"Yeah." Alan was humiliated to feel hot tears in his eyes. He blinked hard. "I guess that's why I said it."

Sam nodded, as though he really did understand. "Tell you what," he said. "I'll make it one way or another."

"You don't need to..."

"Don't worry about it. Just play your game."

"I..." Alan swallowed. "Thanks."

"No problem." Sam nodded toward the back room. "Now get to work."

"Sure." Alan peeled off his jacket and hurried. "Thanks!" he said again, just before the swinging door cut off his view of Sam.

CHAPTER ELEVEN

SAM GLANCED AROUND the crowded bleachers. Unlike the last time, tonight he didn't have to wonder why he'd come this time. He'd volunteered.

Beside him, Rebecca sighed contentedly. "I'm so glad you wanted to be here tonight. I dread meeting Bruce's new wife. Alan says she's way younger than I am. *And* pretty. With you in hand, I don't have to feel like a frumpy old cast-off."

"*You're* pretty," Sam said.

She tucked her hand around his arm and squeezed. "A man of discernment. How did you guess I needed a compliment?"

"I recognize a hint when I hear one."

Her chuckle warmed something inside him. "I wasn't very subtle, was I?"

Sam just smiled. *Subtle* wasn't a word he would use to describe Rebecca. Yet her very openness was one of her most attractive qualities. A man knew where he stood with her.

She continued chattily, "Alan seemed pleasantly surprised when I told him you were coming. This is nice of you, Sam."

"Just curious," Sam said noncommittally. He hadn't told her why he was there and had no intention of doing so. Considering how little he'd had to do with the boy, the surprise was that Alan had turned to him.

"Oh, here they come!" Rebecca tugged him to his feet as she and the rest of the crowd rose to cheer the home team when they ran into the gymnasium. Sam noticed how huge the boys' feet were, how lanky their legs, and thought back to his teenage days.

Alan dribbled a basketball, feinted to one side, then tossed in as nice a jump shot as Sam remembered seeing. With practiced ease, the boys began to run a warm-up drill. The other team appeared and headed for the opposite basket.

Alan executed an easy lay-up and went to the end of the line. He scanned the bleachers and spotted Rebecca and Sam immediately, and for a fleeting second, his gaze met Sam's. Then he turned away to answer something one of the other boys had said to him. A moment later he was back to scanning the stands.

For the boy's sake, Alan's father had better show, Sam thought grimly. From things Rebecca had said, Sam had the impression Bruce Halstead often failed to keep his word. Halstead's promise to come tonight had caused Alan enough grief; he would feel even worse if, after everything, his father didn't come to the game, after all.

Sam was almost looking forward to meeting the SOB. He had developed a cordial dislike for Rebecca's ex-husband.

Sam couldn't tell if Alan spotted his father or not. The buzzer went off and the teams peeled off to opposite sides of the gymnasium.

Alan was a starter at guard, where that dandy jump shot would come in handy. He was the point man who brought the ball up court and waved his teammates into position. As the game progressed, Sam decided the boy had a cool head, unusual in a junior. Another year and Alan would really be something. Sam could see why Rebecca thought her son might be recruited in both basketball and football.

At halftime, with the lopsided score in White Horse's favor, Sam and Rebecca decided to stay put. They talked idly, and she waved at passing friends and acquaintances. The crowd was filtering back into the stands, when Rebecca suddenly stiffened beside him.

"There he is, the jerk."

"Your ex?" Sam hoped his tone hadn't betrayed his curiosity.

"In person. Right there." She nodded toward a couple climbing the bleachers, who apparently hadn't spotted Sam and her.

Sam could see Alan's resemblance to the man: both had solid builds, dark hair and square jaws. He could also see where the resemblance stopped. The father looked more like the classic jock than his son did. Maybe Rebecca's genes had paid off there. The kid's face showed some of the same intelligence and determination she had, balanced by a mouth that seemed made to smile.

The woman was about what Sam had expected: damn near young enough to be his daughter, for sure too young to be Alan's stepmother. Waist-length red hair swayed over a round bottom squeezed into too-tight jeans. About right for an adolescent's fantasy, and too obvious for a man Bruce Halstead's age.

Out of the corner of his eye, Sam was aware of Rebecca giving the new wife a once-over. She finally came to a conclusion.

"She *is* pretty. Now I'm depressed."

"Another hint?"

She made a face at him. "No. Just facts."

"No man in his right mind would choose her over you," Sam said brusquely.

"God, I love you."

He turned his head sharply and their eyes met. Rebecca looked as startled as he felt. The words had obviously slipped out. The question was, did she mean them? Or had they been no more than a flip way of saying thanks?

He opened his mouth without the slightest idea how to respond. *I love you, too?* Did he mean it? Did he even know what it meant?

He was saved by the bell, so to speak. The buzzer sounded, though Sam hadn't even noticed the teams had returned for the warm-up. Rebecca was no longer looking at him, but her pink cheeks betrayed something more than interest in the unequal game. Sam frowned as he turned to watch the boys running down the court. Rebecca had thrown him for a loop in more ways than one.

The game proceeded inevitably and dully to its seventy-eight to fifty-four conclusion. Alan and his teammates thrust triumphant fists into the air. The bleachers clattered as the spectators began to climb down to the polished gymnasium floor.

Sam automatically stood and held out a hand to Rebecca. "Ready?"

She didn't quite meet his eyes. "I suppose I'd better shuffle over and be polite to you-know-who."

"Don't forget you want me in hand," Sam said, his sense of humor restored.

He'd struck the right note. Rebecca finally did look at him. Her eyes smiled, even if her mouth didn't.

"I'm glad you know your place," she retorted.

"Rebecca!" a man's voice said heartily before Sam could reply.

Sam turned to see her ex-husband advancing with his hand out. With a reluctance only Sam recognized, she shook it. "Bruce," she said politely. "Alan tells me congratulations are in order."

"Let me introduce you to Karen."

When he finished the first round of introductions, Rebecca started the second round with Sam. About the time the four adults realized they had nothing else to say, Alan found them.

"Hey, Dad," he said, looking nonchalant. "How's it going?"

Bruce slapped his son on the back. "Hell of a game. How many points did you get?"

"Eighteen. Twenty assists."

"You're going to have 'em begging in another year." Bruce shook his head. "You gave me a scare tonight you remind me so much of myself a few too many years ago."

Sam was pretty sure only good manners kept Rebecca from rolling her eyes. He stepped in. "You made some smart plays, Alan. Give you four or five years, you'll be too high-priced for my store."

Karen smiled, crinkling her nose. "I'm impressed, Alan. Here I thought your dad had some good moves!"

"Oh, puke," Rebecca muttered.

Sam took a firm grip on her arm. It appeared Alan had heard his mother, because he looked gratefully at Sam.

"Alan, do you need a ride home?" Sam asked.

"No, I have my car. I'll see you later, okay?"

Sam nodded. "If you'll excuse us?"

"Of course," Karen said. "It was so nice to meet you."

Rebecca made an appropriate response. Only when they were a safe distance away from her ex-husband did she switch gears.

"Why doesn't he grow up?" she asked in disgust. "Alan can't do a single thing that doesn't remind Bruce of himself at Alan's age. As if he'd been a superstar!"

"Men don't like aging any better than women do."

"Aren't we supposed to be in the prime of life?" she asked.

They exited the gym into the cold night air. Teenagers were gunning their cars out of the parking lot, slowing only for the speed bumps.

Sam steered Rebecca toward his Mercedes. "Some people think twenty was the prime," he suggested.

"But when you're twenty you still have to ask your mother—" Rebecca broke off so suddenly she might as well have hit one of those speed bumps.

Knowing better than to comment, Sam unlocked the passenger door and wordlessly held it open.

They were both fastening their seat belts by the time Rebecca said thoughtfully, "I think I prefer being an adult. Even if the possibilities are no longer limitless."

"I don't know." Sam had started the engine, but instead of shifting into reverse, he reached for Rebecca. One leisurely kiss later, he smiled down at her. "I kind of like the possibilities."

She blinked. The smile that slowly, sweetly, curved her lips twisted something deep in Sam's gut.

"Me, too," she said in a throaty voice. "Right this second, nothing on earth could make me go back to being twenty."

Maybe that was a declaration of love, too. Right this second, Sam had no trouble echoing it.

"WHAT DO YOU DO for dinner all those nights you work late?" Rebecca asked that week during lunch with Sam at the crowded deli. The Wednesday lunch date had become a ritual, though the weather now had kept them away from the park.

In fact, winter seemed to have arrived with a vengeance. The snow level in the mountains had risen steadily and the ski areas were making noises about opening Thanksgiving weekend. Rain had beaten the last of the brown leaves from trees.

This week she and Sam were sitting at a tiny table for two. He set his sandwich down and shrugged. "Sometimes I skip dinner. More often I go in for fast-food."

"Tut-tut." Rebecca looked at him disapprovingly. "You'll develop an ulcer if you don't watch it."

He snorted. "I thought I was going to drop dead of a heart attack."

"Well, something will get you."

He lifted an eyebrow. "What do you suggest?"

"Throwing your cares away. For example, you could come skiing with us Thanksgiving weekend," she said impulsively.

She hoped Alan wouldn't mind. Since Bruce had bowed out of taking Alan, she now had to fill in. Which wouldn't be a hardship if it were March. She liked to ski then—when the snow was perfect and the sun was warm. She hated the sport when it was snowing or—God forbid—raining. Or cold. Or when the hill had been carved into teeth-rattling moguls.

In other words, she was a weenie.

"You want to save me from an ulcer by helping me break a leg, instead?" Sam joked.

"You don't know how to ski?"

"I've been a few times."

"And?"

The crease in one cheek deepened as he smiled at her impatience. "I can turn. Stopping eludes me."

"Gee, you and Alan would hit it off. Alan doesn't believe in stopping. Do you remember Franz Klammer, that downhiller?'' When he nodded, she went on, ''Then you know what Alan looks like coming down a hill. I'd be embarrassed to be seen with him, except I'm such a slow-poke I never *am* seen with him. Once in a while I wave as he goes by in a blur.''

''Why do you ski, then?''

''In this case, because Bruce backed out. Alan could have probably found a friend, but—mean mother that I am—I won't let him drive up by himself yet. As teenage drivers go, he's reasonably responsible, but that doesn't mean he's ready to handle icy roads.''

Without looking wildly enthusiastic, Sam asked, ''What day?''

''Oh, probably Friday.''

''Family get-together on Thanksgiving?'' His expression gave nothing away.

Rebecca nodded. She had mixed feelings about the approaching celebration. She had spoken to her mother twice since her declaration of independence, but neither conversation had been a success. Her mother was clearly angry and hurt. Any improvement in relations would be Rebecca's responsibility.

Of her siblings, only Joe was still speaking to her. He had always been something of a loner. He understood Rebecca's need to separate her identity from the family's in a way Jess and Lee didn't. His support would have been more comforting if he and Rebecca had been close—except that then he would have been part of the problem, too.

For Alan's sake, Rebecca had to show up for Thanksgiving dinner. Besides, maybe the day would give her a chance to show her family that she still loved them, that her determination to stand on her own two feet didn't mean she was rejecting them.

And . . . she missed her family. Rebecca was shocked to feel the hot prickle of tears in the back of her eyes. Damn it, she'd made the right decision! It felt good being on her own. So what was her problem?

She blinked and made a production out of sipping her cola, hoping Sam wouldn't notice. He certainly wouldn't understand, considering that he'd walked away from his own family and apparently had never looked back.

The whole subject of families was one they'd avoided since their fight about hers. Sam had clearly made an effort where Alan was concerned, but he hadn't offered to give Sunday dinner another shot. And it was a cinch she wasn't going to ask him to.

She had been trying not to think about the future at all. She lived day-to-day, week-to-week. She had no idea how Sam really felt about her, whether he had any interest in marriage. He sure wasn't ready to talk about either subject. She could have kicked herself when "I love you" had slipped out. His shock had been plain—just as his silence had spoken more loudly than her foolish words.

Now she could feel him watching her as she took a bite of her sandwich and gathered her composure. At last she met his eyes defiantly and said, "Well? Ready to hit the slopes?"

"If you don't mind picking me up off them."

Her tension dissipated. "I might be spread-eagled in the snow myself."

He grinned devastatingly, wickedly. "The blind leading the lame?"

When he smiled at her like that, she would cheerfully lead him to the ends of the earth, even if she were blind. Or was she hoping to follow? Rebecca wondered.

So much for her vaunted independence, she thought ruefully.

"Something like that," she agreed. "Look at it this way. Alan can rescue us both."

"That comforts me no end," Sam said dryly.

THANKSGIVING ARRIVED on a brilliant, crystal-clear day so cold Rebecca could see her breath as she walked from the car into her mother's house. A glimpse of the Cascade Mountains showed snow-covered peaks shining above forested foothills.

At the door her mother hugged Alan. "Happy Thanksgiving, Grandma," he said, then wandered into the house.

Rebecca tentatively offered a casserole dish of sweet potatoes. "Hi, Mom."

Their eyes met and Rebecca was horrified to feel the urge to cry. Again. She'd cried herself to sleep twice in the past few weeks. Belated growing up was harder than she'd expected.

Her mother's expression was carefully reserved when she inclined her head and said with dignity, "Hello, Rebecca. Why don't you take that to the kitchen."

Rebecca did, finding her sister already there.

Sounding much as usual, Jess said, "You made it. Joe's going to be late. Some idiot decided to take a tree out yesterday and dropped it on the neighbor's roof."

"Oh, dear. They never learn, do they?" She was on the brink of saying more but chose to be cautious. "That smells good. Can I help?"

Jess waved. "Everything's under control. Go tell Steph how gorgeous she looks."

Rebecca couldn't remember the last time she'd seen her niece in a dress. Prebra, at least. When she spotted Stephanie in the living room, she pretended astonishment. "You have legs!"

The eleven-year old shrugged awkwardly. "Mom made me wear this."

"Well, you look beautiful."

"I look dumb," she mumbled sulkily.

"You don't," Rebecca said. "Truly. But you want to know something? I used to feel dumb in a dress, too. I'm still happier in jeans."

"Boys don't have to wear dresses."

"No, but you ought to hear what Alan has to say about ties on the rare occasions he's stuck with wearing one."

Stephanie didn't look impressed. Figuring a change of subject was just as well, Rebecca said, "Your dad here?"

A look of stark unhappiness crossed Stephanie's face. She hunched her shoulders as if trying to withdraw into a shell. "He didn't come," she said.

Biting her lip, Rebecca sank down onto the sofa next to her niece. "You want to talk about it?"

Stephanie shook her head.

"Sure?"

A nod.

"Okay. Where's Sarah?"

"I don't know."

Stephanie's little sister, when Rebecca found her, didn't look any happier, though she was more forthcoming. "Mom and Dad had a fight," she said. "They fight all the time."

"I'm sorry."

Her answering shrug held a cynicism that almost broke Rebecca's heart. "Oh, sweetie, I'm sorry."

Velvet brown eyes gazed up at her. "Why do they fight?"

Rebecca pressed a kiss on her niece's head. "I wish I knew," she said softly.

She looked up to see Lee and his family coming in. He nodded with distinct coolness. Janine pretended not to see her. Their brood separated to find congenial cousins, and the moment with Sarah passed.

Rebecca again offered to help in the kitchen, but the other women insisted they'd trip over one more helper. She tried to tell herself it was just chance that meal preparations were in hand; besides, the kitchen was small. She failed to convince herself.

Not that she was being shunned. When the entire family sat down to Thanksgiving dinner, Rebecca was included in conversations. But there was a difference, a stiffness that had never been there before. She was no longer one of them.

Or so she felt.

She began making her excuses as soon as possible after dinner.

Alan looked surprised but said, "Yeah, I guess I'm ready to go. Hey, see you, everybody."

The cousins chorused goodbyes, and Rebecca sought out her mother, who said, "So early?"

"I'm afraid so. Alan and I are going skiing tomorrow, which means getting up at the crack of dawn."

"Just the two of you?"

Rebecca tried to decide whether that was a loaded question. But, damn it, she wasn't going to lie, as if she were ashamed of Sam.

"No," she said, "Sam's coming with us. He and Alan are getting to be friends."

The pause was barely discernible. "Oh? How nice," her mother said. "Well, enjoy yourself."

Lee she waved at across the room. Tracked down in the backyard, Joe threw an arm over her shoulders and said close to her ear, "In the doghouse, I see."

"I wasn't imagining it?"

"Nope." He grinned. "They'll get over it."

"The question is," Rebecca said, "will I?"

"Their loss."

"Thank you." She hugged him around the waist, quick and hard. "I'll see you, Joe."

Jess was in the kitchen, putting the last few dessert plates in the dishwasher. Rebecca watched her a moment, unseen in the doorway. Her sister stopped once and leaned her forehead against a cabinet, closing her eyes. She looked unutterably weary, scared, alone.

Rebecca took a couple of steps forward. "I'm leaving, Jess."

Her sister straightened, and a practiced mask fell over her face. "It was good to see you. Don't be a stranger."

"I felt like one today."

"What are you talking about?" Jess asked crisply.

"Even Joe noticed."

"You're imagining things."

"Am I?" Rebecca waited for some sign of softening in Jess, but it never came, and finally she sighed. "Never mind. Jess . . . You have two very unhappy kids. Remember, I'm here to talk to anytime you need someone."

This time Jess didn't try to tell her that she was imagining things. Her face crumbled and she turned quickly away. Her voice was just audible. "I'll remember."

Rebecca wanted to hug her, too, but she didn't know if her sympathy was welcome. So she said goodbye and went.

Just before she climbed into her car, she took a last look at the house she had grown up in and wondered if it would ever feel like home again.

REBECCA WAS EAGER for tomorrow to arrive. Honest-to-God adult conversation, an entire day with Sam, no worries . . . What more could she ask?

It had taken a few weeks for her isolation from her family to sink in. She had friends—of course she did. But not close ones. Maybe some of them could be, but she hadn't given them the chance. Friends from her school days had married and moved or taken jobs and moved. Somehow she hadn't needed replacements, because Jess and her mother had been there.

Dozens of times, Rebecca had picked up the phone, longing to talk to one or the other, then put it back down. Without them she had nobody, she realized, nobody she could really talk to. Nobody to listen when she rambled on about her confused feelings for Sam. Nobody to hear her petty grumbles about Alan or her delight at his changing attitude toward Sam. Nobody to hold her if she cried, to sympathize with her soul-searching, to tell her honestly when she overindulged in self-pity or put on an extra five pounds.

Nobody who really *cared*.

Except Sam. She hoped.

Sam had offered to drive. Alan's only comment was "Jeez, what if his Mercedes goes into a snowbank?"

"He's probably less likely to end up there than I would be."

"True," her son agreed unflatteringly. "Do you suppose he'd let me drive partway?"

"In your dreams, kiddo," Rebecca informed him.

When Sam picked them up at seven a.m. on Friday, she was glad she *wasn't* driving. Her eyes weren't quite open yet. By the time they neared Snoqualmie Pass an hour and a half later, the highway was becoming increasingly icy and Rebecca was even gladder she wasn't behind the wheel. Plows had shoved the snow off the road, but the day was as cold as Thanksgiving had been and Rebecca could feel the tires skidding on the black ice. Sam drove with authority, doing none of the foolish, panicky things like slamming on brakes, which would have taken them into a snowbank.

In the huge parking lot, Rebecca groaned as she shoved her feet into the rigid plastic ski boots that came two-thirds of the way up her calves and made her lean forward. She'd forgotten that the miserably uncomfortable equipment was another thing she didn't like about skiing. Out of the car, she proceeded to add layers of clothing, until she felt like a bear ready for hibernation: fat, warm and slow moving.

"Gol, Mom, it's not *that* cold," Alan said, when she grumbled under her breath. "The snow's going to be fabulous! I'm on my way to Seventh Heaven."

"I'd like to start a little less ambitiously," Rebecca said. "Sam, pick your punishment."

"What's the flattest hill?"

"A man after my own heart."

Alan stuck with them long enough for his mother to pay for his lift ticket, before departing for greater things. Sam and Rebecca stamped into their bindings and got in line for one of the lower chair lifts.

Sam turned out to be a better skier than he'd implied, though hardly ready for Seventh Heaven, the steep, mogul-carved run at the top of the mountain. He made it down the slope creditably, though his attempt to side-slip to a stop next to her ended with a crash.

Rebecca swallowed a laugh. "You weren't kidding about not being able to stop."

He picked himself up with a groan and dusted snow off his quilted pants. "I never kid, remember?"

A giggle escaped. She clapped her mittened hand over her mouth. "I'm sorry. You just looked . . . funny."

Sam reached out with a pole and neatly pulled her feet out from under her. She landed hard on her bottom in a patch of unskiied snow. "You rat!" she cried.

"You asked for it." His grin was devilish, his teeth a flash of white in his lean, tanned face.

Rebecca's heart lurched and she felt a rush of sexual excitement. He was hers, all hers. A tiny voice whispered *temporarily,* but she refused to listen. Why should she? Today was real, tomorrow no more than a dream.

Something must have showed on her face, because the amusement faded from his eyes and he said, "You okay?"

She stuck out her tongue. "Yeah, I'm okay. Help me up, will you?"

He obliged, managing to drop a cold kiss on her equally cold lips before they joined the short lift line. When they'd settled onto the double chair and it swung them out above the white slope, Sam said, "I'm glad you suggested this. I'd forgotten how much I enjoyed skiing."

"Did you learn as a kid?"

"Our school district ran a bus and provided lessons. Trouble was, I never got there otherwise."

"Your family doesn't ski?"

He grunted. "Not macho enough. My father called it a pansy sport."

Rebecca turned her head to look at him. "Didn't he ever watch the downhill?"

Sam looked straight ahead, gazing beyond the brilliant white slope crisscrossed by colorfully attired skiers. "Probably not. He'd have been watching the Lakers, instead."

Something grim in his voice made Rebecca bold. "Why don't you ever visit your family?"

He lifted a brow cynically. "My father liked to beat the hell out of me and my brothers. My mother stood by and let it happen."

Rebecca bit her lip. Softly she asked, "Could she have stopped it?"

An angry stare met her troubled gaze. "She could have tried. She could have left the bastard."

"Did he . . . beat her?"

Something shifted in his eyes, and she sensed his anger had become edged with pain.

"Yeah, but not often. Hell, she didn't defy him very often."

"Did she have a job or any way of taking care of all you on her own?"

"No." His tone became harsh. "Do you think it's never occurred to me what a hard row to hoe she would have had? Well, damn it, I do understand, but I also know other women take the risks for their children. My mother didn't."

"I . . . I'm sorry." Rebecca was silenced. He was right to be angry at her sanctimonious intrusion. Right, too, that many mothers, for the sake of their children, refused to accept a brutal man's domination, however scary the future alone might be. Yet Sam was an educated and intelligent man. He would have read about the battered-wife syndrome, would know that his mother deserved pity more than anger.

Still, he had been the child whose mother had been too afraid to protect him. Or had not cared enough. Could the child inside ever really understand?

"No, I'm sorry," Sam said abruptly. "I took my bitterness out on you. And I know damn well my mother isn't the one I should blame."

"You said she calls and writes," Rebecca began tentatively. "Does she ever talk about those days?"

He sighed. "Yeah. Once in a while. But she still defends my father. His dad beat the hell out of him when he was a kid, too. She claims it's the only way he knew to raise boys."

Rebecca didn't dare comment. She was too torn between outrage and understanding—and she doubted Sam would appreciate the latter.

"Here we are," he said. "Better get your tips up."

Rebecca did so in the nick of time. She'd been so absorbed in Sam's story she hadn't noticed they were approaching the lift house. She scooted off the chair and followed Sam down the outrun.

He awaited her at the crest of the hill. "After you," he said, gesturing with one pole.

She saw how closed his expression was and knew that the conversation about his childhood was over. Maybe for good. He wouldn't see any reason to talk about his parents again, much less his buried feelings toward them. Rebecca supposed she should be glad he had trusted her enough to tell her as much as he had. Instead she felt like shaking him.

All she could do was grip her poles, push off and carve her first turn on the gentle decline.

Sam got his message across with a vengeance on their next trip up the chair lift. He talked about work—at first, Rebecca felt sure, to slam shut any opportunity she might take to reopen the subject of his childhood. He continued, though, because he couldn't let go of work, even here on the ski hill.

Rebecca enjoyed the morning, anyway. She was slowly reminded of the things she did like about skiing: the sensation of weightlessness, the slice of a ski edge over the packed surface, the pleasure of a wide carved turn, the delicious tiredness.

Sam seemed to be enjoying himself, too, despite muttered comments to the contrary. They caught glimpses of Alan rocketing by with another boy Rebecca didn't know. When a joyous yodel floated to Rebecca's ears, any concern she'd had that Alan would feel left out because she had brought Sam was eradicated.

Over lunch at the lodge, Sam listened as she told him about the load of lumber she was having delivered tomorrow. The rose arbor was aborning.

"You know, it's the dumbest thing," she admitted, "but even though I could have saved money, I decided not to borrow Lee's truck to pick the lumber up, because then I would have felt I had to justify the whole project to him. As if Lee would care!"

"But your mother would." The comment was dry, not quite a question.

Rebecca's first reaction was to be defensive. Yet she knew that was silly. Here she was struggling to be the independent woman Sam had thought she was, and she was ready to pounce on him just because he'd mildly criticized her mother!

Choosing her words cautiously, she said, "Even Mom probably wouldn't care. But she can never resist offering advice. 'Do you think you can afford it, Rebecca?' 'Wouldn't the money be better put in Alan's college fund?' 'Do you have enough in savings to be spending on frivolities?' I don't think she realizes how I take to heart what's probably no more than a casual remark." Rebecca rolled her stiff shoulders and wriggled her aching toes. "Anyhow, this time I'm doing the project on my own."

"Good for you."

He sounded as though he meant it, Rebecca thought. She cleared her throat. "Well, sort of on my own," she said sheepishly. "I'm still hoping to recruit some muscle for one of these weekends."

Was she imagining a hint of wariness in his gray eyes?

"Alan not interested?" he asked.

"Not very. Though in all fairness, between school, work and basketball, he doesn't have a whole lot of spare time. There's no girlfriend in the picture right now, but he dates. And of course he has friends. So trying to pin him down to a day is like picking up a slug with your bare hands. Slippery. Which is why . . ." She spread her hands.

"You're looking for volunteers."

Rebecca smiled hopefully. "Yup."

Just slowly enough to make her wonder what he was thinking, Sam said, "I won't promise, but maybe one of these days."

"Next weekend?"

"Let me look at my schedule." He wadded up his napkin. "What do you say? Shall we hit the slope again?"

Rebecca wrinkled her nose. "Poor choice of words. My bottom has hit a few too many times already."

"I have a few bruises myself." Sam stood, looking even bigger and bulkier than usual in a heavy fisherman's sweater and quilted pants. His face was sunburned, the squint lines that fanned out from his eyes more prominent as a result, and a scrape decorated his jaw. He was heart-stirringly male, and as evasive as her son.

But he hadn't said no, had he? Sam had managed to fit her into his schedule thus far, so why not this time?

Rebecca groaned, only half-seriously, and struggled to her feet. "All right, you're on."

As she collected mittens, hat and sunglasses, it occurred to her that what she ought to be worrying about was why the damned arbor had become so important to her. Even more to the point, why she was so determined that Sam help her build it.

Face it, she told herself soberly. The rose arbor was no longer a nice addition to her garden. It was a symbol. A symbol of rebellion, of domesticity, of permanence. A symbol of what she wanted out of life.

If only she could be sure Sam wanted the same things.

CHAPTER TWELVE

IF HER ARBOR was symbolic of the future, she was in big trouble. Rebecca gazed sadly at the modest stack of lumber that sat covered with a plastic tarp in the driveway. Christmas was fast approaching, and she hadn't so much as dug a hole for the support posts. Which said something about her ability to live independently.

Sam was coming with her tonight to Alan's basketball game, this time in Lake Stevens. It was the third game he'd attended, all of them his idea. She was glad for Alan's sake; his own father hadn't showed up again.

But deep inside, not quite secretly, she was beginning to feel resentful. Had she been able to get Sam to spend an afternoon helping her with the arbor? Not on her life.

If he was to be believed, he worked every damn weekend. She saw him frequently, but only evenings. Either Sam was so obsessed with work he couldn't put anything ahead of it or he just didn't want to help her build the arbor.

There was no way she'd ask again.

If she was quieter than usual that evening, Sam didn't comment. He seemed tired when he picked her up, and their conversation was desultory during the half-hour drive to Lake Stevens. Unfortunately, Alan had a less than sterling night. He was held to five points, made some bad passes that resulted in turnovers and finally went out of the game for good partway through the second half. His team was soundly trounced, and Rebecca knew he'd shoulder the blame for the loss. After the game, she and Sam waited until Alan emerged from the locker room a little apart from his teammates.

"You okay, kiddo?" Rebecca asked.

He shrugged dejectedly. "Yeah, I'm great. I love losing games because I screwed up."

"It wasn't that bad...."

"Give me a break, Mom. Spare me the pep talk."

"Nobody has a good game every night," Sam said quietly. "Even Michael Jordan is off sometimes."

"Yeah." Alan grimaced. "I guess so. Coach will give me hell Monday, though."

"You'll survive it," Sam said.

Rebecca was surprised to see that he'd struck the right note.

"Yeah," Alan said again, somewhat more cheerfully. He grinned, if wryly. "I'd better go. The bus is waiting for me."

"Are you still spending the night at Geoff's?" Rebecca asked.

Alan was already walking toward the open door of the school bus. "You trying to get rid of me?" he asked over his shoulder.

"I wouldn't dream of it."

"Right," he said, one foot on the first step. "Yeah, I'm going to Geoff's. Don't do anything I wouldn't." The bus door swung shut behind him.

Beside Rebecca, Sam commented, "It's a lucky thing I don't know what he wouldn't do."

"Sometimes I'd just as soon not know what he *would* do," Rebecca said. "I prefer a state of blissful ignorance."

He took her arm. "The ignorance part I can't help you with. The bliss we can go home and work on."

"Is that a proposition?"

"Hell, yes."

"I'll give it some thought," she said, and smiled up at him. Part of her still thrilled at the thought of a few hours alone with him. His kisses, his touch, the intimacy of lovemaking were almost enough to make her forget the more indefinable needs she herself scarcely understood.

During the drive home, she encouraged him to talk about his week. He had finally fired the incompetent manager and promoted the assistant manager, who wasn't quite ready for the responsibility. All of which meant, he said, that he had to put in even longer hours than normal.

"We're remodeling the Lynnwood store," Sam explained. "Knocking out a wall to add some space. While we're at it, I want to experiment with a fancier setup. I want to inspire customers to undertake a project, not just provide the tools once they've decided on. I'm hoping the store itself will do the job—we'll wallpaper and tile, have a couple of sample fences, that kind of thing. Examples of what can be done with the tools, instead of just a bare concrete floor and metal shelves."

Watching him gesture as he talked, Rebecca wondered if she could ever really compete with the work that so absorbed him. She couldn't decide if he actually enjoyed it that much or whether he was consumed by the need to satisfy a powerful inner drive. Money alone didn't seem to be the object, since he was more than well-off.

"Sounds good," she said. "At that speed, you'll be competing against me before I know it."

"Selling wallpaper? Hell, no. In fact, I was hoping I could hire you to do the job."

"Thank you for your confidence, kind sir." Rebecca stretched as he pulled into her driveway. "Home sweet home."

Sam turned the engine off and set the emergency brake. In the darkness she could just see the flash of white teeth as he grinned. "I half expected Alan to decide to come home after all and light the place up like the King Dome on game night."

"No, I think he's resigned to reality," Rebecca said. "Either that or you've charmed him."

Sam gave an oddly mirthless laugh. "Charm's not one of my strong suits."

"Oh, I don't know." Rebecca laid a hand on his thigh suggestively. "You have your moments."

His voice roughened. "I'm glad you think so."

They made it into the house, just. Inside, Sam leaned back against the front door and pulled her tightly against him. His kiss was deep and drugging, his hands urgent. It had been too long, Rebecca thought hazily, the times they could be alone too scarce. If he didn't work so much... But his mouth and touch stole her ability to reason.

The sex, as always, was satisfying. Sam told her how beautiful she was, muttered "God, I needed this," just as he entered her. She shattered around him, her wish for more than physical satisfaction seemingly unimportant at that moment.

Only afterward, as she lay with her head on his sweat-damp shoulder, nestling as close as she could possibly get, did Rebecca acknowledge the longing for something more. For words, perhaps. Instead of *I needed this,* she wanted to hear, *I need you. I love you. I miss you when we're not together. Will you marry me?* Any or all would do. She desperately wanted to know that she *mattered,* that her importance to him wasn't entirely sexual. She wanted to quit feeling on tenterhooks to say what she felt. She wanted forever, no matter what.

In his silence, she found no hope that he would offer any of what she needed from him.

Rebecca was suddenly cold. Since meeting Sam, she had made so many choices. There was no going back from any of them, no matter what happened with him.

She had never realized that she could be so physically close to someone and still be lonely.

Rebecca ran from the realization the only way she knew how. She tightened her arms around Sam and pressed a kiss to his sandpapery jaw. He murmured in pleasure and turned his head to meet her kiss. Oh, God, his mouth felt so good. The desire in his eyes was so potent, she could almost believe she was wrong.

Almost.

SAM WANTED to attend another family gathering at Rebecca's mother's house about as much as he wanted to attach himself to a bungee cord and jump from a tower. And he never had liked heights.

He had spent the morning at the Edmonds store, his least successful, trying to figure out why the store had never taken off. He'd gone over the figures until they swam in front of his eyes, but the truth was, he already knew the answer. Quite simply, he had miscalculated. The waterfront town of Edmonds, just north of Seattle, was a charming and expensive place to live. If you could afford to buy a house there these days, you didn't need to worry about renting a posthole digger or an aerator. You called a good fence company or a landscape firm.

An even more alarming truth was that he didn't give a damn. He was tempted to cut his losses and close the store. That would make one less weight hanging around his neck.

One less excuse to offer Rebecca for not helping her build the arbor.

He told the hovering manager that he was taking a lunch break and strode out. Instead he drove to his place. *His place.* Running the words over in his mind, he snorted in self-disgust. He couldn't even bring himself to say *home.* Home was a cozy place with a wife and children and dinner on the table— No, it was a place where Dad beat the hell out of the children. Home was not a place Sam had ever wanted anything to do with again.

But he was losing Rebecca. He could feel it, as surely as if she were sand that slipped through his fingers no matter how tightly he clenched them. She had become quieter, less likely to say something impulsive. The past couple of times she'd asked if he could spare an afternoon and he had made his excuses, she had only nodded, but he'd seen the hurt before she'd turned her face away. The other day when they'd made love, she had held him close, but she was silent. And afterward, she had looked away.

She mentioned her mother once in a while, but with a constraint that made him realize how much she wasn't saying. He'd wondered how much pressure her mother was bringing to bear on her, whether he had been the cause of a real rift.

A week prior, Sam had cornered Alan when the boy had arrived at work. "Sunday dinner this week?" Sam had asked casually.

Alan shrugged. "We're not going. Didn't Mom tell you?"

Sam frowned and dropped the pretense in favor of bluntness. "Because of me?"

"I don't know." Alan had shoved his hands into the pockets of his letter jacket, and looked down at his feet. "Mom says not."

"But you don't believe her."

"I think maybe she got mad when Grandma..." His cheeks flushed and he glanced up. "Grandma wasn't that crazy about..." His Adam's apple bobbed and he tried again. "I mean, she never likes anybody Mom dates."

That hadn't surprised Sam. It also didn't make him feel any better. Still frowning, he'd nodded. "I'll talk to your mother."

Alan had reacted with quick alarm. "You won't tell her I said anything?"

"No. All you did was confirm what I'd already guessed."

The question now was, what to do about it? Sam remembered all too easily the ugly things he'd said to Rebecca: *I see you letting your mother run your life. I'm too old to submit myself for approval to a girl's parents.*

Worse yet, *Most men are capable of acts of childish rebellion.*

Obviously, *he* was. How mature had it been, asking her to choose between him and her family? How mature had it been to dig his heels in and refuse to help her build the damn arbor, such a small thing that would have made her so happy? Yeah, he ought to know about childish rebellion. Especially now that he'd made himself face the unpleasant facts. He'd been so self-deceiving, he'd thought all those excuses were legitimate —until too many of them piled up. Which was when he began to understand that helping Rebecca with the arbor would have altered the part he'd expected to play in her life.

He had wanted their relationship—*thought* he wanted it—the way it was. Dinners out, passionate lovemaking, a woman who considered him charming no matter how dour he was on occasion. He hadn't wanted to pay the price: providing a *home.*

But a home was exactly what Rebecca wanted and deserved. The kind of home he didn't know how to provide.

Well, there were two things he could do: agree to help
Rebecca the next time she asked and endure another family dinner. Who knew? If Mrs. Hughes decided he was shy
instead of rude, maybe Rebecca could at least regain the
family bulwark she had apparently forsaken on his account.

Sam had never felt more like the jerk he'd heard Alan
call him than at that moment.

IN ANSWER TO Sam's question, Rebecca said, "Oh, we
open presents at home on Christmas Eve." She reached for
a cracker and spread soft cheese on it. "Help yourself,"
she told him.

He was there for dinner at her invitation, which had
come after several rather broad hints from him. At the
moment he sat in the easy chair across the coffee table
from her, watching her with an intensity that made her
nervous, despite the fact that his question had sounded
disinterested.

Since eating was an all-too-easy way to handle nerves,
she reached compulsively for another cracker. "Actually," she admitted, "Alan and I were talking about it the
other night. We were hoping you'd join us."

Sam looked startled. Or was *aghast* a better word to describe his expression? "Good Lord, I don't want to intrude on you. That's a time for you and Alan.
For...family."

Had she imagined the hesitation? Rebecca wondered.
The reluctance to say the word? "To tell you the truth,"
she confessed, "Christmas Eve is just the kind of holiday
that makes us feel a bit lonely. Last year one of Alan's
friends spent the whole holiday with us. His elder sister

was sick and his parents flew to Florida to be with her. It was kind of fun having somebody to help us celebrate. I hope you will this year.''

Seeing the creases between his brows, she thought, *Way to go. Put a little pressure on him, why don't you?*

''Thank you,'' he said, still frowning. ''I suppose you go to your mother's on Christmas Day.''

Rebecca bit her lip but managed to say lightly, ''Most years.'' She'd been trying so hard lately to watch what she said to him, but the next words slipped right out before she could stop herself. ''Why, would you like to join us?''

Now *she* was aghast. Had that sounded like sarcasm? *Was* it sarcasm?

''Is that an invitation?'' Sam asked, lifting one dark brow.

Quickly, before she could have second thoughts, Rebecca said, ''It would be if I didn't know how the idea must horrify you.''

Sam stood up and walked over to the window. Looking out, with his back to her, he said, ''I'd like to go—if you wouldn't be embarrassed to take me.''

He was volunteering? Rebecca rose to her feet and went to him. ''I'd never be embarrassed,'' she said softly, wrapping her arms around him from behind. Under her cheek, the muscles in his back were tense.

''How will your mother feel about my coming?'' he asked.

On the brink of lying, Rebecca hesitated. ''I don't know,'' she finally admitted. ''But all we can do is try.''

''Yeah,'' he allowed wryly. He turned in her embrace to face her, his eyes somber. ''I'd like to try harder.''

Hope sang in Rebecca's blood, scaring her a little. But she was a born optimist and saw no reason to let doubt rear its ugly head now. ''You don't have to do this,'' she said, meeting his eyes unflinchingly. "I should never have pushed you into facing down my mother in the first place."

"What else would I do for Christmas?" he asked.

The loneliness behind his flip answer was enough to sear her heart. She slid her arms around his neck. "I love you, Sam," she whispered, and pressed her lips to his before he could speak.

He groaned, deep in his chest, and met her passion with his own. Later, Rebecca told herself Sam might have responded if Alan hadn't walked in the front door a minute later; she might have heard some of those words that seemed to matter so much.

Well, he'd come close, hadn't he? What else could he have meant by his offer?

THE ETERNAL PESSIMIST, Sam expected to hate every minute of Christmas dinner. If Rebecca's family had seemed cold and unwelcoming to him the last time, this time they would form an implacable wall. How could they help but blame him for their estrangement from Rebecca?

He came close to chickening out half a dozen times before Christmas, but his fear of losing Rebecca was strong enough to keep him committed. Damn it, how hard could it be to sit through another dinner, politely answer questions, maybe even ask a few civil ones of his own? Maybe, if he was lucky, a little Christmas spirit would keep them from making mincemeat of him.

He was equally as nervous about Christmas Eve. He went to Rebecca's straight from work, bearing store-wrapped gifts. It had been so long since he'd had to buy presents for people who were really important to him that he'd agonized over his choices for a ridiculous length of time.

He parked outside, remembering his first visit there. The house was still shabby, but you wouldn't know it from the lights decorating the front and the resplendent tree standing in the bay window.

When he knocked, Rebecca opened the door, her face alit with a smile that reminded him all over again why he had come. Why she mattered so much.

Miniature Christmas ornaments dangled from her ears. She wore forest-green corduroy slacks and a red sweatshirt with an appliquéd Santa on the front. Sam couldn't help but notice how nicely the thrust of her full breasts filled out Santa's form. Feeling awkward, he held out the wrapped presents and said gruffly, "Merry Christmas."

"And merry Christmas to you, too." Rebecca's smile was as soft as her lips when she stood on tiptoe to kiss him. Then she stepped aside so he could come in.

Sam's first impression was that the house smelled the way Christmas should: baking ham and cookies, fir boughs and bayberry-scented candles. A small fire crackled on the hearth, and the tree, which stood somewhat crookedly, glittered with twinkling lights and too many ornaments.

Half of him wanted to settle in like a cat who'd found a warm nook. The other half wanted to turn tail and run.

"Alan!" Rebecca called. "Sam's here."

Size-eleven feet thundered down the stairs. Alan's face shone with the same simple pleasure that illumined his mother's. "Cool. Can we open presents now?"

Rebecca pretended to look thoughtful. "Maybe we should wait until after dinner."

"Mom!"

She laughed. "Let me get Sam a drink first. Mulled wine?"

In short order he was ensconced in a comfortable chair beside the tree, watching Alan root among the packages as if he were still a ten-year-old.

"Here, add Sam's to them," Rebecca said.

"I brought one my mother sent me," Sam said when Alan began piling the additional gifts under the tree. "Figured if I was having Christmas here, I might as well go whole hog." Usually he opened his mother's gift immediately, sent a cursory thank-you note, then put the present away without any more consideration than he'd give a gift from a business associate. Just as he usually sent her a present that didn't take any thought, such as a selection of fancy cheeses. But this year an impulse had overtaken him, and he had chosen diamond earrings for his mother the same day he'd shopped for Rebecca's gift. This year... Hell. He didn't want to examine why this year was different.

He waited like an eager kid for Alan and Rebecca to get to his presents. They handed him theirs first.

From Alan there was a coffee cup that said The Boss. Sam grinned. "Don't forget I'm still the boss."

"Wait till you see it when you pour something hot into it," Alan said cheekily.

"Let me get you some mulled wine," Rebecca quickly offered.

A moment later, Sam watched the cup transform. "The Boss" faded away; "The Tyrant" appeared, instead. He shook his head and laughed. The boy had guts—you had to allow him that.

Rebecca gave him *Cold Sassy Tree*, a novel she loved but he hadn't read, and a pair of lined leather gloves. Sam thanked her. His expression must have pleased her, because she smiled at him saucily and said, "You're welcome."

At last Alan opened Sam's gift, a pair of top-of-the-line basketball shoes. Sam had noticed how worn his were, and how inexpensive to start with.

"Wow," the boy breathed. "Hey, how'd you know what size I wear?"

"I looked in your closet one day," Sam confessed. "I hope you don't mind. If they don't fit, you can exchange them."

"Wow," Alan said again, looking dazed. He kicked off his shoes and shoved his feet into the new shoes, then laced them up. Standing, he pretended to dribble a few steps, dodged an imaginary opponent and came up for a jump shot. "It's like having springs," he exulted. "These are incredible!"

Rebecca smiled at Sam. "Thanks," she whispered.

Sam shrugged and watched her son with a satisfaction he preferred not to examine.

At last she tore open her small package from Sam. She oohed over the sapphire earrings, then peeked in the envelope. Inside was a confirmed order for two old-fashioned roses: Ispahan and Reine des Violettes. Ispahan, the nurseryman had told him, was an ancient rose found growing in the city of Ispahan in Persia, while Reine des Violettes was a rich purple, gloriously double Hybrid Perpetual that was among the first nineteenth-century roses to repeat their bloom.

"I didn't know which ones to buy," Sam said uncomfortably. "So I asked the people at the mail-order nursery. They recommended those. I hope you don't already have them."

"I don't have either," she said. She looked up, tears in her eyes. "Sam, I don't know how to thank you."

Tell me you love me again, he thought, but in front of her son he couldn't say it, so he settled for "Having me for Christmas is more than enough."

He wasn't about to complain, though, when Rebecca leaned forward and kissed him in plain sight of Alan. Then she unhooked the miniature Christmas ornaments from her ears and carefully put in the sapphire earrings. The tiny stones formed the petals of a flower around a diamond center.

"They're just the color of your eyes," Sam said, pleased. "I thought they would be."

She kissed him again. Alan groaned. Rebecca made a face at her son.

"Open your mother's present," she urged Sam. "Alan, where is it?"

With familiar ambivalence, Sam slowly unwrapped the big, squishy package. Inside was a sweater, obviously hand-knit. Sam ran his hand over the nubby twisted yarns. He liked the rust color, and the fact that the sweater was cotton instead of wool which made him itch.

"It's gorgeous!" Rebecca exclaimed, gently touching the intricate cable pattern. "Did your mother knit it?"

He opened the card, and recognized his mother's tiny, slanted handwriting. "I took up knitting this past year," he read silently: "I wanted you to have my first major project. Hope it fits. Love, Mom."

"Yes," he said slowly. "She knit it."

He stared down at the sweater, his throat thick with emotion. How had she remembered so much about him? Why had she wanted him to have her first sweater? Slowly he stroked the bumps and valleys of the design. At last he held the sweater up. He knew at a glance that it would fit. Sam couldn't think of a finer gift, or one that would show more love.

He wondered if he deserved that love.

By the time he folded the sweater again and set it aside with his other gifts, Rebecca and Alan had finished unwrapping their pile. Torn paper littered the floor. Blithely ignoring it, Rebecca stood up. "Shall we eat?"

"I'm starved," Alan announced, jumping to his feet. He dodged ahead of her into the kitchen, bouncing an imaginary basketball beside him.

Rebecca shook her head, but a smile curved her mouth. "Sam, you shouldn't have spent so much money, but I have to admit you couldn't have made Alan happier. Or me."

Sam stopped her with a hand on her arm. "Merry Christmas," he said again in a low rough voice, and pulled her against him. It was a kiss of love, even if he didn't know how to say the words. When he lifted his head, the best he could do was the mundane, "May I help?"

Rebecca tucked her hand through his arm. "You bet. How about carving the ham?" And she drew him with her into the kitchen.

SAM'S EXPECTATIONS for Christmas Day weren't high. He figured the family would be civil to him, that Rebecca would be happily absorbed back into the fold. He wanted at least that much to happen.

He pulled into Rebecca's driveway at noon. Before he'd even gotten out of the car, Alan appeared. He wore a brand-new, stiff pair of jeans and a long-sleeved polo shirt that was just a little large and as obviously new. Bright white, the high-tops made his big feet look even bigger.

Sam rolled down the car window. Alan leaned over to nonchalantly rest his forearms on the door. "Mom will be here in a second. She couldn't find one of her shoes," he confided, "so she's swearing and digging around in the closet."

Sam nodded, hiding his amusement.

"Are we taking your car?"

Sam lifted a brow. "I assumed so."

"Well, then, can I drive?"

"Can you drive," Sam repeated slowly. He was vaguely aware that Rebecca had come out of the house, locked the front door and started down the walk. "You ever been in an accident?" he asked.

"Not yet." Alan gulped. "I mean, no, sir."

Sam exhaled. "What the hell." Opening the car door, he climbed out. "It's all yours . . . so to speak."

The boy's eyes grew wide. "You mean I *can?*"

"Must be the Christmas spirit," Sam muttered.

"Oh, wow!" Reverently Alan took his place behind the wheel. He stroked the steering wheel, caressed the gear shift, studied the dials on the dashboard.

Rebecca stopped beside Sam. She looked from him to her son and back again. "You're kidding."

"I never . . ."

She groaned. "You never kid. I know. I was hoping that you'd changed your policy."

Sam's eyebrow rose again. "That bad?"

"It's only a mile." Her voice lacked conviction.

Sam took her arm and led her around the car. "*I'll* sit in the front," he said. "If you don't mind."

"I don't know." She opened the rear door. "Does the back have air bags, too?"

"Mom!" Alan glowered over his shoulder at her. "I'm a good driver."

"That's a matter of opinion." At his expression, she laughed. "I'm kidding. I do kid."

Sam buckled his seat belt. "Okay. *Very* gently put the car in reverse."

The Mercedes slid, smooth as silk, out of the driveway. There it lurched to a stop.

"You *have* driven a stick shift?"

"Sure." Pause. "A couple of times."

Sam closed his eyes. "A mile, huh?"

"Yep," Rebecca said cheerily from the back seat.

"All right," Sam said again, with patience that struck him as amazing. "Push the clutch all the way to the floor, then hold it there while you *gently* ease the stick forward and to the left."

All told, the boy didn't do too badly. They made it, car and passengers in one piece. The clutch probably wasn't what it had been, Sam figured, but he could afford a new one. It was worth it to see the looks on the faces of Alan's cousins as he drove the Mercedes up to the curb in front of Grandma's house.

The first adult they encountered was Rebecca's brother Joe, who leaned against the porch railing with his arms crossed. He shook his head in awe. "You're a braver man than I am."

Sam let himself smile. "I figure Alan owes me a few now."

"Collect before the glow wears off," Joe advised. He grinned and stuck out his hand. "We didn't talk much last time."

"No," Sam agreed. He propped his shoulder against a porch upright and joined Joe in watching the crowd of teenage boys who surrounded his Mercedes.

When neither man said another word, Rebecca rolled her eyes and disappeared into the house.

About the time the boys lost interest in the car, Joe straightened. "Ready to go in?"

Surprised to realize that he'd acquired an ally, Sam shrugged. "Sure."

Inside, Mrs. Hughes advanced to meet him. A smile firmly in place, she reached for his jacket. "Merry Christmas, Sam! How nice that you came today."

"Thank you for having me," Sam said, inclining his head slightly. Out of the corner of his eye, he could see the living room. Gaily wrapped packages were spilling from beneath a majestic Noble Fir. "I feel as if I should have come with presents."

"Nonsense." The smile warmed a degree. "Rebecca's earrings are lovely. What a thoughtful gift. She told me to admire Alan's feet when he comes in, too."

"Speak of the devil," Rebecca murmured from behind her mother as the teenage boys crowded noisily in the front door.

They succeeded in creating enough of a diversion for Sam to escape into the living room. Not at all to his surprise, there Roy slouched on the couch in front of the television set, remote control in one hand and beer can in the other. He nodded absently at Sam, who hesitated and then wandered over to Jess. Rebecca's sister had her arms around her two girls, her dark head bent as she murmured something to them.

Glancing up, she saw Sam. The smile that dawned on her face looked genuine to him. "Merry Christmas, Sam. Welcome."

"Thank you."

"Go find your cousins," she told her daughters. "Tell Alan how beautiful his feet look."

Sam's mouth twitched. "Rebecca's prouder of those basketball shoes than Alan is."

"I doubt it." Jess's gamine smile widened, and Sam wondered what the hell was wrong with her husband, whose eyes were still glued to the TV set. "She tells me Alan put the shoes next to his pillow last night."

"Good God," Sam exclaimed, half amused and half flattered.

Sam had decided by a couple of hours later that his gifts to Alan and Rebecca had given him an entrée today that he hadn't had the previous time. Or maybe it was the fact that he'd let Alan drive his Mercedes. Even Lee had warmed toward him after listening to the boys' excited chatter.

Still, Sam felt like an outsider as he watched the family opening presents from one another and joking about times he hadn't shared and people he didn't know. Would he ever fit in here? He wondered if his own family was gathered right now. Had his father managed to ruin anybody's Christmas yet?

Sam was strangely pulled between the here and now and the past. The twinkling lights on the tree were the same, as were the smells, the excited gasps, the laughter.... Except he didn't remember very much laughter.

There was the Christmas his mother had sewn him a shirt that even his inexpert eyes recognized as poorly made. He remembered the big stripes he'd thought were ugly, and how they didn't match at the seams. Something on his face must have betrayed him, because his father had roared and leaped to his feet, ordering him to his bedroom until he could learn to be grateful for what he got. Funny, nine or ten years old at the time, he'd seen only the temper. Now he realized that his father had probably been angry because he'd hurt his mother's feelings.

He had other memories of the holiday: awakening on Christmas morning, breathless with anticipation, falling asleep Christmas night with his pillow wet from tears and his stomach in a knot. Sam had always felt as if he were walking a tightrope on Christmas. If he could maintain his precarious footing, he could enjoy the day. But if his balance teetered even slightly, purgatory awaited him.

Now he shook his head, trying to quell the tension that coiled in his stomach because he remembered those Christmases only too well. Hell, there had been good Christmases, too, times he'd either maintained his equilibrium or his father's mood had been good. One year his father had made him a basketball backboard and attached it to the garage so that it was there Christmas morning. He'd been the envy of the neighborhood. Both his brothers had sons now. Sam wondered if they shot hoops on his old backboard. Or was it gone, like the too many intervening years?

Rebecca asked him to admire a delicate gold chain threaded with garnets, which her mother had given her, and he abruptly came back to the present. Alan grinned at him and tossed a wadded-up ball of paper, which Sam snatched out of the air. "Hey, you've got hands," Alan said before ripping open another package.

The Christmas Sam had been Alan's age, his parents had given another present he'd almost forgotten about: a class in small-business bookkeeping at the local community college. He'd wanted to take the class but had been reluctant to pay for it out of his still marginal profits. His father had grumbled constantly about how much time he wasted "slaving in other people's yards." Sam could hear his voice: "Our lawn is a foot high, and you're off mowing some goddamn neighbor's!" Had his father really disapproved? Sam wondered with the value of hindsight. Or had he just not known how to express pride, only dissatisfaction?

Sam watched nine-year-old Sarah open an artwork set from her grandma. His gaze lingered on her face as she lovingly touched the rows of colored markers, the bottles of paints, the delicate tips of the brushes. He couldn't even remember how old his nephews and nieces were. For the first time, he tasted regret. He'd been running for so long he'd forgotten what he was running from. Now he recognized how much he had lost by his chosen exile.

He'd accused Rebecca of immaturity, of clinging to her childhood and family. Seeing her secure in the midst of that family, he had to ask himself, Was she the one who hadn't shaken free of her childhood? Or was he the one who had let his life be shaped by a father he couldn't forgive? Why else had he been uninterested in marrying, starting a family of his own? Why else had he let his life become nothing but the stores?

His pensive mood must have showed, because Rebecca suddenly tucked her hand under his arm and squeezed. Her gaze searched his face, and she asked in a low voice, "Are you all right?"

He wasn't ready to talk about his conclusions—he still had too much to think about. So he schooled his expression to impassivity and said, "I'm fine."

She stiffened, nodded and turned back to her family, withdrawing her hand from the crook of his arm. The warmth had vanished from her face.

He hadn't wanted to share old memories or have her fussing over his emotional state. What he hadn't counted on was that the absence of her touch would leave him feeling so alone again.

CHAPTER THIRTEEN

ALAN REALLY WASN'T looking forward to visiting his dad and his new stepmother. *Stepmother.* Jeez.

Mom had agreed to let him drive himself again, which was something. At least he had wheels, so if he was having a really lousy time, he could take off. As it was, he'd made an excuse so he only had to stay Friday night instead of the whole weekend.

He parked halfway down the block from his father's apartment, then sat in the car for ten minutes wishing he didn't have to go in. Or that Karen wouldn't be there. He wasn't sure which. He was acting like some dumb little kid who didn't want anything to change, he thought impatiently. He wasn't little anymore. What difference did it make to him if his father had a new wife?

He couldn't sit there forever. Grabbing his duffel bag, he finally made his move.

Karen opened the door at his knock, smiled and stepped aside. Her loose red hair swirled around her shoulders.

"Put your stuff in the bedroom, Alan. Your dad ran out to the grocery store. He shouldn't be gone long." She wrinkled her nose. "To tell you the truth, I think he figured we should have a chance to talk without him hanging over our shoulders."

Talk about what? Alan dumped his duffel bag on the bed, then excused himself to go to the bathroom. He stayed in there as long as he decently could, praying for sounds of his dad's arrival. Silence. Finally he came out. What else could he do?

Karen was in the kitchen, puttering with dinner and humming. When she saw him, she nodded at a tray of sliced vegetables and dip. "Help yourself."

His dad had been big on tortilla chips. He probably pretended he liked this stuff.

Alan found himself a pop in the fridge and grabbed a handful of carrot sticks. Meanwhile Karen prattled on, all in this supersincere voice.

"I'm so glad you're here for a visit, Alan. Bruce talks about you all the time, you know. He's so proud of you. I hope you don't mind his marrying me. I promise I won't try to replace your mother or anything like that. Maybe we can just be friends. What do you think?"

"I guess so," he mumbled. *Where was Dad?*

"Tell me about yourself," she said gaily. "The things Bruce never thinks to mention. Do you have a girlfriend?"

He shrugged, realized she hadn't seen him, and said awkwardly, "No. Not right now."

"Is there someone you wish were your girlfriend?"

"Not really." As if he'd tell her.

"Mmm." Her hand stilled above the cutting board where she was slicing meat, as if she couldn't think and cut at the same time. "What do you do for fun?"

He was suddenly grateful for Sam, who never asked him stupid questions. Alan took a long drink of pop, then shrugged again. "Play basketball or throw the football with friends. Go to dances. Just the usual stuff."

"No passionate hobbies, huh?"

Passionate?

"Like your mother's gardening, Bruce says. Or my violin playing."

What else did his father say about his mother? Alan wondered. "I guess not," he said. "How about you?"

"Oh..." Karen drew the word out and her forehead puckered. "Music, of course. I wish I'd concentrated more on the violin when I was in school. It would have been wonderful to be talented enough to play in a symphony. Let's see. I love plays and good restaurants. Your dad and I've been having a wonderful time exploring both." Her smile was sleekly satisfied. "And children. I may go back to school one of these days for a teaching certificate. Although now—" She turned her head. "Oh, here's your dad."

Alan wondered if she was as relieved as he felt. He couldn't tell if she'd really wanted to talk to him or had been put on the spot by his father. And what was this about children?

His dad walked into the kitchen with grocery bags in each arm. "Hey, Alan." He freed one hand enough to offer a thumbs-up. "Sweetheart."

Even before he set the bags down, he bent to give Karen a lingering kiss. Alan looked away.

"So, how was Christmas?" his father asked as he began putting groceries in cupboards. "Get lots of good stuff?"

"Yeah, sure," Alan said. "Sam gave me some really cool basketball shoes. They'll add six inches to my jump."

"Sam? Oh, the guy your mom's dating." When Alan agreed, he said, "You sound like you're getting used to him."

"He's okay."

"Did you get my present?"

"Sure," Alan said hastily. "Thanks a lot. I thought I'd go pick out some CDs tomorrow." Somehow, irrationally, he wished his father had given him something more personal than a gift certificate to Tower Music. He'd have liked to brag about the present from his dad, too.

"Good." His father used that hearty voice that sounded so false. "You can thank Karen for that idea."

When Alan didn't pick up on his hint, Bruce nodded vigorously at her behind her back.

Alan said, "Oh, yeah. Uh, thanks."

Her laugh was a light trill. "I didn't figure you'd like Bach or Brahms. Letting you pick your own music out seemed a safer bet."

"Have you told Alan our news yet?" his father asked.

Something went cold inside Alan, and he *knew*. He knew even before Karen hung on his father's shoulder and said sweetly, "I thought you should tell him yourself."

"You're going to have a brother or sister." His dad looked very serious. "Karen's pregnant. We're excited about it, Alan. I never thought anything this good would happen to me again. It's like starting life all over."

Through a throat that felt raw, Alan managed to say, "That's neat. I'm . . . I'm glad."

"Thanks." His dad's smile was full of real pride this time. "What do you think, am I a lucky guy or what?"

Lucky? Is that what messing around on your wife was? Getting a divorce and seeing your kid once a month? Talking a good line and not meaning any of it? Lucky. Yeah, right.

He didn't have to say anything, because his dad went on, "This was Karen's idea. Hell, I figured I was too old to be a father again, but she talked me into it."

That was the way it went. Everything his dad suggested had been Karen's idea. Dinner was stir-fried with Chinese vegetables Alan didn't recognize, but his father raved about it, even though he'd always insisted he was a meat-and-potatoes man. Every word that dropped from Karen's lips was a pearl of wisdom. Or maybe it was just her lips that he liked so much. Alan couldn't leave the room without coming back to find them kissing. A couple of times his dad winked when he lifted his head and saw Alan standing there. Alan was embarrassed.

In the morning, he woke up because he heard voices, but when he opened his bedroom door, he realized his father and Karen were still in their bedroom. He hesitated. If he flushed the toilet or ran a shower, they'd hear him and know he was up. There was silence for a moment, then a giggle. His father's voice rumbled, Karen gave a cry and the bed creaked. His cheeks hot, Alan went back into his bedroom and eased the door shut. Even there, he heard a keening moan from Karen and his father's shout of triumph.

Alan quietly got dressed, then began shoving rumpled clothes into the duffel bag. He had to stay for breakfast, but after that he'd claim basketball practice started at noon so he had to head for home. He wished desperately that he could just slip out the front door right now without facing them. How *could* he face them without picturing them both naked, kissing each other and touching each other and imagining their *new start,* as if he didn't even exist just on the other side of a wall?

"WHAT DO YOU THINK?" Rebecca asked. "Could you give me a hand tomorrow? I bought the lumber, and it's just sitting there."

"Jeez, Mom, can't you ask Sam, instead?" Alan saw her expression. "Oh, all right," he grumbled. "I'll tell Geoff I can't go to the beach."

Rebecca flung a hand dramatically to her forehead. "The sacrifices children make for their parents."

"Mom!"

"It won't kill you," she said briskly. "Now scoot—let me get dinner started."

"I'm going out later tonight," Alan said.

He didn't offer any explanation of where, when or with whom, and the look on his face was almost defiant. But he was too old for her to question his every move.

Judging this to be a time to step with care, Rebecca did no more than raise her eyebrows and say, "Behave yourself, okay?"

He shrugged. "When's dinner?"

"Forty-five minutes, give or take a few."

"I'm gonna shoot a few hoops outside."

A moment later, she heard the rhythmic thump of the ball hitting the old backboard above the garage. Dicing an onion, Rebecca brooded. Alan had been sulky ever since he'd walked in the door at around noon after the visit to his father. She'd asked what was wrong.

"Nothing," he'd said.

"How was the visit?" she had tried.

"Normal."

"Do anything special?"

"Nah."

She wished that she and Bruce communicated better, so that she could ask him about the weekend and Alan's attitude toward the new wife. Obviously Alan wasn't going to tell her.

Rebecca sighed. Surely going through a period of adjustment was natural after having his father remarry. She should be patient. Alan had a good head on his shoulders. He wouldn't do anything stupid.

On the other hand, she felt increasingly sure that *she* had done something stupid: fallen in love with a man incapable of loving her.

At least she could blame the fact that her eyes were watering on the miserable onion. She was swiping at the painful tears, when the phone rang.

"Damn it . . . hello?"

"That's ominous," Sam said.

"It wasn't aimed at you," Rebecca explained, not entirely truthfully.

"Anything I can do?"

She could think of plenty, starting with her arbor. Being a coward at heart, however, she sidestepped the issue. "Not unless you want to dice some onions for burgundy beef."

"Which sounds a hell of a lot better than the pizza I'm about to eat."

"Where are you?"

"South Seattle, and stuck here for a couple more hours." His voice grew more intimate. "What are you up to?"

"Just the usual." Now she sounded like her teenage son. "How about tomorrow?"

A month ago she would have lied to make it sound as if she had nothing important planned. More than that, she would have considered other plans unimportant compared with spending time with Sam. Now she said straightforwardly, "Alan's promised to help me build my arbor."

"Could you use another hand?"

Rebecca actually pulled the phone away from her ear and stared at it. Had she heard him right? Had he really *volunteered?* First Christmas dinner, now this.

"Rebecca?" His voice was tinny, far away.

Maybe he was changing. Maybe there was hope, after all. She tucked the receiver back in the crook of her shoulder again and asked, "Are you sick?"

He laughed as if she were joking and said, "Just free tomorrow."

"Then consider yourself signed on."

They chatted for another few minutes before Rebecca hung up and went back to her dinner preparations. Her heart felt lighter than it had in months. Sam wanted to help her. That must mean something.

ALAN HAD JUST LEFT that evening, when the doorbell rang. Rebecca opened the door to find her sister waiting on the porch. Jess wore her usual jeans and bright cotton sweater over a turtleneck, but the sparkle that transformed her face from plain to beautiful was missing. Under the stark porch light, the dark circles under her eyes stood out sharply. She didn't smile when she said, "Hello, Bec."

Jess hadn't called her that in years. "Is something wrong?" Rebecca asked, alarmed.

Her sister's mouth twisted. "Depends on your point of view. Can I come in?"

"Of course you can." Rebecca stood back. "Let's go into the kitchen. Alan isn't home. Would you like a cup of coffee or cocoa?"

"I guess so," Jess said without much interest.

"So what's up? Are you okay?"

"Oh, God." Jess's laugh verged on hysterical. "'Okay' does not describe me tonight."

Rebecca faced her. "Roy?"

"Yeah, I kicked him out. Can you believe it?"

Rebecca bit her lip. "Was it hard?"

Just like that, her little sister was in her arms, sobbing her heart out on Rebecca's shoulder. It was ten minutes before she could blow her nose and wipe her wet, blotchy cheeks. "I've been trying to work up the nerve for years," she said miserably. "Isn't that pathetic? I've stayed married to an SOB like Roy just because I'm a coward."

"Hey." Rebecca gave her a gentle shake. "You know it's not that simple. Here..." She pushed a cup of hot cocoa at her sister. "Drink. It'll make you feel better."

They moved to the living room, where Jess curled her feet under her on the sofa and talked. "You were right, what you said that day on the phone. About confession being a two-way street. But I didn't want to talk to anybody. I felt like such a failure."

"Why?" Rebecca asked, puzzled. "For crying out loud, I'm divorced. Sam aside, my record where men are concerned isn't exactly something to bet the house on."

"No, but you're so together." Jess blew her nose again. "You want to know the truth? I knew none of you ever liked Roy, and I hated to admit you were right. Really noble, huh?"

"Mom didn't like Bruce, either."

"Yeah, but that's different," Jess pointed out. "Mom's never liked anybody either of us has dated. You know that."

"True," Rebecca agreed. "But if you felt that way, why—" She stopped. This wasn't the time to get onto the subject of Sam.

"Why didn't I back you about Sam?" She looked away. "I thought he was like Roy. I didn't want you to blow it the way I did." She gave a mirthless laugh. "Funny, because Roy didn't like Sam either."

"Sam's a nice man," Rebecca said. Now was not the time to tell Jess her doubts about him. "Do the kids know yet?"

"No. Thank God they weren't home for the fireworks. Fortunately they're both spending the night with friends. Not that it'll be any surprise to them."

"Jess..." Rebecca hesitated. "Did something bring this on?"

"You mean our separating?" She grimaced. "Just another dumb fight. Roy was ticked off because I had a meeting yesterday evening. John Peters—you know, Peters' Furniture—wanted to talk about us doing their cleaning. Well, Friday is Roy's bowling league. I suggested he take Steph and Sarah with him. I don't like them being home alone evenings. Well, he did, but then he stewed all night, I guess. The minute Sarah and Steph were gone this afternoon, he blew his top. I'm a woman—the kids are my responsibility. He looked like some damned baby-sitter, taking kids with him. He doesn't want to hear about how much money my business makes— I'm just rubbing in how inadequate I think he is." She stopped for breath. "The same old stuff. Only this time, I blew my top, too. So that's it. Finis."

"He was jealous of how much money you made?"

"Yeah, my little business was a nice sideline," she said sardonically. "Until the day he realized I made more money than he did. Then he couldn't take it."

Rebecca bit her lip, watching her sister take a sip of co-coa. She looked so tired, so dispirited. So unlike the woman who reveled in challenges.

"Are you sorry things came to a head?" she asked.

"Oh, Lord, I don't know." Jess let her head rest against the pillowed back of the couch. She closed her eyes. "He has...such a temper. It scares me sometimes. I think if he'd ever hit me, I would have had enough gumption to leave him. It never came to that, but..." She shuddered. "I don't know. I wonder how he's going to take this."

"He won't fight for custody...?"

Jess's eyes flew open. "If he does, he'll be sorry," she said fiercely.

"You know we're all behind you."

"Yeah." Jess smiled wryly. "That's what family is for, right?"

The irony was not lost on Rebecca. "Right," she agreed.

Jess struggled up from the couch. "I've dumped on you enough. I just wanted to say I'm sorry and let you know what's happening. I'd better call Mom when I get home."

Rebecca hugged her sister again. "You can dump on me anytime. And I'm always available as a baby-sitter. In fact, the girls can stay here if you need to be gone overnight or you're worried about Roy."

"God," her sister said. "Life won't be the same, will it?"

"No." Rebecca blinked back an unexpected prickle of tears. "No, it won't."

HELL. Sam struggled blearily out of a deep sleep, summoned by the strident ring of the telephone. The green numbers on his clock radio said 2:06 a.m. Who in God's name...?

He caught the phone on the fourth ring. "Hello?"

There was a hesitation, and he thought maybe the caller was some crank who would just hang up. Then a familiar voice said, in an unfamiliar way, "Sam?"

Sam closed his eyes and groaned. "Alan. What can I do for you?"

"I'm sorry to bother you." The words were slurred. "But I didn't want to call Mom, and...I couldn't think of anybody else."

"You're drunk."

"Jeez, I shouldn't have called."

"Wait!" Sam said sharply. "What is it? Are you in trouble?"

Despite the silence, Sam sensed that Alan was still on the line. "Alan? Talk to me."

"I got blasted, and I just...just didn't think I should drive."

"Where are you?"

"Lakewood."

Sam flicked on the bedside lamp. "Okay, what's the address?"

Half an hour later, he slowed the Mercedes to peer at battered mailboxes along the narrow country road. Twice he stopped and backed up, once using his flashlight to read the faint numbers. Thank God the address was clear when he found the right mailbox, next to a gravel lane that led past a dark mound of blackberry vine.

Lights were on in the small house, and when he opened his car door he could hear the deep thump of a bass guitar. Alan's car was parked between two others beside a shed. The front door opened before Sam reached the front porch, and Alan appeared, calling "See ya" over his shoulder. The boy had to have been watching for him.

"Thanks," Alan said.

Sam nodded. He watched as Alan staggered slightly before he opened the car door and got in. The kid wasn't all that drunk, he guessed, but that didn't mean he could drive. At least he'd had the sense to know that.

Sam didn't try to talk, just started the car and retraced his route through the winding country roads. The boy was just a dark presence beside him. When they had crossed the freeway and were back in more familiar territory, he said neutrally, "I don't think your mother would have minded coming to get you."

Alan must have been sobering up fast, because he sounded more like himself, if unnaturally humble. "She always tells me to call, but I don't usually get drunk, and... Well, she'd have worried."

"That's a mother's prerogative."

"Are you going to tell her?"

"No." Sam slowed for a stoplight. "This is your business."

"Thanks," the boy said again.

"Once I was awake enough to see straight, I didn't mind."

They lapsed back into silence until they were only a couple of blocks from Alan's house. Then Sam asked, "Any special reason you got drunk tonight?"

Alan looked at him, though Sam couldn't read his expression in the faint light cast by streetlamps. "You must think I'm some kind of baby. I've been doing a lot of stupid things lately, haven't I?"

"Calling somebody for a ride home wasn't stupid. It was smart."

"Yeah, but I got drunk in the first place."

Some instinct made Sam ask, "Your dad again?"

"His wife's pregnant." Getting it off his chest must have helped, because his voice changed. "I guess I should have expected it. I mean, she's younger than he is and she must want kids of her own. But he's *my* father. They acted like I should be happy about it or something. But Dad doesn't have time for me now! If he's changing diapers and feeding some baby a bottle, he's *never* going to have time for me."

Sam parked in front of Rebecca's house and turned the headlights and engine off. "I've never had kids, so I can't tell you how he feels. But I doubt if your mother would love you any less just because she had another child."

Alan sniffed, and Sam saw him wipe his nose with his sleeve.

"Yeah, well, that's Mom," Alan mumbled.

Sam nodded. They sat in silence for a moment. Finally Sam said, "Life's a bitch sometimes, isn't it?"

Alan gave a watery laugh. "That sounds like a bumper sticker."

Sam smiled ruefully and clapped the boy on the shoulder. "Seems like I've seen it before," he admitted. "Listen, can you get in without waking your mom up?"

"She hears me come in. She always says 'Alan?' and I always answer 'Yeah, it's me.' I guess she waits up for me."

"That's nice," Sam said. He wondered if his mother had waited up for him when he was that age. Did she still lie awake sometimes, wondering if he would ever come home?

"Yeah, it is," Alan agreed, sounding surprised. "At least with her I'm still pretty sure she cares, even if she does make me mad sometimes. You know what I mean?"

"Yeah." Sam grimaced. "Yeah, I know what you mean."

"Well." Alan opened the car door. "Thanks. Okay?"

Sam nodded toward the house. "Sure. Go on. Get."

Alan quietly shut the door, then headed up the walk. Sam waited until the boy had slipped inside before starting the car again.

The half-hour drive to Everett gave him plenty of time to think about Rebecca's son and his own reaction to Alan's call that night. He finally identified what he felt: he was flattered that the boy had trusted him enough to phone. Sam could never have trusted his own father, and he hadn't had a substitute. He didn't mind feeling that he was one for Alan. In fact, he kind of liked it.

REBECCA SHOULD HAVE awakened Sunday morning with a feeling of anticipation. Today was the big day—Sam and Alan had both promised. But she had slept fitfully, worrying about Jess and her nieces in the long sleepless stretches. She remembered how she had dreaded telling Alan that his father had moved out. Even if Stephanie and Sarah had expected it, the news would be traumatic. As Jess had said, life would never be the same again for any of them.

She showered, and while she was dressing, she heard the bathroom door shut. Good. Alan was up. On the way downstairs, she paused outside the bathroom. "Are you coming to church with me this morning?" she called.

With a sinking feeling, she heard the sound of retching.

"I don't feel very good," Alan said at last.

"Can I do anything?"

"Nah."

More retching.

Flu? she wondered. Or the result of his late night? She'd heard him come in around three o'clock, but he hadn't sounded drunk. Now she looked out the front window. His car wasn't there. And a fine mist made the day gray.

What little anticipation she'd clung to evaporated. She ate her cereal while waiting for the water to boil. By the time Alan appeared, Rebecca was nursing a cup of orange spice tea.

He was pale, and a little green around the mouth. "I'm sorry you don't feel good," she said moderately.

He swallowed. "I'll be okay. I, uh, had a couple of beers last night."

"A couple?"

Alan didn't meet her eyes. "I didn't drive home."

"I hope whoever brought you hadn't had a couple of beers himself."

"No, I called— I mean, he wasn't drinking."

"You know I wish you wouldn't drink at all." Rebecca waited until Alan nodded. "But I'm glad you didn't drive." He nodded again, still staring down at his feet. "Would breakfast help?" she asked.

He lifted his head and dubiously eyed the milk left in the bottom of her cereal bowl. "I don't know."

"Try some food," she advised. Draining the last of her tea, she added, "I'm going to catch the nine o'clock service. I should be home by 10:30."

"Sure," he said.

But when, after church, Rebecca walked back into the house, it was silent. She found a note on the kitchen table: "Geoff took me to get my car. I'll be home this afternoon sometime."

He'd forgotten. She turned around with a sense of fatalism, to see the red light blinking on the answering machine.

When she pushed Play, Sam's voice came out, clear as the sky had been yesterday: "Rebecca, I'm sorry. I just got a call. One of my stores was broken into last night. It was vandalized and money was taken out of the cash register. The police want me to have a look. Maybe next weekend will work better. I'll give you a call."

Her first reaction was to hope the burglary wasn't cataclysmal for Sam. But then a blanket of depression settled over her. So much for her big day. She'd have a few words for Alan when he showed up, but what could she say to Sam? He hadn't wanted any part in this project to start with. He'd probably volunteered because he'd felt sorry for her. As reluctant as he'd been, even a break-in had undoubtedly sounded good to him. She found it hard to imagine that the CEO of a multistore chain had to deal with the aftermath of a burglary. Where was the manager, for crying out loud? Surely he would know the stock better.

But, then, Sam didn't seem to trust any of his managers. Which should have been her first clue. Because he didn't trust her, either—at least not with what really counted: his feelings.

Rebecca sank down onto a kitchen chair and stared at the answering machine, which had rewound and was back to blinking at her. Now what?

Beneath her depression, she found a kernel of anger. She'd learned to do plenty of other things on her own in the scary days after she'd kicked Bruce out. So why not one more?

"To hell with them both!" she said aloud. "I'll build my own arbor!"

She began in a frenzy of energy that kept her from thinking. Digging the holes wasn't too bad, no worse than preparing a new bed for flowers. Her soil was sandy for the first foot, with hard-packed clay and gravel beneath. She chipped it out with the tip of her shovel. By the time she had buried the posts and packed the earth around them, checking over and over with her level to make sure one of them didn't lean, she was wiping sweat as well as drizzle off her face. Unfamiliar muscles ached, and she was mightily tempted to quit, but stubbornness wouldn't let her.

Back in the garage, Rebecca scalloped the ends of the two-by-twelve beams with her jigsaw. Even with the biggest blade in, the saw wasn't really adequate for such large pieces of lumber. It kept getting jammed, and by the time she'd finished the last cut, the blade was bent. Knowing how easy this part would have been with the circular saw, which had been too heavy for her to handle, didn't improve her mood.

The final result wouldn't have stood up to a craftsman's inspection, Rebecca acknowledged, but considering her lack of carpentry skills, she didn't think she'd done too badly.

The damn beams were heavy, though, and long enough to be clumsy. Rebecca carried one at a time around the side of the house and through the backyard. Twice she slammed one end into a gatepost and almost knocked herself out. She dropped the last beam on top of the others with a groan and rubbed her shoulder. She'd probably have bruises.

Now came the good part. She'd nailed little aluminum caps on top of the posts. The beams were supposed to drop right inside them.

The trick, of course, would be getting the wretched beams up there in the first place. Looking at their unwieldy length, she hesitated, but that knot of anger wouldn't let her stop. If she could do this on her own, she could do anything.

One more trip to the garage produced the stepladder. She placed it in the middle of her arbor-to-be, but when she heaved a beam back onto her shoulder and took the first precarious step onto the ladder, the legs sank unevenly into the muddy ground. Damn. She backed off, leaned the beam against one of the posts and moved the stepladder around until she thought she'd found a more stable spot.

Rebecca closed her eyes and pushed wet hair back from her forehead. It would have been so easy to let hot tears join the rain and sweat. She wanted desperately to quit, to go in for a long soak in the tub and a glass of wine and . . . What? A cry? A call home to Mother?

No!

It took everything she had to balance the beam on her shoulder again and start up the ladder. One step at a time, carefully . . . The ladder tilted, but she took the next step, anyway. One more and she could set the beam in place. Then the other one and she'd quit for the day.

On the fourth step she thought she was high enough. She leaned forward and hoisted the beam, her arms shaking from the strain, and eased one end into the cap. Now the other side . . . She missed, leaned farther and fell.

Rebecca hit the ground hard. Then it all happened so fast: the stepladder cracked her on the head, the beam broke loose from the one cap and bounced off her right shoulder, flinging her to one side.

Afterward, she didn't know whether she'd lost consciousness or not. All she knew was that suddenly she was lying with one cheek in the mud and everything hurt. With the one hand that still worked, she pushed herself to a sitting position and scooted painfully to where she could lean back against one of the posts.

The broken stepladder, the fallen beam, the mud... It was all so far from what she'd imagined. The pattern of sun and shadow that would fall on the herringbone brick floor, the heavy scent of roses and the wide graceful faces of clematis flowers. The sense of completion, of accomplishment—

The sense of failure, she thought achingly, and began—at last—to cry.

CHAPTER FOURTEEN

TEARS RAN DOWN her cheeks and she could taste the salt. Her head hurt, her shoulder throbbed and her right arm felt useless.

Even when she leaned her forehead against her knees and sobbed, Rebecca knew that she wasn't crying for the unfinished arbor or because she hurt. It was Sam she mourned. What she had thought they might have. What he didn't care enough to work for.

She should have known. She *had* known what she wanted if she were ever to remarry. She had intended to be so cool and collected: check, he likes to work around the house; check, good with boys; check, there when I need him.

It went to show how little she'd learned from her painful first marriage. *Sexy* had been low on her list, but guess what? She'd quit thinking the minute she'd met Sam. The attraction between them had been so potent that she had refused to face how unlikely it was that Sam would ever really fit into her life. She couldn't even claim there hadn't been warning flags: he was never there when she wanted him; he was no more interested in hearth and home than Bruce had been; Alan had hated him; and the only effort he'd ever made to get along with her family had been at Christmas dinner—and then he'd been polite but guarded.

In other words, she'd deliberately blinded herself.

Well, it was time to face facts. Sam didn't love her, not the way she needed to be loved. And he never would. Work would always come first. He would never share what he felt with her—all she had to do was remember the look she'd seen on his face Christmas Day, and the way he'd clamped down on his emotions the minute she'd asked if he was all right.

No, Sam wasn't ready to share a life with her.

All she had to do was picture Jess telling her about splitting up with Roy to know she couldn't face that again. However hard a break would be now, it would be ten times worse if she let the relationship go any further.

Rebecca sniffed, wiped her eyes on the wet sleeve of her sweater and considered getting up. She should have tried sooner. Her head pounded, her right shoulder and whole side hurt, and now she felt queasy. She was cold, too, shaken with shivers. She couldn't keep sitting there in the rain. She'd done this to herself; she could darn well get herself out of the fix. She wasn't eager to admit to anybody else how stupid she had been.

"Rebecca?"

For an instant she thought she'd imagined Sam's voice. Then she heard it again.

"Rebecca?"

"Sam!" she called back. "I'm ... I'm out here."

He appeared around the house, reassuringly solid. Real. Everything she had ever wanted.

"Good God," he said, and covered the yard in a few long strides. He crouched in front of her, his brows drawn, and gently lifted her chin. Roughly he asked, "Are you hurt?"

She started to nod, and had to close her eyes against the pain that rattled in her skull. "Yes," she whispered. "I fell off the ladder and dropped the beam on top of myself."

"I'll call an ambulance." He started to stand, but she grabbed his arm.

"No!"

She didn't want to tell him how unwelcome the bill for an ambulance would be. She'd have to endure too many years hearing her mother say things like "Oh, dear, I knew you shouldn't have spent the money for this arbor. You should always have extra put away for a bad spot." Rebecca did have money put away; she just didn't want to spend it on an ambulance she didn't need.

With an effort, she moderated her voice. "I've already moved around. If I should have stayed immobile, it's too late now. Will you just drive me to the Emergency Room?"

His intense gray eyes searched her face. "Are you sure?"

"Please," she whispered, hating—now, of all times—to be so dependent on him.

Sam gave a short, decisive nod. "All right. Lean on me."

He wrapped his arm around her so that her head rested against his broad shoulder and eased her to her feet. His warmth enfolded her, but she still felt cold inside. As they moved slowly, with Sam supporting most of her weight, Rebecca seemed to hear his voice, over and over again. *Lean on me. Lean on me.*

I can't, she thought sadly. *It's too late.*

"THEY SAY I can go home now." Rebecca stepped out of the wheelchair.

The nurse gave her a steadying hand. "You will have somebody there to keep an eye on you, won't you?"

"She will," Sam said grimly. He didn't like Rebecca's pallor. He liked even less the way she avoided his gaze.

Rebecca let him wrap an arm around her again as he guided her through the wide double doors of the Emergency Room out to his car, parked only a few yards away. She held herself stiffly, accepting his help, but no more. What he really wanted to do was hold her close, press his cheek to her hair and whisper how scared he'd been. Instead he asked, "What did the doctor say?"

She waited while he opened the passenger door. "That I have a mild concussion and a strained shoulder. I'll be sore for a few days, but I should be thankful I'm in one piece." She settled into the seat and reached for the seat belt.

"Damn right you should be." With barely suppressed anger, Sam slammed the door. He got in, jammed the key in the ignition, started the car. "Where the hell was Alan?"

She showed the first signs of life he'd seen since he'd found her crying in the rain.

"What's that supposed to mean?"

He knew vaguely that guilt was driving his anger, but that didn't mean he had the sense to control it. "You know damn well what that means," he snapped. "You couldn't wait a week? Are you so stubborn you had to do a two-man job alone?"

"Wait a *week?*" Her eyes blazed fire. "Do you know how long I've been waiting? Months! How many times have I asked? Maybe going ahead was dumb, but you sure aren't in any position to chew me out for it!"

"You could have been badly injured!"

Rebecca was staring at him, and he knew the precise moment the curtain dropped, leaving her gaze opaque. Her voice changed, too, becoming listless as she looked away.

"I'm a capable human being. I can't spend my life waiting for a man."

Panic seized him, though he wasn't quite sure what he feared, and he gripped on the steering wheel. "I'm sorry," he said roughly. "I should have been there."

"No." She shook her head. "The arbor was my project, not yours."

"Damn it, I wanted to help you!"

She looked at him, clear-eyed this time. "Sam ..."

His chest was tight. "God, you scared me."

Her expression became sadder, if anything. "Sam, I let this stupid arbor become some kind of...of symbol. I must have thought that if I could get you to help me with it, I would somehow have transformed you into my ideal." She made a face. "Woman's ultimate fantasy. But that's all it is. A fantasy. You're not going to change, Sam. I don't know why I didn't recognize sooner how different we are."

She was going to say goodbye. His panic erupted into full-blown terror. He couldn't let her go! Without her, what kind of life would be left? He knew the answer: another twenty years like the past twenty, loveless, joyless, obsessive.

"What'll it take to prove to you that I have changed?" he asked. "A wedding ring? If that's what you want, we can get married." He heard his own brusque voice and thought, good God, what a way to propose. What happened to roses and candlelight?

Rebecca stared at him in shock. "You think we should get married?" she echoed.

"Why not?"

She stared straight ahead. Her shoulders were rigid and her voice was strained. "A better question is, why?"

"Because I don't want to lose you."

"In other words, I'm pressuring you."

"No, damn it!" He was almost shouting. "We have something good going, Rebecca. You have to admit that."

"No." She shook her head blindly. "There's only one reason to get married."

"You want me to say I love you." Sam drew a deep breath. Three simple words, and his tongue felt tangled in his mouth. Had he ever said them? He *had* to get them out; Rebecca deserved at least that much. He cleared his throat. "I love you."

Rebecca wiped at her wet eyes with her one good hand. "I'm sorry, Sam. It's too late."

"Why? Damn it, *why?*" Raging at the finality in her voice would do him no good; he knew that before he tried. But he couldn't accept it, wouldn't!

She still looked ahead, not at him. "We don't want the same kind of life, Sam. You know it and I know it. Now, would you take me home? I'd like to lie down."

What else could he do? He started the engine and drove the half a mile to her house, all the way conscious of her beside him. He didn't have to turn his head to see her small straight nose, her rounded chin and stubborn, sensuous mouth. He didn't have to look to see the exhaustion in her deep-blue eyes, the mud on her jeans and shirt, the clean white of the sling. He knew he had done this to her, and could not undo it.

Alan's car was in the driveway; he appeared on the front porch when Sam pulled in. Sam turned off the engine and reached for his door handle. Rebecca's hand on his arm stopped him.

"Please. Just let me go," she said, her voice husky, cracking at the end.

"I can't even walk you to your door?"

"Please."

Sam shut his eyes. He had never been closer to crying. "All right," he said almost evenly. "Goodbye."

He heard a ragged breath, then her whisper.

"Goodbye, Sam."

He didn't watch her go, just held on to the steering wheel with white-knuckled hands until his inner turmoil had settled to a sick feeling of loss. Then he started the car and pulled away, allowing himself only one glance in the rearview mirror. Over the picket fence, he could just see the raw posts that should have supported a rose arbor.

"HOW COME Sam didn't come in?"

Rebecca sagged onto her bed, not caring how filthy she was. Her impulse was to lie. Right this second, she couldn't face a discussion. Not that Alan would be upset. He'd probably say "I told you so."

Alan pulled her shoes off and she turned one cheek against the smooth, cool pillow. The pain medication had made her feel dull and tired, but the aches were still there. Including the heartache.

"Jeez, he shouldn't have just left like that when you were hurt and everything." Alan sounded aggrieved.

"I asked him not to come in," Rebecca admitted. "I just . . . wanted to climb into bed."

She prayed that she'd sounded convincing, and knew immediately that she hadn't.

"Are you mad at him?" Alan demanded.

"No, I..." Tears stung her eyes. She blinked them back. How many times had she already cried today? "I..." Rebecca took a shaky breath, then let it out. "I'm not going to see Sam again. I told him so, and he left. And yes, I know you didn't like him in the first place. I guess you were right."

"You're not going to see him again?" Alan sounded so stunned, she forced her heavy eyelids up. His mouth was literally hanging open. "But...but *I* was the one who was wrong!"

"Wait a minute." Her son's consternation penetrated her lethargy. "You could barely bring yourself to be civil. Remember?"

"But that was a long time ago." He stood beside the bed, looking down at her as if she'd sprouted antennae. "I was just...well, maybe I was jealous. Sam's okay. You're not breaking up with him because of things I said, are you?"

Rebecca longed with all her being to pull her blinds and cry herself to sleep, alone in the dim sanctuary of her bedroom. Instead she had to reason with an irrational teenager.

"No," she said. "I'm breaking up with him because..." Because he took too long to say, *I love you.* "Because I needed our relationship to progress. It wasn't. Sam might have been interested in me, but he wasn't interested in my life. Do you understand?"

"No," Alan said stubbornly. "He was nice to me."

"Sometimes," she allowed.

"I called him last night," Alan said. "You know, when I had too much to drink? He's the one who gave me a ride home."

"You called Sam?" She struggled to a sitting position. "I don't understand. Why?"

Alan stared down at his feet. "I didn't want you to know I'd had too much to drink. And I couldn't think of anyone else to call."

"Alan, you know I'd have come."

"Yeah, sure." He grimaced. "I just didn't want to disappoint you."

"You never do that," she said softly.

At that he looked up. "Oh, come on. I did today when I forgot I'd promised to help you."

"You're sixteen," she said. "An occasional slipup doesn't disappoint me."

"Really?"

He looked so hopeful, she had to smile despite everything. "Really."

"Oh. Well. The thing is, Sam was nice. He came right away. He didn't chew me out.... I mean, he could have been my father or something."

A stab to the heart would have been kinder. On a spasm of pain, Rebecca said, "I'm sorry. Oh, God, I'm sorry, Alan. I guess you must have started to count on him. And to think—" She bit her lip.

"That you were going to marry him? Yeah, I figured you were." He hesitated, looking uncomfortable. "Doesn't Sam want to marry you?"

Rebecca closed her eyes. "I don't know. But even if he does, I don't think he envisions the kind of marriage I do. I'm sorry, Alan. I don't know what else to say."

He squared his shoulders, somehow managing to seem both very young and very mature. He said strongly, "Well, I think you should give him another chance. I think you're wrong."

Rebecca shook her head, then let herself collapse back against the pillow. "I can't," she whispered. "I just can't."

Long after Alan had left her in the silence of her dark bedroom, Rebecca lay thinking about family, and about Sam. She had so missed her family—the security, the love, the familiarity. Nobody else would ever know her the way they did. She couldn't blame Sam, who had grown up on shifting sand instead of bedrock, for not understanding. But she couldn't change her decision, either. Home and family were at the center of her life. A man who didn't feel the same wasn't for her.

She simply couldn't face a lifetime of conflict every time her mother called, every time a family get-together neared. She couldn't face knowing that she and her everyday concerns would always come second to the stores. Knowing that Sam would never share his deepest emotions, that however intimate they were sexually, she was part of the world he regarded warily, shielded himself from.

For her, it had to be all or nothing. And Sam, she was convinced, would never give all.

ALAN CLOSED the blinds for his mother, then left her to take a nap. He tiptoed down the stairs. After waiting a decent interval, until he was confident she was asleep, he took his bike and rode to his grandmother's.

She came to the door on the first ring, wearing darkgreen corduroy pants and a fluffy white sweater. As usual, she looked completely unruffled. She must bake cookies or clean house sometimes, but you never caught her looking as though she were in the middle of doing either.

"Why, Alan!" she exclaimed. "How nice to see you. Come on in."

His heart was pounding because he wasn't used to saying stuff to his grandmother that she wouldn't want to hear. He didn't like the idea of hurting her feelings. This time, though, he figured somebody had to say it. Who else was there?

He trailed her into the spotless kitchen, but shook his head when she offered him a pop.

"Well, let me make myself a nice cup of tea," Grandma said. "I just couldn't sleep after your aunt Jess called last night. I can't say I'm sorry that Roy won't be part of the family anymore, but I worry about Stephanie and Sarah."

"What are you talking about?"

"Oh, I thought your mother knew. Aunt Jessie is getting a divorce."

"You're kidding," he said dumbly. He guessed Mom hadn't had time to tell him. This morning he'd been green around the gills, then this afternoon . . .

Which reminded him why he was there.

After Grandma had poured her tea and pulled up a chair to the small table, Alan started indirectly. "You know how Mom's building that arbor out in the back? Well, she was working on it today and she hurt herself."

He listened to gasps and questions and promises to rush right over, then interrupted. "No, Mom's asleep right now. The doctor says she's okay—she'll just be sore for a few days. That's not really what I called about. The thing is..." He took a breath. "She's broken up with Sam."

His grandmother's silence took him by surprise. At last, she said, "Oh, dear."

Here came the hard part. Alan took a deep breath. "I think it's partly your fault," he said. "Mom knows you don't like Sam."

Grandma's back stiffened. In a shocked voice she exclaimed, "Alan!"

"Well, it's true." Honesty made him add reluctantly, "It's my fault, too. At first I didn't like Sam, either. I guess I didn't tell Mom that I'd changed my mind."

"What on earth makes you think your mother's decision has anything to do with either of us? She certainly didn't listen to us three months ago, when she could have avoided a great deal of heartache."

"Because I know she loves him." He met his grandmother's blue eyes, so like his own. "Why else would she break up with him?"

"There are certainly all kinds of reasons. . . ."

"Yeah," Alan said angrily. "You know the one she gave me? Sam isn't interested in her life.

"Well, that's bull. I know it is! What she means is, she had to choose between the rest of us and Sam. It's just not fair."

"What is it you think I should do?"

"Quit making Mom feel guilty for dating someone you don't like."

"I only wanted what's best for your mother," Grandma said self-righteously.

"Yeah?" He knew he sounded rude but didn't care. "What's that?"

She hesitated a second too long. "Certainly not turning against her family."

Alan stood up. "Mom never turned against you. She never would."

He was shocked to see tears in her eyes. "These past few months have been . . . very difficult."

"You can change things," he said quietly.

His grandmother gave herself a little shake, straightened her shoulders and lifted her chin. "What do you want me to do?" she asked again.

This time, he knew she wanted an answer. "Act like you want Sam there when I invite him to the next Sunday dinner."

"I can't imagine that he'd come."

"I bet he will," Alan said.

She gazed at him, almost unseeing, for a moment, then sniffed, "Very well. If that's what it takes, I'll do it."

For the first time, he felt self-conscious. "Uh, thanks."

She didn't tell Alan he was welcome. Instead she said stiffly, "I miss your mother."

He surprised himself by saying, "Yeah, well, all of you keep telling me that how Mom and Dad feel about each other, or Karen or Sam or any other adult, doesn't have anything to do with how they feel about me. The way parents and their kids feel about each other is different, remember?"

There was a moment's silence. His grandmother's mouth tightened, showing the tracery of lines around it, then twisted into an almost smile. "I guess I needed reminding," she said so softly he knew she was talking to herself. "Perhaps I was foolish."

He left her there at the kitchen table, gazing out the window at the winter-bare yard. He didn't know whether he had done any good. Maybe it was too late. But how else could he make up to Mom for being such a jerk? Funny, he'd been so sure he knew who the jerk was.

MAYBE CHANGE had to start at the beginning, Sam thought. He sat in his car, looking at the house where he had grown up. He didn't want to get out and walk up onto his father's front porch, knock on the bastard's door, shake his hand.

Well, nobody had ever said change was easy.

Damn. He was tempted to start the car again, forget the whole thing. If he was trying to redeem himself in Rebecca's eyes, he might as well admit that his chances would not likely be helped by this visit. She'd said goodbye, not "Call again someday, once you've reconciled with your family."

Sam had phoned one of his brothers first, the one he'd been closest to. Doing that had been easier. It shouldn't have hurt when Mel didn't even recognize his voice. Trying to sound humorous, Sam had to say, "Remember your long-lost brother?"

"Sam?" His brother had sounded...shocked. "What's up?"

"Just . . . saying hello."

To Sam's eternal shame, Mel was obviously delighted.

"Damn, it's good to hear from you! We were just talking about you. Something about Christmas makes you think back."

"Yeah," Sam had said gruffly. "That's why I called."

"So, what are you up to?"

Sam brought his brother up-to-date on his life, then heard all about Mary's gallbladder surgery and the two boys, eight and ten years old, who were real hell-raisers, according to their proud papa.

"Christmas or no Christmas," Mel said, "they're both grounded. Tied a sparkler to the cat's tail. Scared the bejesus out of it."

Sam seemed to recall a similar escapade when he and Mel had been about the same age. Which had ended with a whipping.

"How's Mom?" he'd asked.

"Getting younger every day," Mel said. "She's dragging Dad to ballroom-dancing classes. Can you believe it?"

"No," Sam said bluntly.

There was an awkward silence. "Dad's mellowed," Mel had said. "I think maybe he regrets the way he raised us."

Sam's voice was hard. "I'll never believe that."

"You know, he wasn't as tough on Larry and me. Maybe even then he recognized his mistakes."

Bitterness roiled in Sam's stomach. "Maybe he just wore his arm out on me."

"You're not going to forgive him, are you?"

"No," Sam had said without apology. "But I want to see the rest of you."

"Mom?"

"Yeah. Especially Mom."

"She misses you."

Sam had to clear his throat before he could continue. "I miss her, too."

Now, still sitting in his car, Sam tried to remember how many years it had been. Too many to make going home again easy.

He got out of the car at last, slammed the door and started across the street. The neighborhood hadn't changed at all. The houses were still modest, well cared for, with signs that most were occupied by young families. Only a few blocks from Green Lake, his parents' small frame house was still painted white with black trim, the edge of the lawn was still ruler straight, the film of lace curtains still guarded the front window. The basketball hoop was a little askew, but the backboard was freshly painted. Bushes and trees were bigger, and a carport had been added to the side of the house.

He felt as if he'd stepped into a time warp. He automatically reached for the familiar brass doorknob, before he stopped himself and rang the bell.

Sam could hear footsteps coming, light and quick. His mother's. Despite the cold day, he was sweating inside the heavy sweater she had knit him. Why hadn't he called first? Met her at Mel's?

Why hadn't he done this a month ago, when he could have brought Rebecca with him? She would have known what to say.

The door opened and a woman stood framed in the doorway, behind the haze of the screen door. She was of medium height, with short curly brown hair softened with gray. Her face was round and gentle, her eyes gray. An apron covered her ample bosom, and she was wiping her heavily veined hands with a dish towel.

"Yes, what can I do for—" She drew a sharp breath and stopped, clutching the dish towel to her chest.

"Hello, Mom," he said quietly.

"Sam," she whispered. Her eyes filled with tears and she stepped back. "Come in. Please. Not that I have to invite you. This is your home, too."

No. Never again. He knew that, even as he crossed the threshold. The umbrella stand still stood in the entryway; even the smells were the same. His memory traveled up the stairs—he knew exactly where the third one squeaked. The carpet was the same, though more worn than it had been. Down the hall, his bedroom was the second on the right. Half of him wanted to climb those stairs, step into the past; the other half was terrified to do so.

His mother was wringing her hands now. "Your father is home."

"That's all right," he said.

"He loved you, you know," she said almost inaudibly.

Had his father loved him? Sam wondered. Did he give a damn anymore? He shook his head. "It's too late for that. But I've finally realized how much I missed, never coming home. You and Mel and Larry. And knowing their kids. I figured maybe it wasn't too late for that much.''

He braced himself even before he consciously heard the back door slam.

''Helen?'' his father called brusquely. ''Somebody here—?''

His father stopped dead in the kitchen doorway, his face registering nothing. He was the first to speak. ''So. Decided to come home again, have you?''

Sam inclined his head. ''In a manner of speaking.'' His father was still a big man, Sam saw, his memories hadn't deceived him there. But the years showed in the deeply carved lines on his face and the beer belly, the gray bristle on his jaw that needed shaving, the steel gray of his hair and bushy brows.

''What, you need a loan or something?''

Amazingly, Sam felt the stir of amusement. ''No. I don't need anything.'' *Not from you,* he thought.

''Expect us to welcome you with open arms?''

''No,'' Sam said again. ''I don't expect anything from you.''

The heavy brows knit. ''Then what the hell do you want?''

''To talk to my mother.''

He was sorry to have upset her; out of the corner of his eye he could see her hands worrying away at the dish towel. But he wasn't sorry to have confounded his father, whose thoughts were visibly working as he scowled at Sam.

''Might have done more good ten years ago,'' his father said at last. ''Now you'll just get her crying again.''

''I don't think so,'' Sam said without inflection.

''I suppose you want me to disappear.''

Sam shrugged. "I don't care either way." He was vaguely astonished to realize he meant it, that he was completely relaxed, that he honestly *didn't* care. That he was free.

The beefy shoulders shrugged, and his father said churlishly, "Go on in and sit down, then. Doesn't matter to me."

Maybe it didn't, but he came, too, settling into his sagging recliner, which might have been the same one that was there twenty years ago. The TV remote control lay on the arm; he always had wanted to control what was watched. An empty beer can sat on the end table.

He turned on the TV to some game show, though the volume was so low he probably couldn't hear what was said. Sam and his mother sat on either end of the couch. Her smile was shaky as she looked at him.

"The sweater fits you."

Sam glanced down. "Yeah. You remembered that wool makes me itch."

"How can a mother forget something like that?"

He pictured Rebecca, cheering Alan on, fussing over him, teasing him, her eyes always loving. "I don't know," he said. "I guess I figured you would."

They both knew he wasn't talking about itchy sweaters. "Never," she said quietly, and he nodded acknowledgment.

The moment of silence that followed was awkward but not strained. He wasn't surprised when she asked, "You're not married?"

Sam shook his head. "I've met a woman, though."

His mother's face brightened. "Tell me about her."

Sam did, throwing Alan in for good measure. "I don't know whether it'll work out," he said finally. "But I'm going to do my damnedest to see if it can."

"Don't swear," she said, but laid her hand on his. "I'm sure I'd like her."

He clasped her hand in his. "Yeah. I'm sure you would."

"Can you stay for dinner?" his mother asked.

"Not today," he said. "But I'll be back."

Sam stood, nodded to his father, who glowered back, and said, "See you, Dad." At the front door he gave his mother a quick, hard hug. "I'm sorry, Mom," he whispered.

Her tear-filled eyes met his and she said in a low voice, "No. I'm sorry. I should have done something. I shouldn't have let your father—" She broke off and pressed her lips together. "But I didn't know what to do, how to support us. And then it was too late."

"Well, I survived," Sam said. "It just took me a while to realize I had."

"Will you come to dinner soon? Maybe on a Sunday?"

Sunday dinner. A family tradition. He was surprised to hear himself say, "Sure. I'll call."

Another hug, a kiss on her soft cheek, and he escaped. The hardest part was over. He felt as though the crushing weight he had carried for too many years was suddenly gone. He had faced the ogre and his own anger, and found neither to be as formidable as he had imagined.

Maybe he could talk about both now. If it wasn't too late.

CHAPTER FIFTEEN

HALF A DOZEN vehicles already blocked the gravel driveway leading to Joe's house when Rebecca arrived for Sunday dinner. Alan's was there, she saw; he had spent the previous night at his father's and come directly. Another beater belonged to one of Lee's boys; there was Jess's van, and Lee's car.

She still didn't move to get out of her car. Today would be bittersweet, a return to the circle of her family, a pretense that nothing had changed. But things *had* changed. Too much. And not just for her, she thought, her gaze lingering on Jess's van.

Joe owned a magnificent, modern home with a spectacular view of the Cascade Mountains and ten acres of mixed pasture and woods. Of all the siblings, he had made the greatest success of his business. Yet he had never married and had no children, despite the string of pretty women he'd dated. Funny how her life and her siblings' lives had turned out, how set the patterns were. Look how she'd fought to escape hers and in the end had turned back to embrace it. Did Joe ever regret the solitude he had chosen? she wondered.

And did she care right this minute whether her muleheaded brother ever got married?

"The truth is," she muttered, "you don't want to go in."

Once she'd acknowledged her reluctance, Rebecca collected the dish of scalloped potatoes from the back seat and headed up the drive, her back hunched against the cold. The drive was icy, and she had to walk carefully so as not to slip. Idly she tabulated who was there and who wasn't from the vehicles parked bumper to bumper. She didn't see her mother's car; somebody must have picked her up. Joe's pickup was parked in front of the garage doors, and next to it—

Rebecca stopped dead. Next to it was a Mercedes-Benz. A gray Mercedes sedan.

It couldn't be Sam's. Nobody would have invited him. He wouldn't have come if he *had* been invited. Would he have?

She felt as if she were babbling, and she hadn't even opened her mouth. She momentarily closed her eyes, took a deep breath and continued on up to the porch. Sam didn't drive the only Mercedes-Benz in the world. Maybe Joe had invited a friend. Or Lee. Or...

Rebecca didn't believe herself. She knocked, then went in the front door. The slate-tiled entry opened onto an enormous living room that overlooked a deep ravine. Rebecca had always felt as if she could step right out the wall of glass at the other end and plunge into the valley.

Today she didn't notice. Her gaze went no farther than the man who stood solidly beside the stone fireplace facing her. Tall, dark and sexy. Lean face and hooded eyes, a mouth that gave nothing away. Shoulders so broad she had thought they could protect her from the world.

Sam.

Some emotion showed briefly on his face, but Rebecca jerked away before she could identify it. She stormed into the kitchen and dropped her casserole dish unheedingly on the tile counter. Her mother, Jess and Janine all turned to stare at her.

"Who invited him?" Rebecca demanded.

Her mother played innocent. "Him?"

"Sam." The name came from between gritted teeth. Her stomach was doing flip-flops, undecided between fury and anguish. What was he doing here?

"Why, I think Alan invited him."

"I'll kill him!" Rebecca snapped. "Where is he?"

"Alan?"

She almost lunged across the kitchen.

"Down in the family room, I think," Mrs. Hughes said hastily.

Rebecca stormed out of the kitchen—and came up against a wall. Sam blocked her way.

His voice was a low rumble. "Can we talk?"

"I have nothing to say," she shot back.

A muscle twitched in his cheek. "I can't accept that. Damn it, give me a chance, Rebecca."

"Don't you think this is kind of underhanded?" She had to press her lips together to gain some measure of control, before she could go on. "This is *my* family. You have no right...!"

His eyes were dark and intense. "Was there a better way for me to show you I was serious when I said I loved you?"

"This isn't a game."

"Do you think I don't know that?"

Her chest hurt worse than the time her car had been rear-ended and she was flung against the steering wheel. Why was he doing this to her? Why now, when she had given him so many chances before?

Rebecca summoned all her self-possession. Lifting her chin, she said bleakly, "Sam, I'm too old to fall into your arms because you say you love me. Bruce loved me, too. Once upon a time. The truth is, love doesn't stand up to real life whittling away at it. There has to be more. As far as you were concerned, I was light entertainment for Saturday nights. You didn't want anything to do with my family. No matter what we'd planned, work always came first. Either you have a problem delegating or else you *want* it to come first. Either way, I'd have been living with a man who dropped by when he could manage it. No." She shook her head with painful finality. "That's not for me, Sam. I'm sorry."

"I can learn," he said roughly. "Until I met you, I didn't know I had anything to learn."

She made a sound that should have been a laugh but wasn't. "Learning isn't that easy. Sam, I want a partner who is enthusiastically present. Not one who figures he has to show that he's willing."

His eyes smouldered with emotion. In a seeming non sequitur, he said, "I went to see my parents."

For the first time, Rebecca really looked at him. She saw suffering to equal her own carved into the haggard lines of his face. She saw a forty-year-old man who had nursed his bitterness for more than half his lifetime, yet who had now—suddenly—healed the fractures that were partly of his own making.

"Why?" she whispered, and waited for his answer with more hope than she had felt in weeks.

"Why do you think?" he said impatiently. "I figured it was the only way I could prove I'd changed."

Her hope died a quick death. "Wrong answer," she said, and tried to step around him.

His hand closed hard around her upper arm and his jaw clenched. "Damn it, Rebecca, what is it you want?"

Desperately she looked for Joe, who stood in the living room, watching them. He was at her side in seconds.

"Rebecca," he said calmly, "I didn't hear you arrive. Come and see my new big-screen TV. Assuming I can pry the kids away from it."

She sounded almost normal when she said, "So that's where Alan is. I wondered."

Sam's expression closed in that way she knew so well. She thought it was what scared her most about him. She must look the wreck she felt, while he now appeared completely unmoved.

"Isn't it just another toy?" Sam said.

Joe pretended to be insulted. "Hell, no, it's a necessity of life."

To Rebecca's eternal gratitude, Sam didn't follow when she left with Joe. On the way downstairs to the family room, Joe asked, "Everything okay?"

Answering that would have taken a week. Instead she went right to the point. "Did you know Sam was coming?"

"Nobody ever tells me anything."

True enough, Joe *was* the last to know family gossip. In this case, however, she recognized an evasive response when she heard one.

"You knew," Rebecca accused.

Joe stopped in the doorway to the family room, his gaze on the huddle of teenage boys surrounding the enormous television screen. "Yeah. I knew." He shrugged. "I figured Alan knew what he was doing."

She couldn't even be mad. "Have you met a sixteen-year-old yet who knows what he's doing?"

Joe was startled into a grin. "Now that you mention it..."

Rebecca let the subject drop. She hid her turmoil and duly admired the high-tech television set, allowing her gaze to meet her son's only once. That was enough.

Hastily Alan said to his cousins, "Hey, uh, let's go make some popcorn."

To a chorus of agreement, four of them disappeared up the stairs.

Rebecca half hoped that by the time she went back upstairs Sam, too, would be gone.

No such luck. Sam stayed to the bitter end. Every time she turned around, he was *there*. Sipping a beer, laughing at something Joe said, talking to Janine, listening with bent head to Jess, who otherwise kept much to herself all afternoon. It was enough to make Rebecca scream even to see her mother chatting amiably with Sam.

Later Rebecca couldn't remember a single thing she said, heard or ate. She didn't even know whether Jess had talked about Roy or how Stephanie and Sarah were taking the breakup. She knew only one thing: every nerve end had been pricklingly aware of Sam's presence.

If she could have fled with any dignity, she would have. Instead her gaze had been drawn inexorably to his. Sometimes the look that met hers was inscrutable, the gray eyes dark and watchful. Twice he smiled, that slow, sweet, sensuous smile that had once melted her and now seared her insides as though she'd drunk battery acid.

If this was a battle, Rebecca surrendered. After informing her darling son that they would have a little talk later, she quietly made her excuses to Joe and her mother, then eased into the kitchen to collect her casserole dish. Maybe if she just slipped out, he wouldn't see her go.

Unfortunately, the front door was within view of the living room. Sam was back where he was when she'd first come in, leaning against the massive fireplace mantel. He straightened when he saw her shrug into her coat, but some of her panic must have registered, because he didn't move. He didn't have to move. The fact that he was there at all was devastating enough.

Feeling hot and cold, and more frightened than she'd ever been in her life, Rebecca left alone. She drove on automatic pilot, her thoughts consumed by the man she was trying to shut out of her life.

The man she loved.

The man who'd accused her of letting her mother rule her life, and who was now using her family to undermine her.

The man she would have sworn was unwilling to change, but who had to be trying.

Somehow, despite the icy roads and her distraction, Rebecca made it home. Five o'clock in the afternoon, and it was already dusk. She wished she'd left some lights on. The house looked dark and cold, an unwelcoming refuge.

I love you, Sam had said again. Rebecca picked her way up the walk and unlocked the front door.

Maybe he meant it, she thought. Maybe she was wrong not to give him a chance to prove it. Was a clean break now really better than years spent hoping for what he couldn't give her? Wasn't *some* hope better than none?

She honestly didn't know. Her certainty had fled in the face of Sam's determination, and without it she knew herself to be vulnerable. Waiting was hard, but what else could she do? If Sam tried again to prove that he meant what he said, maybe she would have her answer.

One way or the other.

SAM HAD TO FIGHT to keep himself from going after Rebecca. When the door closed behind her, he cursed under his breath.

He'd had his chance and blown it. She'd given him an opening—one last one—but instead of taking it, he'd been a coward yet again. He wasn't used to talking about how he felt. Maybe he'd thought she could read his mind, that his mere presence would be enough. Maybe he'd expected Rebecca to fall penitently into his arms, apologizing profusely for ever trying to get him to talk about anything that really mattered.

He'd desperately wanted her with him when he'd visited his parents. Afterward, memories had ached to spill out. Today, when Rebecca had asked why he'd gone home again, all it would have taken was the truth: because you made me see what I was missing. But that would have been too close to the bone, he thought acidly. It would have left him naked. So what had he done but try to put the onus on her. *See what I did for you?*

He'd gotten what he deserved. So he was probably ten kinds of fool for feeling hopeful despite everything. But damn it, she'd *wanted* him to give the right answer. She hadn't said goodbye to him lightly, and she hadn't walked away again easily. The principle had been right; only the execution had left a little to be desired.

So what next? Sam glanced around, to find that he was the object of several wary glances. Alan's expression was the friendliest. The look on Rebecca's mother's face was the closest to hostile.

Jess wasn't watching at him at all. Her gaze was internal. Sam had heard enough lowered voices today to know why. If he was going to offer any sympathy, he'd better do it now. Before somebody kicked him out.

Sam joined her at the window, where she pretended to look out at the gray and white vista of a forested valley and the mountains beyond, all losing focus in the gathering dusk. She glanced over at him without much curiosity.

"I hear you and your husband have separated. I'm sorry," he said.

Her smile was twisted and painful. "Thanks, Sam."

"How are the girls taking it?" He nodded toward her daughters, who sat together on a couch, nibbling on peanuts. Except for being unusually quiet and seeming to cling to each other, they didn't look too bad.

"Oh, well, I suppose." She gestured ineffectually. "I think in the end it'll be a relief. Having your parents fight constantly is scary."

"Yeah." He touched her arm. "If there's anything I can do..."

"Thanks, Sam." This smile was an improvement. "Do something for Rebecca, instead."

He grinned himself. "I'm trying."

Sam left her alone then, to stare sightlessly out the window. Intending to leave, he thanked Joe, then went to Rebecca's mother to politely say goodbye. She would probably be thinking, *good riddance*. But before he could say anything, Alan appeared at his elbow.

"What happened?" the boy asked.

Sam's first instinct was to squelch the teenager with a cool word or two. The disappointment on Alan's face stopped him. Besides, that kind of instinct was what had gotten him in trouble in the first place.

"I blew it," Sam admitted.

Rebecca's mother cleared her throat. "It would help if you didn't always look so... unemotional."

Good God. Now he had to submit to analysis by his future—he hoped—mother-in-law.

He was further disconcerted when Alan, too, studied him. "Yeah, you do have kind of a stone face. Maybe that's why I used to think you were a..." He swallowed the last word.

Sam supplied it. "Jerk."

The boy flushed. "Uh, yeah. You knew, huh?"

Sam clapped the teenager on his back. "Yup."

Alan had the grace to look Sam in the eye. "I'm, well, I'm sorry."

"It's okay. I probably was one."

"Which is neither here nor there," Mrs. Hughes said tartly. "Unless Rebecca thinks you're one."

Sam raised a brow. "Wouldn't you prefer it if she did?"

She didn't even blink, just inclined her head slightly as though acknowledging of a hit. "I have begun to think I might have been wrong. Alan's fondness for you is one reason."

Fondness? Sam didn't even have to glance at the boy to know she was right. And that he returned the feeling. He was probably too old to become a father himself—he couldn't imagine Rebecca wanting to start over with a baby who would be born about the time her son graduated from high school. But thanks to Alan, Sam knew what fatherhood might feel like.

As usual, he didn't know how to find the right words. But he tried. "Then I'm luckier than I deserve to be," he said levelly, and Alan flushed again.

"What do you plan to do now?" Mrs. Hughes inquired.

"I don't know," Sam admitted.

"Maybe you should buy her something pretty," Alan offered.

"She'd probably accuse me of trying to buy *her*."

Rebecca's mother frowned in concentration. "Possibly, but the idea has merit."

It struck Sam then how bizarre this council was. If Rebecca could see them now, conspiring against her, she'd be steaming. Family was security to her, a solid wall at her back. This wall had caved in, welcoming a wolf into her enclave.

"Something tangible," Mrs. Hughes continued musingly. "The earrings were nice...and the roses, of course."

Just like that, the answer hit him. "Roses. That's it!"

"What's it?" She and Alan asked almost in unison.

"The arbor." Rebecca had said it was a symbol, and he'd use it as one.

"Hey, cool," the boy breathed, and Mrs. Hughes nodded once, decisively.

"Alan, do you know what her plans were?" Sam asked urgently.

He frowned. "No, but she had a picture cut out from a magazine. There was a blueprint, I think. And she talked about bricks—you know, to match the patio."

"Can you find the blueprint?"

"I can," Mrs. Hughes announced. "I take it you intend to surprise her? When?"

With a spark of amusement, Sam likened their consultation to a football team huddling on the field. He was tempted to wrap his arms around both of them while they hunched over their plans.

"Let me think," Mrs. Hughes murmured. "I have a friend who's considering redoing her living room. I'll have her make an appointment for Rebecca to bring samples to her house. Perhaps two or three o'clock in the afternoon. Yes, that would do it. Rebecca would never leave the store in the morning, so it should be safe for you to work then. With my friend's help, you should have the whole day. You *can* take the day off?''

He shouldn't, but Sam agreed without hesitation. "Can you give me a hand, Alan?"

The boy glanced at his grandmother, who nodded. "I don't believe missing one day of school would hurt."

"Sure!" Alan agreed.

"Then we're on for Wednesday?" Sam glanced around at his co-conspirators. To Mrs. Hughes he said, "You'll find the plans and make sure Rebecca stays busy all afternoon?" When she agreed, he looked at Alan. "I'll meet you at your place about 9:30."

Rebecca's son gave a thumbs-up. "Let's do it!"

WONDERING WHY Mrs. Tillinghast had been so insistent that she come today, Rebecca spread her carpet samples out on the floor of the immaculate, formal living room. The present carpet, cream colored, was as pristine as if no one had ever set foot on it. Although Rebecca wouldn't have chosen such a light color, she couldn't imagine why her mother's friend wanted to replace it.

"I brought samples of various blinds, too, though you might prefer drapes...?"

"No, I believe I'll stick with pleated blinds," Mrs. Tillinghast said. "They're modern but still give such a soft effect, don't you think?"

"Yes, and without looking as heavy as drapes. I'm considering some pleated blinds with a lacy pattern for my own windows, even though mine is an older home."

"Why, that sounds pretty." The older woman sat beside her on the couch. "Did you bring a sample of those?"

They spent a satisfying two hours discussing carpet, blinds, the possibility of reupholstering furniture, even stripping the dark molding and whitewashing it. When Rebecca asked why Mrs. Tillinghast wanted to redo her living room, the attractive older woman said blithely, "Oh, I'm just tired of it. Ted isn't fond of so much white, either. And with our grandchildren visiting, light carpet is a constant worry."

Rebecca had gotten as far as packing the samples she wasn't leaving, when Mrs. Tillinghast glanced at the clock and asked, "Dear, would you mind taking a peek at my kitchen while you're here? I'm tempted to make a clean sweep and replace at least the countertops. A friend just did hers with tile, and the room is so charming. What do you think?"

Rebecca discussed the pros and cons of tile versus laminated surfaces, admired the bleached-oak cabinets and ventured the opinion that the deep rose color Mrs. Tillinghast was considering for carpet could be continued into the kitchen. At 3:30, she finally escaped. She was grateful now that she'd talked Mrs. Tillinghast into a one o'clock appointment rather than the later one the older woman had preferred.

Rebecca felt drained and her shoulder ached. She should be delighted by the possibility of an order as sizable as this one; Lord knew, she could use the income. Business always slowed around Christmastime. People overspent on gifts and didn't even contemplate remodeling until spring made them take a good look at their yards and houses. So she ought to appreciate Mrs. Tillinghast's early restlessness.

Of course, Rebecca knew perfectly well why she didn't. The symptoms of depression were easily recognizable. She'd suffered it once before in her life, thanks to her ex-husband. If she'd been smart, she would have learned her lesson and sworn off men for good.

As if she could have resisted Sam.

Her thoughts began the familiar, vicious circle. Sam loved her in his own way. Couldn't that be enough? Was she really better off alone? Surely with time Sam would learn to trust her with his feelings. He was good with Alan. So what if he wouldn't always be there when she wanted him? So what if he wasn't interested in remodeling a house or gardening, and hated family gatherings? So what if he wasn't anything like her ideal?

That always brought her up short. It wasn't that she'd thought she could take a shopping list down to her local K mart to pick out a new husband. But this time around, she'd known what was important to her.

It was the distillation of what she'd learned during her first, unhappy marriage. Sexual compatibility was all very well, but a man who was ready, eager and willing to fix the toilet that wouldn't quit running was even better. Romance might stir the soul, but it didn't endure through constant disappointment. Alan liked Sam now, but how would he feel when his stepfather didn't show up at his basketball games any more reliably than his father did?

To Rebecca, love no longer meant candlelight, wine and roses. It meant caring enough to change, to compromise, to *try*. If Sam loved her enough to do all those things, why had three more days passed without a word from him?

Back at the store, she put away the samples, checked in a couple of wallpaper books, returned three phone calls and nagged a manufacturer yet again about an order of custom blinds that was two weeks late. At four o'clock, she turned on the answering machine and closed up shop.

Thinking about what she could cook for dinner, Rebecca turned onto her street. She was still a block away when she recognized Sam's car, parked at the curb behind Alan's. Her pulse fluttered, then accelerated. If Sam wanted to talk to her, why would he have come by so early? He knew she usually worked later than this. Was something wrong? Had Alan tried to call her when she was out and, when he couldn't reach her, turned to Sam again?

Rebecca grabbed her purse and rushed up the walk to the house. She usually called hello the minute she opened the door, but today she stood just inside the entryway and listened.

Silence. Gray afternoon light left the living room dim. Her panic rising, Rebecca hurried into the kitchen. It was deserted, too, but the light was on and unwashed plates and glasses were piled in the sink. Where on earth were Sam and her son? What had they done, snacked while they waited for the ambulance?

And then a flash of movement, a bright color, caught her eye. She set down her purse on the table and slowly went to the window. She'd found it too painful to look out these past weeks. The raw bones of the unfinished arbor reproached her with her inadequacy and her stupidity. What if she'd really been hurt, so that she'd been unable to work, even for a few weeks? What would she and Alan have done?

Now, through the wavery glass, she could see the backyard. Flower beds were muddy, stubbly expanses; the trees were bare of leaves, except for the small cedar. Out in back, where she had labored and fallen and cried, stood an arbor. Rebecca pressed her fingertips to her mouth and stared.

Alan and Sam were still at work, Sam with a shovel, Alan on his hands and knees. She couldn't quite make out what they were doing, but she saw Sam pause and say something, then Alan laugh.

Rebecca felt as though she were in a dream. In that unreal state, she went out the back door. It slammed behind her, and man and boy looked up. She followed the gravel path in its curve through the garden. Ahead of her, Alan stood up and Sam leaned the shovel against the arbor.

The arbor. *Her* arbor, just as she had imagined it in every detail. The slatted top and sides, the circular bench inside, the roses, now brown sticks emerging from the ground. The path flowed right into the brick floor of the arbor, with its elaborate herringbone pattern.

Her eyes were filled with tears by the time she looked at the two men in her life. Sam, muddy and sweaty, awkwardly laid his arm around Alan's shoulders. The two grinned in triumph.

"What do you think?" Alan asked eagerly.

"It's absolutely beautiful," she said, still feeling as though she would wake up any minute. It was as if they had read her mind. She remembered in her frustration and disappointment shoving the plans in the bottom drawer of her desk, where she wouldn't have to look at them. "How on earth did you know...?"

"Your mother dug the plans out," Sam said. "If you'll excuse the pun."

There was something different about his voice. He sounded unsure of himself, but also spontaneous. His usual reserve was gone.

"And the roses...?"

"They're your mother's doing, too."

Alan nodded. "Grandma said to tell you they're an early birthday present."

"She talked an old-rose nursery into sending them by overnight mail," Sam added. "She's a hell of a negotiator. Maybe I should hire her to manage one of my stores."

In other words, all of this—her arbor—was a conspiracy. A family one.

"Thank you," Rebecca said tremulously. "I . . . I can hardly believe it."

Sam dropped his arm from Alan's shoulders and came to Rebecca. With one big hand, he lifted her chin so her eyes had to meet his. His voice was low, scratchy. "You said the arbor was a symbol. Can it still be one?"

She was smiling through her tears. "That's a silly question."

"I can change," he said roughly. "I need a home again."

"I've been a fool, haven't I?"

"No, I've been the fool." His eyes held nothing back. "I thought I'd left home years ago. It took you to show me that I'd carried it with me. All that pain and anger didn't let me make a new home. But I can do that now. With your help."

"Oh, Sam." She flung her arms around his waist and held on for dear life, her cheek pressed to his chest. His arms closed around her just as tightly, and she felt him nuzzling her hair. "I love you," she said. "And here I didn't think it was enough."

"It wouldn't have been if I hadn't recognized what I was missing. If I hadn't realized how much I love you, too." He lifted his head and stepped back. "Hey, Alan. Come here."

Her son came. Through her blur of tears, he looked so tall and yet so young. When Sam held out his arm, Rebecca did the same. In a rush, Alan was hugging them both, tears on his cheeks.

"I love you," Rebecca said again. "I didn't deserve this."

"Sure you did, Mom." Alan's grin wobbled only a little. "Aren't you the one who says mothers live a life of sacrifice, and they deserve a payback every once in a while?"

Now Sam was grinning, too. They must look ridiculous, Rebecca thought, and gave them both another fierce hug. "What do you think of garden weddings?" she asked.

"Depends on whether we have to wait for flowers to bloom," Sam said.

"You know," Rebecca informed him, "some of the earliest bulbs will be blooming in a month. Do you think we could make a bouquet out of crocus?"

Sam laughed. He suddenly looked younger, too, she thought, more carefree than she had ever imagined him.

She reminded herself that it wouldn't always be this good, this easy. But, then, few worthwhile things were. After all, even the best gardeners had to battle weeds. Not to mention black spot and mildew and aphids.

"We can wait for spring," Sam said. "That'll give me a little time to sell a couple of the stores. With luck, my weekends should be free after that."

Rebecca tried to look guileless. "So we can build a pergola, and maybe a little entry court in front, and a grape arbor would be nice, and—"

Alan was ignoring her. He talked fast. "You guys aren't going to have a baby, are you? Did I tell you Dad is? That's bad enough, but at least I can see why somebody as young as Karen might want one. But think what a hard time the guys would give me if my mother was pregnant!''

Rebecca punched him in the stomach. "Kindly don't say 'my mother' in that tone of voice. And no, I have no immediate plans to get pregnant." She ventured a look to see how Sam was taking this. What she saw surprised her. It also sent warm blood rushing to spots she shouldn't be thinking about in front of her son. "Give me a little while," she said, and she wasn't talking to Alan anymore. "You never know."

"Jeez." Alan glanced from her to Sam and back again. He sighed. "I guess maybe you guys would like to be alone for a while. I'll go by Geoff's and see what I missed at school today. Just don't do anything I wouldn't."

As they watched Alan go, Sam said thoughtfully, "Seems like I've heard that before."

"Yes, and he'd better not do what I assume we're going to."

"And what, madam, might that be?" Sam gently turned her to face him. Hands on her hips, he eased her up against him, where she fit as effortlessly as the right puzzle piece.

She smiled up at him. "Wasn't it you who pointed out that we have something good going? I've heard it put more romantically, but the phrase seems apt. The 'good' part isn't hard to figure out—" she wriggled just a little, kissing the hollow at the base of his throat "—and 'going,' well . . ."

Sam shook his head. "Hold everything. Now that we're getting married, we should wait until our wedding night."

Rebecca leaned back in his arms to stare up at him in shock. "What?"

"Just kidding," he said, deadpan.

"But... you never kid."

He swung her up into his arms. The grin he flashed was devilishly sexy—and had always been her undoing. "I told you I could change, didn't I? Right now, I'll practice carrying you across the threshold. Maybe by our wedding day, I'll have it down pat."

She recovered enough to say archly, "Not to mention a few other things."

In her bedroom, Sam gently laid her on the bed. He braced himself above her, the expression on his face changing. "God, I love you," he said, his voice raw.

Rebecca touched the side of his face, savoring the hard, rough line of his jaw, his warmth, the tenderness of his mouth as he pressed a kiss into her palm. "I love you, too," she whispered. "I don't intend to let that ever change."

"Never," he agreed roughly, just before his mouth covered hers.

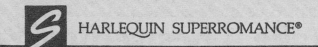

Take 4 bestselling love stories FREE

Plus get a FREE surprise gift!

Special Limited-time Offer

Mail to Harlequin Reader Service®

> 3010 Walden Avenue
> P.O. Box 1867
> Buffalo, N.Y. 14269-1867

YES! Please send me 4 free Harlequin Superromance® novels and my free surprise gift. Then send me 4 brand-new novels every month, which I will receive before they appear in bookstores. Bill me at the low price of $2.71 each plus 25¢ delivery and applicable sales tax, if any.* That's the complete price and—compared to the cover prices of $3.50 each—quite a bargain! I understand that accepting the books and gift places me under no obligation ever to buy any books. I can always return a shipment and cancel at any time. Even if I never buy another book from Harlequin, the 4 free books and the surprise gift are mine to keep forever.

134 BPA AJJC

Name _____ (PLEASE PRINT) _____

Address _____ Apt. No. _____

City _____ State _____ Zip _____

USUP-93R   ©1990 Harlequin Enterprises Limited

HARLEQUIN SUPERROMANCE®

THE MONTH OF LIVING DANGEROUSLY

LIVE ON THE EDGE WITH SUPERROMANCE AS OUR HEROINES BATTLE THE ELEMENTS AND THE ENEMY

Windstorm by Connie Bennett pits woman against nature as Teddi O'Brian sets her sights on a tornado chaser.

In Sara Orwig's *The Mad, the Bad & the Dangerous,* Jennifer Ruark outruns a flood in the San Saba Valley.

Wildfire by Lynn Erickson is a real trial by fire as Piper Hillyard learns to tell the good guys from the bad.

In Marisa Carroll's *Hawk's Lair,* Sara Riley tracks subterranean treasure—and a pirate—in the Costa Rican rain forest.

Learn why Superromance heroines are more than just the women next door, and join us for some adventurous reading this September!

HSMLD

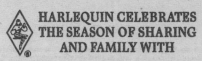

**HARLEQUIN CELEBRATES
THE SEASON OF SHARING
AND FAMILY WITH**

Friends, Families,
Lovers

Harlequin introduces the latest member in its family of
seasonal collections. Following in the footsteps of the popular
My Valentine, Just Married and *Harlequin Historical Christmas
Stories,* we are proud to present FRIENDS, FAMILIES,
LOVERS. A collection of three new contemporary romance
stories about America at its best, about welcoming others into
the circle of love.... Stories to warm your heart ...

By three leading romance authors:

**KATHLEEN EAGLE
SANDRA KITT
RUTH JEAN DALE**

Available in October, wherever
Harlequin books are sold.

Fifty red-blooded, white-hot, true-blue hunks from every State in the Union!

Beginning in May, look for MEN MADE IN AMERICA! Written by some of our most popular authors, these stories feature fifty of the strongest, sexiest men, each from a different state in the union!

Two titles available every other month at your favorite retail outlet.

In September, look for:

DECEPTIONS by Annette Broadrick (California)
STORMWALKER by Dallas Schulze (Colorado)

In November, look for:

STRAIGHT FROM THE HEART by Barbara Delinsky (Connecticut)
AUTHOR'S CHOICE by Elizabeth August (Delaware)

You won't be able to resist MEN MADE IN AMERICA!

Where do you find hot Texas nights, smooth Texas charm and dangerously sexy cowboys?

HEARTS AGAINST THE WIND

Strike it rich—Texas style!

Hank Travis could see himself in young Jeff Harris. The boy had oil in his blood, and wanderlust for the next big strike. There was nothing for him in Crystal Creek—except a certain marriage-minded Miss Beverly Townsend. And though Jeff seemed to have taken a shine to the former beauty queen, Hank wouldn't make book on Harris sticking around much longer!

CRYSTAL CREEK reverberates with the exciting rhythm of Texas. Each story features the rugged individuals who live and love in the Lone Star State. And each one ends with the same invitation...

Y'ALL COME BACK...REAL SOON!
**Don't miss *HEARTS AGAINST THE WIND* by Kathy Clark
Available in September wherever Harlequin books are sold.**
